BEYOND KILLOUGH CREEK

J. L. ANDERSON

Cover photo of Killough Creek by J.L. Anderson

Published by Anderson & Sons

Jacksonville, Texas

What lies behind you and what lies in front of you, pales in comparison to what lies inside of you.

- Ralph Waldo Emerson

KILLOUGH FAMILY TREE

Issac Killough Sr. (twin to James Killough of Killough Planation in Alabama), married to Ursula (Urcey)

Their Children:

Patsy Killough (remained in Alabama)
James Killough (remained in Alabama)
Polly Killough, married Owen C. Williams (brother to Sarah Jane, Barakias, Elbert)
- children, Elizabeth, James H., John C.
Second marriage - Jefferson Wallace – no children
Issac Killough Jr., married Sarah Jane Williams (sister to Owen C. Williams, Barakias, Elbert)
- one child, stillborn
Nathaniel Killough, married Orleana Deaver - children, Eliza and Julia
Second marriage - Bethanena Fisher - no children
Third marriage - Lockey McKee - children, Nathaniel Jr. and Orleana
Samuel Killough, married Narcissa Norris - one child, William
Allen Killough, married Elizabeth Brasher - two or three children
Jane Killough, married George C. Wood (Woods) - four or five children

Elizabeth Killough, engaged to Barakias Williams

AFTERMATH OF THE MASSACRE

Known Dead from the Massacre

Issac Killough Sr.
Issac Killough Jr.
Samuel Killough
Allen Killough
George Wood (Woods)
Barakias Williams

Known Survivors of the Massacre

Ursula Killough
Polly Killough Williams
Owen Williams
Elbert Williams
John H. Williams (child)
James C. Williams (child)
Nathaniel Killough
Orleana Killough
Eliza Killough (infant)
Narcissa Norris Killough
William Boykin Killough (infant)
Sarah Jane Williams Killough

Missing after the Massacre

Elizabeth Williams
Elizabeth Killough
Elizabeth Brashers Killough
Jane Killough Wood (Woods)
Six to eight young children

This is a work of fiction, based on historical events. As always, some recollections may vary.

PROLOGUE

In 1837, the family of Isaac Killough Sr. emigrated from Alabama to the new Republic of Texas. They settled on a piece of land in East Texas within the boundaries of Cherokee Indian territory established by the unratified Houston-Forbes treaty.

On October fifth, 1838, the Killough compound came under attack by a group of renegades, including Caucasians, Blacks, Mexicans and Native Americans. Six men of the Killough community were killed: Issac Killough Sr., Issac Killough Jr., Allen Killough, Samuel Killough, George Wood, and Barakias Williams. Twelve survivors were accounted for in the days following the tragedy, five of whom were adult women, and four young children. Approximately twelve women and children disappeared, presumably killed or abducted by the assailants.

Seventeen-year-old Elizabeth Killough and fifteen-year-old Elizabeth Williams were last seen following other family members, going hand-in-hand to hide in the canebrake.

Although Nathaniel Killough declared in his petition to the Republic of Texas that both Elizabeth Killough and Elizabeth Williams were deceased, none of the other survivors noted such loss in their recollections. On the contrary, Narcissa Norris Killough Sammons, one of the survivors, stated the Indians who accosted them during the massacre assured them that none of the women or children would be harmed, presumably at the direction of the leader(s) of the attack. Some years later, Reverend James Parker claimed to have spoken with Elizabeth Williams while searching for his niece, Cynthia Ann Parker, mother of the Comanche chief Quanah Parker.

BOOK ONE
MOLLY

1

There is a tiredness that seeps all the way into the marrow of my bones and is reflected back into each and every drop of my blood, plodding through my body with heart-wrenching effort. I have lived through yet another October.

The years between then and now, like day and night, childhood and age, have passed, sometimes with undue speed, others, lethargically. But those who say time heals all wounds are wrong. Time simply passes, no less and no more. That is all time does.

I was born Mary Elizabeth Williams, called Molly by family and friends. I am a survivor of what is now called "The Killough Massacre". I am a white woman by birth, a Texian by allegiance, and an Indian by choice. This is my testament, not of captivity, but of freedom.

I arrived in Texas from Alabama in the spring of 1837,

not yet a woman but more than a child, awkwardly placed in a family of uncles, aunts, cousins, my parents, and my brothers, with my maternal grandparents ruling over us all. We carried letters of introduction and recommendation from men of good reputation, including Mother's cousin, Reverend John Killough, a Cumberland Presbyterian minister in Alabama. In Nacogdoches, we made camp for a spell while the menfolk sought the counsel of established residents in choosing a site for our new homes. After riding through the county for many days, my uncles Allen Killough and George Wood purchased a half league of land between the Neches and Saline Rivers from Reverend Sumner Bacon. As a woman-child, I should not have been witness to certain events, but my presence was unnoticed as Grandfather and a Mr. Archibald Hotchkiss talked outside the courthouse, where the transaction was registered. Mr. Hotchkiss told Grandfather that he and the late Mr. Ben Hawkins had, in the last year or so, negotiated with the Creek Indian nation and their chief, Opothleyahola, to purchase the very same land, for the relocation of their people from Alabama and Georgia. Mr. Hotchkiss declared the Muskogee Creek might still be willing to pay several thousand dollars for the land, now that Houston's land grant treaty with the Cherokee had been tabled by the Texas legislature, and most assuredly would not be ratified. Grandfather calmly informed Mr. Hotchkiss that his sole intent was to provide a home for his family, not to speculate in land deals, but I noticed Uncle Nathaniel, who was nearby, took close note of Mr. Hotchkiss' words. I thought little of it at the time, but it was a scene that would come back to haunt my sleepless nights.

The homestead secured, we journeyed west on the Saline Road to the home of Mr. Martin Lacey. Mr. Lacey had built a small stockade for the protection of his family and neighbors. Fort Parker, a community four or five days' travel further west, suffered great losses the year before with several men killed, and women and children abducted by wild Indians. After an evening's entertainment and night's rest, we traveled north on the same trace, arriving at our new homesite in the space of three days. Grandfather and the uncles immediately set about preparing fields, planting a cash crop of corn, and small subsistence gardens, before turning their hands to building cabins. Father did not do much on account of having a new supply of 'medicine' for his rheumatism, a sore spot in our close knit community. None of the homes were particularly large or comfortable, compared to our former establishments in Alabama, but proved serviceable and kept most of the wet, wind and cold at bay. Women and children – those who were able – tended to the livestock of chickens, pigs, and two milch cows, all of which we had procured in Nacogdoches. The younger children made a game of helping clear the fields of rocks and other impediments to plowing, and the women and girls fell to the general work of housekeeping – washing, sewing, cooking, cleaning, spinning, weaving, and all the tedium that makes up daily life.

We found ourselves in the midst of Cherokee Indians led by an assortment of chiefs, elders and leaders. Foremost among these were The Bowl, who lived nearby, and Big Mush, who kept camp betwixt our homes and the Lacey's. Sam Benge was another notable name but was notoriously unreliable in temperament and attitude toward Americans, although he was most nearly a white man himself. His kinsman, Utana, commonly known as Tail, adamantly opposed the Republic and white civilization, and was known for quickly being provoked to violence and brutality. Another attached to Benge was referred to in the company of women and children as "Dog Shoot", but I overheard the men having a good laugh over his real name, which was similar in pronunciation, but of a more vulgar vein. Grandfather said that a name like that just went to prove what his fellow Indians thought of him.

The first year passed uneventfully. For the most part, our Indian neighbors treated us civilly, and often with kindness and consideration. That the land we occupied was theirs by a proposed treaty with President Houston, and by possession for the past twenty years, was a point of contention. Tension increased when, in December of that year, the Texas Legislature refused to ratify the treaty. President Houston met with the Cherokee leaders around us, and even stopped by our little settlement, in the aftermath of the legislature's decision. He was a grave and solemn man, holding little hope for helping his Indian friends. Grandfather and the uncles expressed relief that their titles to the land were secure and backed by the full faith of the Republic, and jubilation they could now publicly assert ownership. I thought it was a miserable thing; I worried over what might become of our good Indian neighbors since they would not be allowed to own the land where their crops grew, their livestock grazed, and their children played so happily. Nothing about the decision seemed fair; I dared voice that opinion while the President was in our midst. Grandmother pulled me sharply aside and whispered that such dealings were not for young ladies' voices, but I saw a faint, sad smile descend upon the President's visage, and he nodded. "Madam, a young miss possessed of a sharp mind and good heart is a Texas treasure." He bowed in my direction, a stately gesture forever imprinted upon my memory.

In the latter part of the spring of 1838, we began to hear rumors of unrest. Some stated the Mexicans intended to retake the Republic; others claimed the Indians plotted massacres to drive the white men from Texas. Even though neither fully trusted the other, there were charges that the Mexicans and Indians had a secret agreement between them, based in part on a report by Mrs. Plummer, a former captive of the Comanches from the raid on Fort Parker. By August, Grandfather and the uncles felt keenly the unpredictable nature of the situation, and we packed our wagons, hurriedly retreating to Nacogdoches.

Weeks passed. The crops at home were nearing maturity; Grandfather and the uncles anxiously paced back and forth as they considered the alternatives. Leave the crops to wither and die, lose the potential income and provisions for winter, and set up new homes in town and open a mercantile, or risk returning and harvesting what crops remained – the discussions continued, day after day, night after long and dark night. Emissaries, in the form of Mr. Goyens of Nacogdoches and Uncle Allen, were sent to negotiate with the Indians. The talks were encouraging; our representatives returned with assurances our persons would be unmolested whilst we tended to the harvest, tempered by the warning to finish our tasks and remove ourselves permanently by the first white frost. Mother's youngest sister, Elizabeth Isabelle – Izzie - and I listened covertly as Grandmother, Mother and the aunts whispered among themselves that the men were foolish to trust and confided in one another about quiet yet futile conversations with husbands and brothers, counseling the men a loss of a crop was of no consequence compared to a loss of life. The fear of a renewed war for Texas was palpable, and all indications predicted our homes would be the center of the maelstrom. Men, however, will do what men will do. As September drew to a close, we repacked the wagons and returned to the lonesome cabins.

On October fifth, 1838, my family was attacked by an assortment of rogues, ruffians, brigands, and highwaymen; Indian, Mexican, Negro, and White. Hiding in the canebrake, Izzie and I observed the band included Tail and, to our surprise, a former neighbor of ours from Alabama, Mr. Hawkins. It seemed to me most of the mounted assassins were Mexican or White, wearing Indian paint on their faces and dressed roughly in the manner of red men. My grandfather and most of the men of our family were killed outright, with the notable exception of my Uncle Nathaniel Killough, and, I heard, my father and his youngest brother, Owen and Elbert Williams.

Although hidden in the canebrake from the barbaric assault, Izzie and I saw clearly the horrible depredations perpetrated upon our family. When the attackers took leave of the smoldering waste of cabins and crops, we sought shelter within a cabin with an untouched loft, spared by God's grace and green logs. Therein we passed the night, resolved to set forth for the Lacey's fort on the morrow, to seek the company of Christians, with the hope the women and children of our family would likewise find their way to safety. We held no illusions about the fate of my beloved grandfather, Izzie's father, having found his earthly remains beneath quilts in front of his cabin, or of Izzie's betrothed, Kias, for we saw with our own eyes his demise at the hands of a scoundrel. Likewise, I bore the horror of seeing the mortal remains of Uncle Isaac lying murdered in a creek bed, and Uncle George viciously felled beside his own home. In the space of a single afternoon, we had felt more agony than a soul should bear. Little did we know how soon we would find anguish surpassing the grim grasp of Death.

We were awakened the next morn by a clamor in the yard below our hideaway. We heard the voices of strangers, men, and the sounds of furniture and household goods being shuffled about, horses whinnying, and all manner of commotion. Above the noise, we heard the familiar voice of Uncle Nathaniel. To this day, I cannot recall if our excitement gave away our hiding place, or if we willingly made our presence known. Either way, we were discovered and stood before that same kinsman, the thrill of rescue giving way to indescribable fear. Among the motley crew of men, Uncle and Mr. Hawkins were standing toe to toe, quarreling. Angrily, and loudly, Hawkins demanded payment, in gold, for "services rendered", making it quite clear the "service" was responsibility for the murders and assault upon our homes. Uncle professed not to have any coin, pled poverty, and proffered a meager assortment of change bills. Hawkins insisted he must have something more valuable than scraps of paper. Uncle gave a cursory glance to his sister and me, devoid of any humanity, compassion or familial tenderness. He jerked his head in our direction, offering us up with a curt word as if we were slaves on the auction block. Mr. Hawkins grinned in the most lewd manner, eyeing us from head to toe with a lecherous gleam. Uncle cast his eyes aside but did nothing otherwise. Hawkins allowed he would be satisfied with the terms of the deal, for the time being. I was fortunate: Tarrapin, a mixed-blood Cherokee Indian well known to us, rode into our midst at about this time and bargained for my salvation. Mr. Hawkins would not permit him to redeem my dear cousin; we parted with great sorrow.

I was only vaguely aware of the rhythmic movement of the horse beneath me and how I was unashamedly clinging to my savior. My mind wanted to churn a hundred different thoughts at once, but I was too fatigued to think, and even with my hands unbound, I had no wish to escape. In silence, we followed paths through dim woods and bright meadows, down one hillside, up another, across a creek, thorough a wider stream, the grasslands, trees, springs, and red dirt pathways all blending into a dream from which I could not awaken.

At length, we stopped. We had traveled to the southeast a good many miles, to a point where the earth rose in a gentle knoll beneath two enormous black walnut trees, not far from a gurgling stream.

Terrapin dismounted, and lifted my tired body from the horse, setting me on the ground with great gentleness.

He led me to the stream, where he pointed out the spring that fed clear, cold water into the creek. I drank gratefully. My senses slowly returned and I looked around curiously. The landscape was peaceful, the sun was setting soon, and no sinister shadows lurked in the treeline. "Where are we?" I asked. "Is your village near?"

Terrapin nodded. "My home is near. The village, further."

"You live alone?"

"I live as needed. My elders have a home where I am welcome. I can take you there, or I can take you to Lacey's fort."

"Taking me to the fort would be dangerous for you."

He nodded in assent. "It could be dangerous for you also." He paused as I absorbed his words. "I saw the man riding away from Hawkins. And you. And the other girl. He did not help you. He is your family." It wasn't a question, it was a statement of fact.

I hung my head, ashamed for Nathaniel, ashamed for myself, hurt, wondering what I had done to deserve my uncle's disdain.

"There are men who will do anything to acquire land, money or position."

"Yes," I said quietly, "but I never thought my uncle was one. Until today." I looked at Tarrapin, seeking some sign of compassion, understanding – and maybe even forgiveness. "I think it was all about the land. He wants to sell it all to the Creek Nation, now that Lamar will be president and the Cherokee expelled."

He had a sorrowful smile. "Perhaps. Your people do not want us here, Cherokee or Creek, Keechi or Kickapoo, Caddo or Coushatta, Shawnee, or Delaware. Our young people are driven away. Our old people follow, if they can. If they cannot..." His voice trailed off into sadness. "We are too few to fight, but some will fight, and they will die with honor. The Raven was our friend, but now he cannot live in both worlds. You know what happened to your family was not the work of my people, but they will be blamed, and they will suffer." He saw as Daniel the writing on the wall and knew the days of Indian freedom in Texas were at a close; those who could move away, must, and those who could not, would die at the hands of vigilantes unless they could succeed in claiming to be white or loyal Tejanos, for the tide of Texian favor had turned irrevocably against the Indian and Mexican.

I turned this over in my mind. In my heart, I knew his words to be true. And yet, there had been Cherokee attackers – Tail, and others. But I knew the Cherokees who had been our neighbors and friends would not have harmed them.

As I turned over my memories of the horror, I realized it had been perpetrated by a motley gang of hate-filled, blood-thirsty savages from all races. Pondering further, I knew he spoke of General Houston, his lifelong friendship with the Indians and his position as President of the Republic of Texas. It must be a very difficult task, even for a man as great as he, to keep peace in this new country. If only I, a girl of fifteen, barely a woman, could only find a way to help avoid more bloodshed and grief... a small, still voice within me said "you can."

"What about you?" I asked. "Will you go away or will you stay?"

"I will stay as long as I can and care for my elders. They should not have to leave their home again."

I turned my gaze to the open meadows that held no signs of human habitation. "Where is their home?"

"Why?"

I drew a deep breath and straightened my back. My decision was quick, my heart unfettered by ties to family or race, having just witnessed the treachery of my own kind, the pain a raw wound upon my soul. My thoughts turned to Ruth, making her way with Naomi to a foreign land, and I drew strength to face a new sunrise. With one simple declaration, I set the course of my life. "I wish to help you care for them."

2

I will pass over the details of my days and months following, as I became an adopted daughter to Honey and Poppa, the parents of my dear deliverer. Honey was half White and half Cherokee; Poppa was Mexican who had lived with the Cherokee almost all his life. We lived in near isolation, a hard two days journey from my former home. Few visitors passed our direction; fewer neighbors lived within walking distance. Striker's Village, a Cherokee town to the east, was easily reached by horseback, but had dwindled to a few families, most of whom disappeared as time passed, slipping away into more remote territory by the light of the moon, as the fervor for 'Indian Removal' became widespread. Our little family learned to communicate, by an amalgamation of English, Spanish, and Cherokee. The farm was small yet provided basic needs, and blessed us with luxuries of sweet berries, abundant nuts, and good water. My friend came and went, and went and came, often in the dimness of the new moon, slipping from one shadow to another, bringing news of the outside world, some glad, some grim. Mostly grim.

Of my parents and brothers, he had heard nothing indicating their whereabouts, only that they had escaped the massacre without injury. I did my best not to care; Mother and I had not been pleasant to one another for quite some time, not since I overheard an argument between her and my father wherein he called me a "misbegotten changeling" who cursed Mother's womb as I was born. I had asked a multitude of impolite questions afterwards, and my role as the family servant became more pronounced as I realized both parents held me accountable for the many unborn and still-born children that came after me, and worse yet, the few born with yellowed eyes and glossy skin who lived but a few hours or days. When two healthy sons – John, followed a year later by James – did finally arrive, I was pushed further aside, while they formed a perfect little family of four. The pain of that exclusion did much to inure me to the pain of loss.

What Tarrapin did learn was the fate of Grandmother and Aunt Sarah Jane, who was great with child, and Aunt Narcissus, along with baby Billie. They had made it safely to Lacey's fort, by the fortuitous intervention of Little Bean and his kinsmen. In quick succession, General Rusk attacked Kickapoo Town, believing the band who attacked my family harbored there. Tail was killed, which was probably well deserved – The Bowl even said as much. President Houston turned over his office to Mr. Lamar, sealing the fate of the Indians in Texas. Lamar harkened to nothing less than eradicating all Indians from the Republic. Sarah Jane's poor babe arrived and quickly passed from this world; Sarah Jane, Grandmother, Aunt Narcissus, and little Billie fled back home to Alabama. Uncle Nathaniel applied for restitution from the Republic for the loss of homes, household goods, livestock, wagons, and human lives, conspicuously noting Izzie and myself among the deceased. Upon this latter intelligence, I bit my lip as anger blurred with fear. Did she live as I, hidden away, or had she succumbed to the embrace of an unmarked grave?

Spring arrived, summer tagged along behind, sultry and ill-tempered, an equal match for the Texians and Indians. Lamar ordered the Cherokee and others to remove to the Arkansas territory; who could blame them for not wanting to go? Lamar huffed and puffed, sending General Rusk, with Burleson and Landrum, to enforce his desires upon the Indian towns. The brave soldiers burned homes, destroyed crops, slaughtered men and rendered women and children destitute. Had the roles been reversed, public outcry would have declared an unspeakable atrocity, and Texians would have been chomping at the bit for revenge. But there was rejoicing. The burned-out homes and ravaged crops were simply an expedient means of clearing the finest land for the ingress of civilization, and the slaughtered men, homeless women and children were nothing more than savages who had no place in a proper society.

Honey and Poppa debated what to do. Poppa thought although none of us were truly full-blood Cherokee, we were considered such in society, so perhaps we should go with the Cherokee; Honey refused to leave her home. In my eyes, neither were in any condition physically to undertake even a journey to Nacogdoches.The decision was made for them when Tarrapin arrived, declaring The Bowl lay dead on the field of battle, and bearing the wounded body of a young brave, fair skinned, with dark hair and hazel eyes. He would need weeks, if not months, of dedicated nursing and time to recuperate. Travel was out of the question. To be Indian was out of the question. To be Mexican was out of the question. From that moment on, should anyone question us, we were Black Dutch, which was only slightly better than being Indian. Above all, we were proud – albeit reclusive - Texas settlers.

The fall harvest and good hunting stocked our storehouse well and we settled into a long and cozy winter. Our patient recovered physically more quickly than we had anticipated; his spirit, however, seemed irrevocably damaged by the travails of loss – his home, his livelihood, his family, his friends, his leaders. He would sit for days on end, staring into the fire, saying nothing, taking little food or water. I feared the lack of human interaction would only serve to drive him further inward, so I began reading aloud each night, by the light of a Betty lamp, from old copies of Godey's which Tarrapin had so kindly brought from his earlier journeys, following with a Bible reading, beginning with Genesis. (The Bible had been left with Honey many years earlier, by an itinerant Methodist preacher, in the days of Mexican rule, when the only accepted religion was Catholicism.) Little by little, the man emerged, and we found he spoke fluent English as well as Cherokee, and understood more Spanish than he spoke. He longed for news of his mother and worried she and his young brothers and sisters would not survive the trek to Arkansas and Indian Territory. I silently shared a similar heartache for Aunt Janie, Aunt Bessie and the seven children who had not been heard from since that fateful day. Rumors swirled that they were abducted and traded to any Indian who wanted them; a clear possibility, because there were handsome profits at Coffee's Station and other trading posts for those bringing in captive women and children for redemption. As for my dearest Izzie, I feared her fate might be even worse, at the mercy of that reprehensible Hawkins man.

I ventured forth into civilization for the first time in the spring of 1840. More than a year and a half had passed since the attack on my former home; I had difficulty recalling it as my home, although I remembered each and every detail of the cabins and my loved ones. It was as if remembering a dream world, where the characters were real, yet there was no sense of reality. I set out with Tarrapin and our long suffering patient, who called himself John, on Trammel's Trace southward to Nacogdoches, to trade for goods and hopefully hear good news of the world. I was resolved to see and be seen, and if it caused Uncle Nathaniel consternation, so be it. He had certainly caused enough for me.

I knew from past experience the store of Roeder and Parmalee would not deign to trade with anyone who was not blessed with a fair complexion; I was perfectly happy to stay far away from their establishment, for in addition to dry goods, they sold whiskey by the glass and housed a billiards parlor. It attracted a rather unsavory crowd, in my opinion, despite the fact Uncle Nathaniel was always delighted at the prospect of trading there. He claimed that he and Parmalee were both "young men with brilliant prospects." I had my doubts. There was something about Richard Parmalee that was unsettling; I recalled his odd behavior the first time Izzie and I saw him in 1837. He had openly stared at Izzie; his face turned white and his eyes widened. He ventured a single word - "Nelly!" - and nearly tripped over his own feet turning to hurry away from us.

Tarrapin traded with Frost Thorn's mercantile, where Cherokee Indians in particular were not only welcome, but encouraged. He exchanged hides and furs for cash and goods, and concluding his business, left to meet with Mr. Goyens, while Mr. Thorn and I bartered. I had spun yarn over the winter, and Honey had prepared a good supply of homespun cloth, sending the excess with us for trade. I received a new Godey's, a bone tatting shuttle and cotton thread, and some yellow on blue calico for a new dress for Honey. As I prepared to take my leave, the bell of the shop door chimed. I heard an audible gasp; a woman's voice and from the corner of my eye, saw a delicate hand flutter to a snow white pelerine crowning a blue and white striped day dress, with a delicate white ruffle dusting the floorplanks. In a moment, my heart fluttered wildly then beat steadily again; I had been discovered by a friend, not a foe. "Mrs. Killough," I declared as cheerfully as I could muster the courage for speech, "how delightful to see you today." I smiled and bowed her direction. As I hoped, she was speechless as I hurried to her side to catch her elbow. "Do let us go out and talk for awhile. It has been so terribly long since we have seen one another."

With those words, Sarah Jane allowed herself to be maneuvered from the mercantile and onto the broad sidewalk. I always had a special place in my heart for my 'double aunt' – Sarah Jane never failed to remind me she had to be my favorite aunt because she was my aunt twice over, by blood and by marriage. "After your mother married my brother," she would tease, "I had marry her brother Isaac just so I could be loved twice as much by my favorite niece!" But she somehow forgot to remind me of that on that particular day.

"I am dead, you know," said I companionably as I tucked my arm through hers.

"So Brother Nathaniel says," she replied acidly. "But you feel warm to the touch and I do believe I see you breathing, so either I am dreaming, or Brother Nathaniel is sorely mistaken." She stopped suddenly, voluminous skirts swaying indignantly as she turned to study my face. "Mary Elizabeth, my little Molly dolly, it is you! I am not dreaming! How have you come to be here? Where have you been? And where, dear God, is Izzie?"

The final inquiry stuck me as a flaming arrow to the heart, for I had no answer. I had hoped, for a moment, she might know my dear one's fate, but she was as blind as I.

We continued our promenade down the street until we discovered a quiet spot to sit and talk with neither prying eyes nor curious ears to intrude. I told her bluntly of the morning after the raid, how Uncle Nathaniel treated us as common chattel to be traded, and how Izzie slipped from my sight. I assured my dear aunt of my contentment in my current arrangements, and though she begged me to join her household, I could not bring myself to depart from those who needed and loved me, who sheltered me in my darkest hours, as the final seasons of life turned them ever homeward bound. It was, I felt, my Christian duty to abide with them and give them comfort, to the best of my ability, prayerfully and with the guidance of the Almighty.

Some hours later, we parted with love, many embraces, kisses, and fond caresses of care and concern.

Sarah Jane avowed her intention to remarry within a
month's time, a fine fellow, John N. Sullivan, her "Angel
of Mercy" in the mournful months that nearly consumed
her will to live after losing husband and child. He was the
reason she had returned to Texas after a brief respite in
Alabama, where she had sold what little property she still
owned. She took leave of me, resolute in determination to
live well whilst keeping watch over Nathaniel and doing
everything in her power to deter his political ambitions.
He had made known his intention to be a candidate for
Congressional Representative next fall, and fully
expected to win the seat. Sarah Jane had long suspected
there was something amiss in his character, due in no
small part to his alacrity in claiming remuneration for
losses after the raid, and his avoidance of those who
offered to help seek the family members believed to have
been taken captive by Indians. Now with what she knew
to be blatant lies about the fate of Izzie and myself, she
felt her her deductions sound. She asserted vehemently
she would not be lulled into a false security again in this
life, and most especially not by him. But she would have
to be patient. He was the Justice of the Peace for their
section of the county, often in the company of men
known to be Freemasons, powerfully placed in
government, and an award of restitution from the
Republic of Texas for the loss of family, livestock and
material goods had made him wealthy. We agreed
cunning, good timing and his own conscience, if it
existed, would be the best tools to reveal his true nature.
She must have effected some small triumphs in the
community; he was roundly defeated at the polls in the
autumnal election.

My life continued, falling into comfortable routines
with Honey, Poppa and Tarrapin, whose mysterious

journeys grew less frequent and of briefer durations. John elected to go to Nacogdoches, where he found work with Thorn and Company, carrying goods for trade between towns in Texas and Louisiana. Mr. Thorn paired him with the little old yellow-bellied Frenchman, Louis Rose (the appellation "Moses" chidingly applied due to his age; perhaps Methuselah would have been more appropriate, but it did not rhyme with Rose as well as Moses did), who, despite the tide of public opinion long turned against him for his boast of not crossing Colonel Travis' holy line, continued to hold the respect of his employer. From time to time, they would pass our way, stopping to spend a night and bring tidbits of news from travels triangulated by Nacogdoches, Natchitoches, and Logansport. During one of these informative encounters, Monsieur Rose inquired if any of us recollected the massacre of the Killough family, nigh on six years past. I turned my head quickly toward the blazing fireplace, lest my eyes betray some spark of intimacy.

"Yes," I answered, feigning some measure of uncertainty, "we heard there were a number of folks either killed or taken off, but it was a good while back. Why do you ask? Texas is annexed to the United States now. Surely, there's not another rebellion brewing?"

"Ah non, mon chere! Mexico, she is not happy with the States, but eet ees not for war I ask. I hear the children of that sad family, there are those who live. Some with Comanches, some elsewhere." Was it my imagination, or did he smile knowingly and wink my direction? "Les petits garcons, et fille Parker, they are seen with Noconi Comanche."

"I was given to understand there were two young ladies in the Killough family. What of them?" I hesitated to ask, but my curiosity to discover some word of Izzie overwhelmed my desire for secrecy.

He caught my eyes for a moment, gazing steadily, then turned away, shrugging. "Monsieur Killough, he say l'mademoiselles sont morts. What might a poor Frenchman perceive their kinsman not?" I nodded. Nothing more was said of the matter.

3

Thus it came to pass Tarrapin and I made our way to seek the Comanche campgrounds. For weeks we followed traces, rivers and streams, making discrete inquiries wherever possible, trusting old Moses' words as if, as his namesake's, they came from God Himself.

When we reached the confluence of the Arkansas and Missouri rivers, fatigue, long delayed, overtook my mortal shell. I conceded to the rigors of the trail and begged respite. We took lodging with a small band of Indians known in earlier days to my dear companion as friends. I rested for many days, a fortnight and then some, ministered to by a blue-eyed Indian, barely into womanhood, who spoke no English, but whose face showed kindness and compassion. As I began to recover, I became aware of some distress on her part. I tried to make her understand by signs that I wanted to help her, as she helped me. One evening, I implored Tarrapin to translate for us; she was painfully reticent, to the point of fear, and refused to speak with him.

The next day, as she and I took our morning meal, a sturdy young warrior, handsome after the fashion of his people, came to our lodge with Tarrapin. A white man was in town, seeking a girl who had been taken captive many years ago. My nursemaid, Naduah, entreated the warrior with frantic eyes and flying words in their native tongue; epiphany burst forth unto my mind, and I knew she was the poor captive – only, her true captivity lay in her heart belonging to this man and these people. I arose, placing my hand upon her arm, and said "Present me to the gentleman instead." I led her to a pile of buffalo robes, pressing upon her shoulders until she was seated, her wide blue eyes calming as I smiled and brushed a hair from her forehead, shaking my head to and fro to say "no". The young warrior's stoic manner nearly cracked for a moment; he loved her with an equal passion. With a quick word to her, he and Tarrapin escorted me to an audience with the stranger.

Wearing a simple calico shift, I met Reverend James Parker. He sought some familiar feature in my face; finding none, his shoulders slumped and his countenance registered defeat. I feared this was not the first time he had encountered such disappointment. He bade me share my Christian name. I obliged. He quickly connected me to what he termed "the Killough Family Massacre". I assented to this conjecture. Immediately, he offered to redeem me from my captors. I refused. He must have thought me senseless, for he pressed the question, declaring with all the zeal of a circuit riding preacher the absolute will of God Almighty was the reunification of families torn asunder by the heathen hordes. I was equally resolute in my affirmation that God Almighty had placed me according to His will, and that I chose to follow Him while continuing upon the Indian path. "Mr.

Parker," I concluded, "I trust with all my heart that I am where God intends me to be, with the family He directed me to join. If, someday, you find your Cynthia Ann, I pray you will recall my situation, and if you find her likewise, leave her to the connections to which she is willingly bound." Clearly, my words fell on deaf ears. I turned and left, never seeing him again.

Before we left the Noconi camp, the young warrior, Peta, beckoned to us, and pointed to a group of boys playing at a distance. "Red Hawk", he said to Terrapin, who translated for me. Several youngsters were mounted on ponies, learning the skills they would need to survive on the Great Plains, as they followed the buffalo herds. I watched, puzzled for a moment. A familiar gesture from one child caught my attention. A healthy, happy, whole boy, who looked a bit like Uncle George and had Aunt Janie's wavy hair, leapt upon a galloping pony, paused a moment, then somersaulted to the ground, graceful, unhurt. I wanted to run and catch him up in my arms, rejoicing. Instead, I compelled myself to turn to Peta and smile with thanks and understanding. This was my young cousin's home now. He was one of their own. What I had vowed of myself and pleaded for with Mr. Parker, I now had to accept for my own blood kin, and trust that he was upon the path God intended. I have never been so heartbroken in all my life.

Once more at home with Honey and Poppa, we spent a warm and cozy winter by the fireside. Age was showing in Poppa's gait, and Honey had more than one spell that frightened us, growing short of breath and unable to speak. Rest and hot broth effected recovery, but with each episode, she lingered in bed longer and could manage less upon arising. One chill afternoon, as I stoked the fire, she called softy "Daughter," I straightened, hastening to her bedside, pulling a stool close so I could sit and hold her hand. "have you given thought to what you will do with yourself when Poppa and I are gone?"

"Honey, please..."

"Daughter, you must."

I knew she was right. I entered this household a dependent woman-child, quietly tortured by despondency over the events which forced me from the family of my birth and nearly turned my heart to stone. As the years passed, the despair and paralysis of emotion relented to an inner strength and growing affection for all the inmates of our modest domicile - Honey, Poppa, Tarrapin. A flush colored my cheeks, which she discerned by the flickering firelight.

"You should marry him."

How could I? For all my good and noble intentions, my heart still harbored a childhood aversion to the swarthy complexion, the hawkish nose, the high cheekbones, and the long dark hair which framed his face. And yet – how could I not? From the moment I mounted behind him and rode away from Uncle and horrors, I had felt a fond tremble at the sight of broad shoulders, strong arms, clear eyes and confident manner. Still, he was nearly old enough to be my father, and had never, by word or deed, approached me as a suitor might. Or had he? The trip back from Arkansas had been dreadful; one night, I had given over to great sobs and hot tears, thinking of what might have been for myself, Izzie, and my cousins had Uncle not betrayed us by hateful greed. He held me close in my distress, heavily muscled arms pulling me against his chest, never saying a word to reproach my fragility, reluctant to release me even when my cries subsided. What but love could render such comfort?

In the Noconi camp, I had witnessed the bond between Peta and Naduah, and knew without a doubt if they were ever parted, each would perish without the other. I tried to imagine my life without him and failed.

I squeezed Honey's hand with gentle pressure. "Would he want me?" I whispered.

"Would you have him?"

"Yes."

Within the week, Tarrapin brought a deer, freshly killed, and presented it to me with great formality. His eyes met mine, hesitant for the first time since we had met. I searched their depths and saw the man, abiding in love, uncertain of my response, cautiously hopeful. I bestowed a smile of tenderness and gratitude upon him. At eventide, I placed the roasted venison upon the table before him, my head bowed demurely.

And so, after the custom of his people, he had proposed marriage. I, in turn, had accepted.

The question of how to be married disturbed me greatly. I desired a full and legal union, but that desire was tempered by an equal desire to continue our blessed anonymity, for fear of being removed from our home because of my betrothed's bloodline. The Republic was soon to be a State, but that did not change our position; if anything, it created greater peril, because the United States' treatment of Indians was harsh, riddled with broken promises and broken lives. The tales we heard of removals and reservations were harrowing. Likewise, we had no desire to flee to Mexico, as so many others had before us. All I wanted was a normal life for us, in our own home, on our own land. I considered seeking a sympathetic minister or justice of the peace, but I knew in my heart that each would be bound by law to record our marriage in a county ledger, and I would not endanger us all by my penchant for propriety. The only route to peace of mind was to forego convention, church and law. Adam and Eve were not joined as man and wife by man, but by God, and I saw no reason why man should be concerned with our marriage. Marriage is for two to be joined as one, passing through life, help mates one to another, to love and comfort through good times and bad, a commitment to renew daily, as the sun rises and sets, willingly and cheerfully.

A frontier marriage it was to be. One spring morning, we announced to Honey and Poppa our intention to live, from that day forward, as husband and wife. They responded with blessings and best wishes; Honey had a tear in her eye as Poppa clasped Tarrapin's forearms.

"Son," Poppa interjected among the congratulations, "you must take a new name for this new life. Your wife, and the sons and daughters to come will be best served by a Texian name."

Honey agreed. "Borrow a name from one of our friends, perhaps. Louis Rose, Frost Thorn, Haden Edwards, George Bays, Elijah Debard?"

Tarrapin thought for a moment. "I would not want you calling me Louis and thinking of the little Frenchman", he teased, "so open your Book and choose a name to write, and that is the name I shall answer to when you call."

I opened the Bible and the pages fell to the Book of Matthew. "Matthew." I felt the word on my tongue, trying it and finding a natural fondness for the syllables.

He considered it for a moment, thoughtfully, then nodded. "You will remain Molly Williams, will you not? And I shall be Matthew Williams, if it pleases you."

I was surprised to find myself comfortable with retaining my maiden name, and with his appropriation of my surname. I had no particular affinity to being a Williams; my parents had long ago erased whatever affection I had for that familial association, but as I reflected, I resolved that this Williams family would carve its own path, and any children we might be blessed with welcoming would be loved unconditionally.

I blushed with joy as I penned our names within the Bible – Matthew and Mary Elizabeth Williams, united in marriage, March twenty-third, in the Year of Our Lord, eighteen hundred and forty-five.

In the evening, enveloped in his arms, I felt a deep peace previously unknown. I breathed deeply and pressed closer against his chest. I sensed his lips brush against my hair. A deep desire awakened within me. I turned my face upwards to his; I called his newly given name. "Matthew." Our lips met; we were truly wed.

Samuel Houston Williams arrived in this world the morning of February nineteenth, 1846.

4

Sam was a fair skinned babe, with light brown hair and blue eyes. I bowed my head and gave thanks for his health and his appearance, grateful his path in life would be easier because of the lack of shadow to his skin.

He was a little more than a year and half old when I chanced to see Sarah Jane again, this time in Gum Creek, a new community which had arisen in the gently rolling hills of pines and pasture about ten miles west of our farmstead. A Mr. Jackson Smith and wife Evalina had recently settled the area, where he established a blacksmith's shop and was placed in charge of the postal services. A handful of families from Alabama, Georgia and the Carolinas established homes nearby, with ambition for businesses as well as farming. A modest dry goods shop, smelling of freshly milled wood, stood a short distance down the lane from the smithy.

"Mrs. Sullivan?" Startled, she nearly dropped the tin of fine French soaps, delicately scented with lavender, that she had been inspecting with a longing gleam in her eye. "May I introduce my son, Samuel Houston Williams?" I must admit, I was beaming with pride.

Sarah Jane raised her eyebrows. "Williams?" she questioned, suspiciously.

I blushed, drew near, whispered in her ear, then stepped back and said simply "Yes. Matthew Williams is my husband."

I left her for a moment to digest the news, while I turned to a stack of newspapers, newly arrived from New Orleans. There were papers from New York and Boston, not too long past dated, and more recent editions from nearer locales.

I scanned the New Orleans Bee. The salacious details of the Paris murder of a Ducesse, by her husband, for the love of his supposed mistress, the recently dismissed governess of the murdered woman's own children, followed by his suicide before standing to account by his peers, captured my attention, mostly old news but with the added speculation that the Duc had survived. Jane perused the details alongside me, drawing a shocked breath now and again as the intrigue grew of the nobleman's supposed absconding and rumored sightings of him in New Orleans, where he had relations. "Can you imagine a man being the hand of such evil in his own home?" Jane exclaimed.

"Of course I can imagine, and so can you," I hissed. "At least, this poor fool acted on his own behalf, rather than hiring out the evil deed, and had the decency to remove himself from this world in atonement. May God have mercy on his soul."

"May God have mercy on him, but I pray He will show no mercy to Nathaniel." Jane's bitterness resided securely in her heart. Her countenance shifted, she looked at me curiously. "He received a letter from Mr. Parker some time ago, reporting you had been found with the Comanches."

"I was", I replied calmly.

"Whatever were you doing with Comanches? They are bloodthirsty savages! You know what they did to the Parkers, the Gotchers, the Websters, that poor Matilda Lockhart..."

"Perhaps from their viewpoint, circumstances were different." I spoke quietly, with conviction. I did my best to explain to her the circumstances of our journey, and told the tale of finding Janie's son.

Sarah Jane listened with tears glistening. "If only there could be some justice in this world, that I could witness, I would be somewhat consoled. If Nathaniel knew you lived, happily, and that Janie's little ones were healthy and strong, I think it would be punishment greater than any court could render. Nothing will change the past, but if his days were haunted, I would think righteousness had been served. Will you show yourself to him?"

"I am not ready to face Uncle. I may never be." The truth was, I was afraid of him. Still. Sarah Jane could wish for his days to be haunted, but it was my nights that were haunted by terrifying dreams of murder and families ripped apart. I held my Samuel a bit closer, the softness of his baby hair against my lips, as if I could press a million kisses upon his little head and protect him forever from such monsters.

To change the subject somewhat, Sarah Jane talked of the McKee family, newly arrived from Tennessee, headed by a slave-holding minister. Nathaniel had even purchased a slave of his own, a young man to help with the farming, while Nathaniel tended to other ambitions. They had grand plans, the McKees and Nathaniel, to create a new community. Larissa, they were calling it, after the birthplace of Achilles, with a fancy college, church, and even a Masonic lodge. She would like nothing better than to see those plans go awry.

As I understand, a scant year later, her opportunity to spoil the noble vision arrived.

The inaugural classes had barely begun at the temporary home of the ambitious college when a finely attired gentleman from Alabama presented himself on Sarah Jane Sullivan's doorstep, the very same doorstep she had claimed as Sarah Jane Killough. By local standards, he looked rather outlandish in a fashionably tall silk hat, a black frock coat, finely embroidered gray waistcoat, linen shirt, vibrant red silk cravat, and striped trousers. For a moment, she was self-conscious of her simple, shapeless house dress, but quickly recalled he had appeared uninvited, without any forewarning, and the shame, if there were any, should be his for such impertinence.

He introduced himself as one Jesse Duren, formerly of Alabama, lately of New Orleans, and inquired if indeed she was Mrs. Sullivan. Cautiously, suspiciously even, she affirmed the query. He doffed his hat in a grand and graceful manner and motioned to the carriage discretely paused a short distance away.

The carriage door opened and a vision of pink, brown and cream plaid descended. Delicate slippers peeped cautiously from beneath a decidedly full skirt, topped with a ruffled bodice and puffed sleeves edged with ivory lace, a trim waist nipped in a pronounced 'v'. A pink silk bonnet trimmed with wide cream ribbons gently framed a demure face with blushing cheeks and rosebud lips.

"Izzie!" Sarah Jane managed to exclaim, as Mr. Duren gallantly caught her as she fell into a faint.

I was not there to witness the reunion; my own would come in the due course of time.

5

I spent the first sixteen years of my life with Izzie, the next ten not knowing what had become of her, and then reunited, after a fashion, for sixteen final years. Whatever happened during that lost decade must have been beyond the limits of human suffering, for she returned as an illusion of beauty and refinement fitted neatly over a single-minded, vengeful passion. Upon our first meeting after her homecoming, she was her old self for a bit. "Remember when we came to Texas?" she asked. "Nathaniel and George sold their store to Cousin Abner, and Cousin Abner's partner, Mr. Grace, gave us some books to help pass the time on the trip? Waverly novels, some poetry by Lord Byron, and Mr. Lytton's "Paul Clifford" in two volumes? That was your favorite, the fatherless orphan living in two worlds, finally finding love and a new life in the new world. It was a wonderfully romantic story then, and now, look - I brought you a new copy. It's a single volume, which makes it much nicer for reading." Izzie was glowing with excitement as she proffered the tome, running her fingers along the three-quarter leather bindings on the marbled book boards, appreciating the texture of the leather corners protecting the the smooth covers. I opened the book and gaped at the intricacy of the engraved frontispiece. Enthralled, I shifted my eyes to the opposite page. The familiar words jumped out: "It was a dark and stormy night; the rain fell in torrents..." I closed the book and clasped it to my breast, the gilt page tops reflecting in our eyes as we shared so many unspoken joys. The next time we met, her joy was gone, replaced by a bitter glint in her eye and malicious tone to her voice as she recounted having surreptitiously entered Nathaniel's home – what had been her home with her parents on the day of the massacre – while he and his family were away. She had pulled aside the old stones in the hearth and found her grandmother's jewelry and spirited it away – for which, I could not find fault with her, because knowing Nathaniel he would have not given it to her willingly. But what disturbed me greatly was her description of how she went through the house, now appended with additional rooms, and collected small items belonging to her brother. She seemed to have the idea of using them for some nefarious purpose. I dare say it sounded like some sort of witchcraft, employing methods she had learned in New Orleans. She was not herself; something had been born out of that horrid day that twisted her mind now and again. And yet again I do not find fault in her. I find the fault only in those who perpetrated the horror.

I barely recognized this incarnation of pain and anger, although she tried to be the sweet girl I loved so well before the tragedy. Izzie shielded herself from the shame of her widening waistline, fabricating a tale of marriage and untimely widowhood for the community well before her fatherless child's arrival. She glossed over her time in Louisiana in brief references to nursing or taking in sewing and laundry to supplement her work in an orphan's home, dwelling more on the kindness of her employers in providing her with books for pleasure reading. Only Sarah Jane and I ever knew the truth, and I sincerely doubt we were told the whole of it.

Sarah Jane, for her part, seized the opportunity presented by Mr. Duren and sold him her homestead, and she and John bought Narcissa's former home, as it was a bit larger and better suited for the couple plus Izzie and a baby. Mr. Duren, for his part, proceeded to build upon his new property a devil's playground, christening it Talladega. A race track, gambling saloon, and bawdy house were the nascent establishments, providing no end of consternation to Nathaniel's and the McKee's efforts to establish their vision of Larissa as an epicenter of refinement, academic excellence, and moral pre-eminence. Sarah Jane was just tickled to death to have a hand in spoiling their pompous self-righteousness.

For awhile, it seemed Izzie might find some peace in her soul and a quiet life on this earth. William was born in due time, but she was not well suited to motherhood. Sarah Jane gladly assumed the care of the boy as Izzie retreated into some dark recess of her soul. She spoke in feverish whispers of seeing the dead, particularly her father and Kias. Being in close proximity to the site of their deaths, lodging with Sarah Jane in what had been Samuel and Narcissa's cabin, preyed upon her wits and drove her to fits of despair and melancholy, relived only by frightening intervals of giddy interactions with unseen spirits.

When William was still quite young, the traveling ventriloquist, a Mr. E. L. Harvey, made his way though the area, as he was accustomed to making a circuit entertaining from San Antonio to Shreveport, then New Orleans and back into Texas. Izzie caught his eye, or he caught hers, and she behaved well enough, long enough, to make a quick marriage. Little William was left with Sarah Jane, a temporary arrangement that was understood to be permanent. Her letters, although infrequent, were lengthy and spoke of delving deeper into spiritualism, of the Reverend Jesse Ferguson, and as war overtook the South, séances to reunite mothers with sons lost to far away battlefields. Although her obsession with the departed had not abated, she at least no longer seemed consumed by melancholia.

I suppose Izzie and Eben Harvey would have continued traveling from one community to the next for a lifetime, had her husband's life not been cut short by a band of guerrillas in Missouri. For the second time, Izzie witnessed the violent, brutal death of her love, and this time, there was no hope for restoring her to equanimity. She made her way home, alone, heavily burdened by death and desire for vengeance. What she did once she returned is between her and the Almighty, may God rest her soul.

I ached for her; I still do in the dark night when sleep eludes me, and my thoughts turn to our heavenly Father. I pray she has found peace and forgiveness. I pray she forgave herself, as well as those who wronged us so badly. I trust she had no sins for God to forgive, for her sins were of her madness, and not of her own true nature. Had the tragedy never been incited, she would have wed Kias, borne a multitude of children, built a home, and enjoyed the love and respect of family, friends, and community. Indeed, both our lives would have been very different. She lost her life that day as surely as

Grandfather, Kias, and the others, just as I gained a life I could have never imagined, for which I am eternally and humbly grateful.

As I enter my sixty-fourth year, I can affirm without reservation my life has been blessed. My children have brought forth children of their own, my husband loved and honored me until Death claimed his mortal body and God claimed his immortal soul. Soon, God willing, we will be reunited.

In the past week, I have met the son of Naduah, who appeared at the Fair in Dallas. Quanah is a very impressive gentleman, not dissimilar to his parents in demeanor and grace. Like his father before him, he escorted me to view the dancers from his nation and beckoned one to his side. I caught my breath sharply, and time stood still, dissolving years into a dim mist, as recognition leapt betwixt my eyes and Red Hawk's. Here at last was Uncle George and Aunt Janie's boy, grown to full manhood, wearing a feathered headdress, boned breastplate and moccasins! He spoke little English, but happy faces are the same in all languages. I found he recalled our family names and he had missed his parents greatly for a long while. He did not hold any Indians to account for their loss; he made himself clear that a Mexican man, Manuel, had taken him that fateful day, and his Indian parents had been kind and loving. Too soon we had to part; I wished him well, and my prayers follow him as always.

Izzie has been departed from this life some twenty-four years now; she passed only days after her brother Nathaniel, in that terrible month of April 1864. We buried her - Sarah Jane, John Sullivan, my son Sam, my dear husband and I - in private, by the moonlight as she had wished, her resting place unmarked, alongside the cairn of iron ore stones marking the resting place of her beloved Kias. In the days before her death, She entrusted to me a sheaf of papers along with her heirloom jewels, to be held for her son, hoping he would return safely from the War (he had lied about his age and gone away to fight the Yankees with Captain Lovelady of Jacksonville). Though true motherhood had slipped through her fingers, she loved him after her own fashion. Izzie dreamed William would someday marry and have a family of his own, the kind of family she had only been able to give him by leaving him with Sarah Jane and John. John has been gone from this world for many years; Sarah Jane slipped from this world not long ago. I am the only one left with first hand memory of the massacre and the terrible after-effects of that day.

William has fulfilled Izzie's dreams and more, becoming a respected farmer, a good husband and beloved father. The oldest of his three girls, Jemima, is set to be married to a gentleman lately arrived from South Carolina. As a wedding gift, I assembled the brooch and ear bobs Izzie had hidden so long ago in the fireplace into a shadow box and fastened the sketches she penned of her life, as well as those of Sarah Jane and these of my own, between the backing boards. Someday, some curious soul may prise them apart and discover our stories, but it is still too close to be told without starting gossip and rumors which might compromise certain opportunities in life for her son, his daughters and the grandchildren yet to come.

BOOK TWO
IZZIE

1

Mama and Papa named me Elizabeth Isabelle when I was born. Papa said I was named after two great queens, Elizabeth who ruled England and made it a great country, and Isabella, who sent Christopher Columbus to the New World for the glory of God and country. Mama explained privately that both these ladies were much smarter than the men around them, and if I ever felt that the boys or men in my life were treating me unfairly, to remember who I was named for and that I am just as smart or smarter than they are. I have never forgotten Mama's words about living up to the illustrious names I carry. In my most desperate moments, I have had to resolve time and again to be the smarter, the more cunning, and wilier than the men who have tried to mold my life to their will. Of course, Elizabeth Isabelle is quite a mouthful for a little one, and I had trouble getting all the syllables out clearly. Mama told me that when I started talking, and they were trying to get me to say my name, all I could manage was "Iz Is", so my eight older brothers and sisters began calling me "Izzie". The new name stuck.

The way I got my nickname is not really a memory of mine, but one of my parent's memories passed down to me. My first memory that is all my own is of my sister Polly placing her newborn baby in my lap. I was barely three years old. Mama made me sit on the floor, cross legged, and Polly put a chunky bundle of blankets in my lap, wrapping my arms around them. She pulled back a bit of the top blanket, and there was a round, beet-red, scrunched up baby face, eyes squeezed tightly closed, wisps of damp hair curling every which way on her head. Then she opened up her tiny little mouth and screamed at the top of her lungs. That was my introduction to Molly.

On my first day of school, I wore a blue dress patterned with tiny white flowers and a freshly starched pinafore. That was to be my school dress until I outgrew it, which took some time, because Mama had made it with wide seams and a deep hem, "room to grow". She had to reset the sleeves any number of times, to keep up with my growth spurts, but the dress wore out before I actually outgrew it. I had a simple brown-gray homespun shift for chores at home, and a pink frock fancifully trimmed in brown taffeta and ivory lace for Sundays. The brown taffeta and lace was left over from making Mama's Sunday dress; the pink was leftover from my sister Janie's Sunday dress, so after a fashion, we all matched at church services. Mama's dress rustled with every step she took; the taffeta felt pleasantly crinkly when I pressed my face against her skirt. She always smelled of lilac water on

Sundays, and sometimes in the summer she would let me put a splash on my neck. I never cared much for the Sunday preaching but going to school during the week was a delight.

School was a welcome change from helping Mama with cleaning and cooking, washing and mending. From the time I was able to wield a dust rag, I was put to work doing whatever chores she deemed necessary, sometimes a bit beyond my ability, but never a challenge I could not conquer with a bit of ingenuity and gentle guidance. All the same, I was not fond of housework. It was repetitious and repetition was boring! School gave me the opportunity to do something new each day, even if it was a bit similar to what I had done the day before, and the day before that.

When I came home from school in the afternoons, I practiced being a teacher. Molly was my erstwhile student and she learned to read alongside me. Together we developed a great love of books, even writing little adventures for ourselves and 'publishing' them for distribution among the family. One of the most exciting stories we wrote was about our barn cat, Delilah, and her kittens. Delilah was a calico with hardly any white on her. She regularly produced litters of four or five kittens, and she taught them all in swift order the family business of catching mice. Delilah's kittens were in great demand; all the neighbors clamored for one and everyone said they were the best mousers in the whole state of Alabama, or at least, in Jefferson County. Mama and Papa indulged us in our endeavors, and made sure we had paper and pencils, and even watercolors and brushes for illustrating our little tales. Perhaps that was the first seed of putting pen to paper to make this record of my life.

My school years passed quickly. Molly joined our class in due time, well ahead of others her age in reading and writing. Her sums, however, were not unlike mine. Addition and subtraction were easy enough for us, as long as we had enough fingers and toes, but we were both hopeless when multiplication and division were introduced; fractions and percentages were far beyond our comprehension. History and geography occupied the same category as reading and writing, though, and we fell into a bit of a competition in reciting the states and their capitals, imports and exports, and the order in which they entered the Union. We were both deemed graduated in 1836. I was fifteen, Molly was nearly thirteen. Upon our graduation, I was offered a position teaching the youngest students, which I gladly accepted. Mama and Papa were happy to see me happy, and even more so, to know that I was learning to earn my own keep. Mama still needed my help with the housework, though, so I felt as if I actually had two jobs – only one did not pay! Molly simply went home to help her mother with the new baby, and took over most of the housekeeping duties, as Polly had a difficult pregnancy and childbirth. There had been many babies that had never reached birth between Molly and this new little boy, and the few that did, had not lived more than a few days, sometimes only hours. At least this one seemed to be destined to live.

Mr. George Wood, the schoolmaster, married my sister Janie about the same time I started school. By the time Molly and I graduated, my now-brother-in-law George had moved on from teaching to running a mercantile with my brother Nathaniel, the better to support a growing family. There were four girls in our family – Patsy was the oldest, then Polly, Janie and finally me. Patsy was a full twenty-one years older than I, and Polly twenty years my senior. Janie came closer to my age; she still lived at home when I was young. My brothers were fairly well spread apart in age as well, James being the eldest boy, born right after Polly. Junior was next, two years younger than James. Then, there was Nathaniel, Allen, and Samuel, just five years older than I. George and Janie started having babies before they had been married a full year. By the time we moved to Texas, there were four little ones, and then one more in Texas. A baby seemed to appear every other year, always in the spring.

My brother Isaac – he was Junior, because Papa was Isaac Senior - was the brother who always looked out for me, even though he was much older than I. Mama said it was on account of his being a natural born protector. Junior kept trying to take care of everyone, instead of simply taking care of himself. I wonder, now, if he ever even thought of himself as anything other than an extension of Papa and our brothers. He married Sarah Jane Williams just before we emigrated to Texas. Sarah Jane's brother Owen was married to my sister Polly.

Owen had two brothers who went with us: Elbert and Barakias, the latter called 'Kias' by one and all. Kias was five years older than I, quiet and shy. Most people would consider him tall and thin, rather like a beanpole, but you would be mistaken if you took his thinness for weakness. He had more strength in his arms than any of the men in our family. His hair was light brown and wavy; his eyes were grey-green, always dancing with a sparkle of mischief. His lips were thin, like the rest of him, but a healthy pink, and he kept trying to grow a beard and failing miserably. Whatever facial hair he managed to grow simply looked like the scraggly underbrush we encountered walking in the woods. The best thing about Kias was that he was smart; he could read and recall clearly what and where he had read on any subject, and he could connect one reading to another and draw conclusions that, once stated, were clear, but had not readily apparent to others. He just needed a little encouragement when it came to being ambitious, and I had enough ambition for the two of us. By the time we reached our new settlement, we had an understanding that our future was to be together. Mama and Papa, though, insisted that we wait until I turned eighteen to wed, and so we set our wedding date for the day after my eighteenth birthday, November seventeenth, 1838.

I am not sure what possessed Papa to decide to pull up stakes and move to Texas. He was well past sixty years of age when we set out, and Mama just a bit younger than him. I suspect it may have been Mr. Williamson Hawkins, who was a bit younger than Papa, but still an older gentleman, feeding him stories. Mr. Hawkins' nephew was the great Davy Crockett, who was lost, with so many other brave souls, at the battle of the Alamo. Mr. Hawkins kept telling Papa what a wonderful place Texas must be, for his nephew to find it worth fighting for, and dying for. He regaled Papa with letters describing the wonders of abundance, that a man had no need to work in Texas, that all that manner of sustenance would be just outside his doorstep, ready for the taking. And the Republic of Texas was giving out free land to anyone who would come and settle. At least one of Mr. Hawkins' sons had already set out to seek a fortune in Texas, although it was widely speculated that not much would come of that, for a couple of his boys already had a certain type of reputation. One rumor was one or another had fallen in with a bunch of wild Indians and taken up their heathen ways; another suggested a not-so-prodigal son was riding with Mexican outlaws. But that was just gossip.

Papa was intrigued with the tales. With such riches to be had for the taking, we packed up trunks and the boys loaded them into wagons. We sold off or gave away most of our livestock, except for our horses. There would be plenty more livestock in Texas, as well as anything else we might have need of, according to Papa. Of course, Papa had to have Jack, his little fice dog come with us. Jack had a soft, smooth white coat of short hair, with brown markings around his eyes and on his forehead, and he was just as good a mouser as the barn cat Delilah had been, plus he was an excellent squirrel hunter. Papa would have been loathe to part with him. Mama and I were not as certain as Papa was that Texas would be the land of milk and honey that folks were making it out to be, but we would not – or could not – sway him to stay in Alabama, so off we went, Mama, Papa, Nathaniel and his wife Orleana, Samuel and Narcissa, Allen and Bessie with their three little ones, Junior and Sarah Jane, Janie and George and their four children, Polly and Owen with Molly, John and James, and Owen's brothers Elbert and Kias, and me.

The most expedient route was south to the gulf coast, where we loaded our horses, wagons, and household goods onto a schooner, along with ourselves, having found one sailing from Mobile to Galveston. From Galveston, we traveled again by wagon north to Nacogdoches, which seemed to be the very center of Texas civilization.

2

Nacogdoches was a pretty little town, with gracious homes and bustling businesses. There were a number of "Indian mounds" in the area; no one knew who built them or what their purpose was, other than to remind us that like those who came before, our time on earth is fleeting. An immense two story building of stone with a second floor veranda running its length served as the courthouse, and this is where George and Allen concluded the transaction with Reverend Bacon to purchase land to the north on the twenty-third day of May in 1837.

While the men were busy with 'men's business', the 'girls' tending to the little ones, and Mama and Narcissus calling on some of the well-connected ladies in town, Molly and I browsed the Roberts, Allen and Company mercantile, purchasing some sewing notions and writing papers. Leaving the shop, we made a pretty pair, if I do say so myself. Blonde-haired and blue-eyed Molly was wearing a dark blue day dress with pale blue flowers embroidered at the neckline and sleeves; I had chosen a deep emerald green frock with a white fichu, the edges embellished with entwined pink and yellow roses, which set off my chestnut hair and green eyes to a great advantage. A gangly young man, no more than twenty years of age, with a wide forehead and sharply pointed chin, with curly brown hair and deep set eyes, handsome in a foppish fashion, exited the stone house at about the same time, and in that moment, our gazes met. The young gentleman's eyes seemed to bulge, and his pale complexion became even paler. Looking straight at me, he called out "Nelly!" The fear in his voice was palpable. I was taken aback. Surely he had mistaken me for another. But what woman would frighten him so? For he turned quickly, and nearly lost his balance completely, and strode away at such a brisk pace that it could almost have been called a run.

I remarked to Papa about the queer young man and his odd reaction to me. Papa shrugged it off, saying perhaps I simply reminded him of someone he would rather forget, probably someone far away - maybe a sister he left behind, or a love affair that ended badly. He allowed my description of him sounded familiar. He had met so many people over the past few days, and he thought he recalled being introduced to a young clerk named Richard at the courthouse that could be the young man. I made little note of it, and thought no more on the fellow, for I had no interest in pursuing any young men. Kias and I were engaged and he was the only young man I wanted.

Three days later, our wagons were loaded, the horses harnessed, and our new livestock was ready to be driven to the parcel of land over which George and Allen waxed poetic. They had ridden there with a local fellow, a Mr.

Norris, and saw for themselves the wide spring fed creek, the ample selection of timber for building cabins, and the tall sugar cane that grew wild. They glimpsed the abundant wildlife for hunting and the open land suitable for planting and pasturing livestock, all nestled into rolling hills where a welcome breeze seemed to flow continuously. Mama and I were still doubtful about the abundant wonders, but Nacogdoches had done much to convince us there was at least a bastion of civilization to which we might return should the unsettled wilderness prove unconquerable.

Our first stop was grandly named "Fort Lacey". In truth, it was a small stockade surrounding a cabin and a handful of outbuildings. The Indian Agent, Martin Lacey, offered us a share of what creature comforts he had in stock. We dined on corn mush with a bit of salt pork in each bowl, and a gentleman sharing the hospitality of the Lacey's with us produced a fiddle after dinner, supplying some merry tunes before we bid goodnight to one and all.

We journeyed northward, reaching an Indian village the afternoon of the first day. Truly, there was little to distinguish it from the rougher settlements of white men. A few wood huts, some tents, open fires with cook pots hanging above, children tussling about, women working, men sitting and smoking while they talked. The women's dress was about the same as any ordinary farm woman, but the men were arrayed in fantastic combinations of deerskin breeches, fancy dress vests with bright embroidery, silk cravats – sometimes worn two or three together - and elaborately trimmed beaver hats, often adorned with feathers. We were welcomed warmly, and introduced to Little Bean, the head man of the community. We saw some Negroes mingling in the camp, and I could not be certain if they were in servitude to the Indians, or if they lived among them as equals. One or two acted as translators from time to time over the course of the evening. A mulatto woman had been assigned to assist the women in our group, and a dark skinned man was never far from our menfolk. Apparently, this was to facilitate to our comfort, but it made me a bit uncomfortable. I was quite glad to be on our way again in the morning, although I must confess, I looked behind us for several miles, wondering if we were being followed and might be ambushed.

The second night found us in a rough camp beneath some sweet gum trees. The trace we followed meandered close to the stream that supplied water to the Indian village, and for the most part, was on even ground. George and Allen cautioned us that the next day's journey would be the most difficult, because we would be going mostly uphill. The gently rolling hills were not gentle when riding in a heavily loaded wagon! Mama decided she would walk as much as she could the next day, saying it would be easier on her back. She rarely complained, but when she did, it was the small of her back that ached the worst, followed in short order by her upper back. The only thing that seemed to bring her any relief was to lie completely flat without any cushion beneath her. I could not see how that helped; it seemed to me that it would only make things worse, but she swore by it.

George and Allen were quite right. The next day was difficult. More than once, I feared the wagons might get stuck, or tilt off kilter, but Providence provided and we arrived at the top of a grass knoll, surrounded by trees of pine, pin oak, sweet gum, and black walnut. The sky was bluer than I had ever seen it before, with dainty clouds making lace patterns over our heads. Papa insisted that we kneel and give thanks, and ask for blessings upon this land and our endeavors to make it fruitful for the glory of the Almighty. Looking back, I do not believe the Almighty was paying much attention to us that day.

3

We camped for the first few days, living out of wagons and tents. The novelty of camping quickly wore thin; Polly and Mama were sharp with each other, Narcissus did her best to boss everyone, Bessie did her best to boss Narcissus, Orleana and Janie tended to the children, and Sarah Jane, Molly and I just tried to stay out of everyone's way. The men set about exploring the acreage, deciding on building sites, studying the soil to see where crops would be best suited, and figuring where livestock could be pastured. Before the second week had passed, a work crew arrived to assist in building our first cabins.

The crew consisted of a foreman and a dozen strong men. Some were slaves owned by Mr. Lacey, including Cage, who was the foreman. The others were owned by Mr. Goyens, a free colored man who owned a large sawmill in Nacogdoches. Cage was a likable fellow, and the workers heeded his instructions without hesitation. They did, however, give him a bit of ribbing, which he took with an easy grace. "Hey, Cage" one hollered, "I think they's an Injun ova yonder! Better git yore rifle!" All the crew began to laugh. Papa and Samuel looked around, not knowing if they should be alarmed.

Cage laughed himself, then caught Papa's eye. "Ain't nuttin' to worry ova, Mist' Killough," he said. "Dem boys jus' havin' fun wid me." He shuffled his feet, abashed. "T'other day, I kilt a deer. I wuz bringin' it back to the fort, when I spied an Injun. Skeered me so, I dropt the deer off mah horse. Thought fer sho I'd shot at the Injun, an den dropt my gun. but when Mist' Martin went out, he done fine my rifle still loaded, but de deer done gone. Dey be joshin' me bout dat evah since."

With the Indian question settled, the work crew, along with our men, felled trees, stripped and notched the logs. Within a space of about three days, we had serviceable living quarters for everyone. Each cabin was pretty much the same as the next – a simple square or rectangular building set about a foot or more off the ground, with a mud and stick fireplace lined with iron ore rocks from the creek at one end of the cabin, and a window opposite. A short covered porch ran the length of the front, with a door either within a few steps of the fireplace or else centered along the length. Mama and Papa's cabin had extra windows, for cross-ventilation, and the loft spanned three quarters of the space overhead. Mama wanted stairs for getting up to the loft, but Papa convinced her that a ladder would do for now, and leave her more space in the cabin.

Space in the cabin was rather limited. Mama and Papa had a rope bed in one corner; I slept in the loft on a feather mattress. Papa promised me a bedstead when winter came. We had two large trunks – one was in the loft, the other was by Mama and Papa's bed – that held an assortment of necessary items and beloved treasures.

Mine contained a number of books given to me by my cousin Abner at the outset of our journey, a few trinkets from childhood, an extra quilt for winter, and a stash of fabric and trimmings for when I would need a new frock or two. The reminder of the cabin furnishings consisted of a rough bench and rocking chair by the fireplace and some shelves on one wall. Mama's spinning wheel and loom took up one side of the room. A small table, set near the bed, held an ewer and a wash basin. A looking glass hanging above provided a spot for Mama and I to tend to our hair and as we endeavored to remain as ladylike and neat as possible in the wilderness.

Polly and Owen were the first to expand their cabin, the one to the furtherest west of our settlement, since they had to accommodate Molly and the two boys, plus Elbert and Kias. The men built a second pen, connecting the two roofs, leaving a breezeway betwixt the cabins. Elbert and Kias took possession of the second pen, leaving the first for Polly and Owen, and the loft for Molly and the boys. I know Molly was dissatisfied with that arrangement, but she would never voice her displeasure to her parents. Molly despaired of ever being able to have her own home; she feared she would never find a suitable suitor living as far away from others as we did. She felt duty bound to be meek and subservient with her parents, for she would be living with them for a very long time. She accepted her role with more grace than I could have mustered, but as my wedding plans progressed, she became melancholy.

I tried to cheer her up, suggesting that after Kias and I married, young Elbert might well decide to swap spaces with her, leaving the new addition as her private retreat. The idea was met with a bittersweet smile. As much as that thought cheered her, she considered that living further apart from her family would only encourage her to treat her even more as a servant and less as a daughter and sister. Thinking quickly, I suggested that once Kias and I were married, she could make her home with us. She clapped her hands and laughed. "What fun that could be!" she exclaimed "But do you think Mother and Father would allow me? Who would take care of the boys and tend to the housekeeping?" She sighed, quietly resigning herself to what she had often confided she felt was God's will for her life: to always be the caretaker, never the cared for. I wondered if there would ever be anything – or anyone – who could dissuade her from that conviction.

Nathaniel and Orleana selected a building site tucked into a hillside, several steep yards up from the creek, to the southwest on the opposite side of the creek from all the other homesteads. The choice sharply underscored the sentiment that Nathaniel was 'set apart' from the rest of the family, a feeling held by both Nathaniel and the others in our little community. I felt sorry for Orleana; I never was convinced Nathaniel had made a love match, but rather had found a woman willing to overlook his faults in exchange for the security of marriage. Orleana had a romantic streak in her; her first action when their cabin was finished was to dig up and transplant a cedar seedling to stand guard near her front door, telling me that the evergreen represented the undying love she and Nathaniel shared. I did my utmost to not let on that I felt her love was not reciprocated, but the sadness in her eyes told me she already suspected as much. She simply hoped that someday, something might change and his heart would match hers, beat for beat.

Junior and Sarah Jane, Allen and Bessie, Samuel and Narcissa, George and Janie – each couple had a cabin in turn, scattered between Mama and Papa's and Polly and Owen's. Once everyone was housed, efforts turned toward plowing and planting. George and Allen had brought plenty of cotton seed, seed corn and sweet potatoes in their wagons; the cotton seed was the first to go into the ground, then corn, and finally, sweet potatoes. Corn would be a reliable cash crop, they reckoned, and cotton, even if it never produced enough to take to market, could at least be carded and spun at home. Sweet potatoes would provide sustenance should our family gardens fall short in production of other vegetables, and would be a welcome addition to the incessant Texican diet of corn, corn, and more corn.

Molly and I tended to the chickens, fed the hogs, milked the cows every day, and brought up fresh buckets of water from the spring. When our morning chores were done, we joined Mama over the cook-fire to help with preparing the noon meal, usually a stew made from whatever the men had hunted most recently. Dinner at noon was a communal event. Papa and Samuel made two long tables with benches on either side, and it accommodated us all. I cannot recall the food not ever being less than plentiful, or as bland as we had encountered at the Lacey's, so overall, we were doing well as settlers.

Thus was the foundation of our days at Killough Settlement.

4

The spring and summer of 1837 passed quickly, as we stayed busy with building, planting, and, as crops started to come in, harvesting and putting up excess against the coming winter. We had no idea what sort of weather to expect in the coming months, and when we asked those who had been there longer than ourselves, we were told "Welcome to Texas. You just never know what kind of weather you are going to get." So, we prepared for the worst and hoped for the best. In May, Orleana confided to Mama that she was in the family way. Orleana was thrilled; Mama was happy for her, but quietly told me she hoped this would change Nathaniel's attitude toward his wife. He worked at presenting himself as a good husband, but it rang hollow in his words and actions. He was condescending to her at every turn, finding fault where there was none, belittling her every step, even when she was following his directions with exacting preciseness. If any woman ever walked on eggshells for a husband, it was Orleana. The babe, named Eliza Jane, made her appearance on November seventh. Nathaniel gave the infant a withering glance, shook his head, and walked out of the cabin. He had wanted a son.

Nathaniel and Orleana were not alone in procreating. Junior's wife Narcissa had given birth in September, a chubby tow-headed boy named Billie. Bessie, Allen's wife, had birthed another boy to match their two- and five-year-old sons in mid-January. George and Janie were expecting another baby as well; she figured it would arrive around Easter or thereabouts. She was close; the fifth of the Woods' children, the third boy, was born in March 1838, a month before Easter. George was delighted, but it would not have mattered a whit to him if it had been another girl. "The more, the merrier" he proclaimed, and kissed Janie's perspiring forehead. Having three new nephews did not do much for Nathaniel's demeanor.

In between the arrival of babies, word reached our little colony on Christmas Eve that Congress had officially declared the Houston-Forbes treaty with the Cherokees null and void. As of the sixteenth of December, 1837, we had full legal rights to our property. Papa was delighted, and declared that henceforth, we will remember Christmas Eve as the day we truly became settlers on this land. What a wonderful Christmas gift for us all! It was just like back home in Alabama, in January 1834, when we received the news that we could legitimately settle on the land in Indian territory that Mama and Papa had owned for over a decade. We had quite the celebration then, and now again, although Papa gravely cautioned us to ensure that should we ever be asked about our settlement, we should always reply that we "arrived" on December twenty-fourth, 1837. He worried that our claim to ownership might be challenged if it was widely known that the land had been part of the treaty territory. Accordingly, the births of babies which had arrived between spring and winter were entered into the family Bible as having been born back in Alabama, as 'proof' of our official residence. I thought it all rather absurd, but since it did not have any bearing on the plans Kias and I had for the future, I did not bother considering the matter any further.

As the mild winter progressed into planting season, Papa laid out grand plans for more crops and expanded pastures. By then, our two milk cows had become ten, and we had a bull and eight calves, in addition to mules and horses. Papa decided to plant more corn, squash, peas, and beans, and he planned to cut some of the sugar cane in the fall, pressing it for syrup. There were some maple trees to tap as well and Bowl, the local Cherokee chief, had gifted us a half dozen peach tree saplings not long after the cabins had been built. Papa looked forward to creating a garden paradise, just as Mama looked forward to getting as many of the comforts of civilization as possible. She had talked him into getting a cast iron stove for cooking on, setting up a cane press, digging a root cellar, and building a spring house and a smoke house. Ostensibly, all those things were for the use of everyone in the family, but in truth, it was mostly for Mama.

I was happy for Mama as she bustled about, creating the best home for Papa possible in the confines of our wide open swath of countryside, but I knew I could never be happy living within a stone's throw of every single one of my relatives for the rest of my life (except Molly, of course!). I began to plant some seeds of my own, as Kias and I talked about our future together.

The infrequent forays into Nacogdoches had stirred a

desire in me to have a life away from plows and fetching water from the spring every morning. The homes of the Sterne's and others, nice clapboard affairs without mud chinking logs or insects crawling out of the bare bark, with a handy well in the yard and a cook in the kitchen – therein lay my inspiration. I appealed to Kias' intellectual side, flattering him with my estimation of his talents and abilities, then subtly guiding him to a vision of our future home, surrounded by our precocious children, providing them with comfort and a good education instead of toiling in fields and mucking cow sheds. The examples of his brother Owen's work-induced 'rheumatism' and the discontent of Janie's husband George at becoming a farmer after having been a schoolmaster and running a successful mercantile business served as cautionary tales about a farmer's life; the early gray hairs and lines on Bessie and Narcissus' faces were equally potent. He felt he could not bear to see my youthful bloom decay under the burden of being a farm wife, and agreed that city life would be better all the way around for us. He declared that after the fall harvest, he would take his share of the crop money, making us a nest egg for marriage and independent living. I was quite content with having led him to that decision.

5

I think July and August are probably the worst months in Texas. It is hot and humid and just downright miserable, and I think all that misery just makes people act ugly. At least, it did in 1838.

We had been going along nicely all year, the planting was done, the crops were coming in abundantly. There had been just enough rain and the right amount of sunshine for everything to grow and produce aplenty. The Cherokees around us, Bowl to the north and Big Mush to the south, were friendly and did not seem overly concerned about the situation with the nullified treaty. I did not pay a lot of attention, but I overheard enough to get the impression that most of the Indians intended to continue living as they always had, where they always had. They would defend their homes, of course, if need be, but the wisdom of the elders was to avoid aggression. The Mexicans, however, were another story.

News was a rarity in our little outpost; we relied on other settlers passing through to share what they had seen and heard in their travels, and to occasionally pass along a newspaper. The Telegraph and Texas Register was a reliable source, when a copy could be obtained, and anything heard at Frost and Thorn's store in Nacogdoches was equally reliable, by county standards. Through these channels, we heard about Vincente Cordova's attempt at insurrection against the Republic.

Cordova was quite a prominent figure in Nacogdoches. A proud Mexican, he was loyal to the Constitution of 1824 and sought to restore Texas to Mexico. He had a fair number of followers, including Mexicans and Indians, and Negroes, the latter of which were mostly runaway slaves from the United States who had fled to Texas when it was under Mexican rule in order to live as free men. Cordova had sought to ally with the Indian nations, promising them legal title to their lands. Bowl and others had been courted by such enticements before, and experience had shown them that such offers were nothing more than insubstantial dreams. The only Indians who chose to ally themselves were those who were young and trusting, or who simply hungered for war. Between these groups, we heard that between one to four hundred men had been swayed to affiliate themselves under his leadership. In July, they started planning a rebellion; in August, they took action.

The uprising was short lived, but we did not know it at the time. Cordova was reported to be advancing toward Chief Bowl's village just a short distance from our settlement, which was worrisome. While Papa trusted the chief and many in the village, there were some who had shown by word and deed that they were aggrieved by our presence, and would have us removed. After some discussion, we decided as a family to temporarily take

leave of our homes in late July and repair to Nacogdoches
until the situation settled.

To keep ourselves occupied, Mama and I took
advantage of being in town and bought a supply of dress
goods. Together, we began sewing a trousseau for me.
Molly, my sisters, and sisters-in-law joined in
enthusiastically. I selected a grey wool for winter; we
fashioned a skirt and two bodices, one trimmed in
aubergine velvet, another plainer but with pin tucks and
cording to provide some embellishment. A lightweight
lawn, white with tiny pale pink flowers, again, a skirt
with two bodices, was quickly stitched up for the warmer
months. I insisted on cutting one bodice to be used for
evening wear, with a berthe for balls and a ficu for
afternoon wear, should I need a good dress to call on
ladies or receive them, and the other for Sunday
meetings, with detachable sleeves and a matching
pelerine. Two simple day dresses, a practical apron with
pockets, a new chemise and two petticoats finished my
trousseau. The scraps we set aside for piecing a quilt.

While we were busy sewing, the men worked at
engineering a plan to get us back home. With the
assistance of Mr. Goyens, acting as both a negotiator and
interpreter, George and Allen reached an accord with the
Indians. The agreement promised safe passage and peace
in which to reap the harvest of the land "until the first
white frost." When that would be, and what came after
that would be anyone's guess, but the men assured us
God was guiding the affairs of mankind, and that He
would see that we prevailed over the red heathens. For
my part, I wondered why God had ever created Indians, if
He was so determined that we should be annihilating
them at every turn, but I dared not voice that question.

6

The men had kept the wagons and carriage at the ready, so little time was wasted in preparing for the trip to our small settlement. Kias and I made arrangements for our upcoming nuptials. We would be wed at the home of Mr. Sterne the morning of Saturday, the seventeenth of November. From there, we would depart to a boarding house, where we had made arrangements for our living quarters. Kias had secured the promise of employment with Mr. Edwards, and I was offered a teaching position at a small, private female academy. We were both delighted with our prospects; the only thing that dimmed my joy was the lurking shadow of Richard Parmalee, Clerk of the Court.

After our first encounter, where Parmalee accosted me as "Nelly", I found every time we were in town, he was nearby. He never ventured so close as to be threatening, but close enough to be intimidating and cause me great discomfort by staring at me. His eyes bored into my silhouette; he seemed to be at every turn.

He never spoke, and rarely bowed. He simply stared. For the life of me, I could not fathom his actions. Kias assured me there was naught for concern; as my husband, he would deal with Mr. Parmalee, if necessary, when we became Nacogdochians.

Once we returned to the cabins mid-September, the men began harvesting what they could of the crops, and Mama and I started planning my wedding in earnest. I decided to wear my new grey wool with the velvet trim for our wedding, if the weather was turned cold. Mama offered to loan me her earrings and brooch, all that remained of her mother's demi-parure of amethyst set in gold. Molly busied herself crafting a bridal bouquet of paper flowers, delicate forget-me-nots with just a tint of indigo. My sisters and sisters-in-law each brought a gift from their own household goods for starting our new city life and to remember them by when we were apart. Their generosity and thoughtfulness knew no bounds, although I knew not when I would have a home of my own in which to use crockery and kettles.

I spent my afternoons on the porch of our cabin, piecing blocks for a memory quilt. Mama had given me a bag of remnants to add to those from my trousseau, and Polly and Sarah Jane had offered up bits from their scrap bags as well. I smiled as I worked, thinking of the pleasures Kias and I would have recalling the origin of this square or that, as the years passed. Most evenings, Kias would come and sit with me as I finished a block, and we dreamed aloud our hopes for the future. He was eager to begin working for Mr. Edwards, and hoped to follow his lead in the business and social world. He wanted very much to become a Mason, like so many of the important men in Texas.

The evening of October third, the family gathered at

George and Janie's place, the full moon almost bright as daylight. To a person, we were in good spirits; all the cotton had been picked, the squash and pumpkins which had avoided the foraging wildlife were harvested, almost all the corn was in, and we had friendly relations with the neighboring Cherokees, in particular, Sleeping Bear and his mestizo wife, Sophronia, who lived a short distance to the southwest from Nathaniel's home. That selfsame couple joined us in our meal that night; we feasted on the fruits of our labors and roasted venison, as Elbert had taken down a buck deer the previous day.

Sleeping Bear spoke seriously of troubling news, however. Sam Benge's village had been visited by members of the Cordova gang, mostly Kickapoo, Shawnee and Biloxi Indians along with a few Negroes, all of whom had managed to avoid arrest unlike their Mexican leaders. These malcontents were not so motivated by allegiance to Mexico as they were dedicated to causing mayhem among the increasingly American born Texian population such as ourselves. Chief Benge had listened to their complaints and plans for conquest, and, in the fashion of other Cherokee chiefs, declined to ally himself with one side or the other. Papa, George and Allen pressed the question of our security; Sleeping Bear allowed he was uncertain; he felt these "young troublemakers" were more inclined to drink and talk rather than take action, but under the right circumstances, they could turn ruthlessly violent. In his opinion, they did not have a strong leader among them, only followers with no one to follow, now that neither Cordova nor his lieutenants were guiding them. Nathaniel offered nothing to the conversation, which was unusual for him. I observed as his eyes studied first one man, then another, and another, until it seemed he had taken a full measure of each and every male in attendance. Yet he declined to speak.

George reiterated to the assemblage our intention to observe the agreement to remove ourselves at the first frost, which would probably be in about a month, perhaps a bit more. Kias took my hand at this and squeezed it gently, with a little smile. The first frost for this year, then the first Texas wedding for our family! "After our lovely little bride and her handsome groom are settled, I propose we each consider our futures carefully. This land of ours is a foretaste of Heaven; it has proven fertile and abundant. Personally, I do not foresee difficulty from this so-called rebellion, and I would suggest we plan to continue with our colony in the spring. However, there is wisdom in remaining away during the winter months; Allen, Elbert, Nathaniel and I can always ride out here from time to time, to ensure the sanctity of our homes, that they remain unmolested until our ultimate return. Then we shall establish, permanently, a settlement to grow into a fine community and even, with God's blessing, a thriving town." George's words resonated with wisdom, prudence, and optimism. I almost regretted our decision to make our lives away from this place, but not so much as to have a change of heart.

7

Friday, October fifth, 1838 was the end of our world. Just after clearing the tables from our noon meal, it happened. In so many ways, this was the last day of my life. Every day thereafter was spent in purgatory, awaiting my final disposition.

I was in the cabin I shared with my parents, packing a trunk for our trip to Nacogdoches. This trip was to be our last for quite a while. I would marry Barakias Williams next month; Father had arranged for Adolphus Sterne and his wife Eva to host our wedding in their home. In addition to my generous trousseau, there was a particularly lovely gown of pink, set aside before we ever left Alabama, trimmed with embroidered roses and twining vines in three shades of green, with cream lace work at the bodice and cuffs. I was so eager to wear that dress as my second day dress, the first dress I would wear as Mrs. Barakias Williams.

The memory quilt was finished with piecing just the day before, and we planned to baste together the top with batting and backing this afternoon. I was lost in thought, staring out the window of the cabin. I remember twisting a loose lock of hair back into place and securing it with a carved whalebone hairpin. I remember thinking about Papa's insistence that 'the Indian question' would soon be settled in the favor of 'good Christian men' and the future held naught save the promise of the rewards of perseverance and the sweat of our brow. In my seventeen years, I had never doubted the words of my father. Yet there was a certain stillness in the woods beyond the clearing that gave me pause. I inched my head slowly through the window, the better to hear the eerie silence.

To this day, I am not certain what came over me. For no reason, I felt as though was in a dream. I felt as if I was floating on air, between two worlds, and I had no control over where I was going or what was happening. I only knew in that moment my life was changing drastically. I heard the crack of a rifle shot, and I snapped out of the dream, scurrying backwards in alarm. Whatever was happening outside was clearly not an accident.

Time was of the essence. Only a few items of any true value were in the cabin. I moved into action, securing what I could. Already the war whoops of rampaging savages were growing near and the gunshots rang out ferociously. A Bowie knife had been left on the rough hewn bench; I grasped the hilt and resolved to use it as necessary, when necessary. I spied the amethyst earrings and brooch I intended to wear on my wedding day. Snatching up the jewelry, I pulled a loose stone from the hearth, shoving the pieces into the space beneath. Quickly, I dropped the hearth stone into place and bolted from the cabin.

The rifle shots and war whoops grew closer. I

gathered up my skirts, still clutching the knife, and ran out the door, calling to my brother Allen and sister-in-law Bessie. She had her youngest in her arms and the two older boys, James and Samuel, trailing close behind her. We had long ago decided as a family that the best course of action, should we be attacked, was to run and hide rather than stand and fight, for we numbered far more women and children than men. Allen and Bessie were headed for the canebrake, a veritable forest of wild sugar cane growing deep along the creek, more than twice as tall as the average man and thick as two day old corn mush. If we could get into the heart of the canebrake and stay quiet, we would have a good chance of waiting out the raid, escaping the Indians and avoid being scalped.

Running towards us were Polly and Molly. Molly made the fateful decision to go with me and Bessie, to help with the children, leaving Polly to continue toward her cabin, her boys, her husband, and horses. Polly had never been one to go along with the family plan.

Crashing into the canebrake, our little group slowed at a spot deep in the growth where we could huddle together. Janie and George were already there with their children.

"Should we pray?" asked little James, who had been taught from the cradle to seek the guidance of a Heavenly Father.

"Yes, dear," whispered his mother, "but not out loud. This time, we must pray quietly, just words inside our hearts and minds."

James squeezed his eyes shut, his lips moving but without a sound. Molly and I held hands tightly; Bessie, holding her toddler daughter in one arm, gathered her sons close to her side. The sun, almost directly overhead, seemed to stop moving across the sky, and the longest hour began to creep in slow shadows among the cane stalks.

More rifle shots, war whoops, screams – every time the cane rustled, we trembled. Horses whinnied, some near, some far. Concealed in the canebrake, our little group was blind to what was happening in the clearing, in the fields, in our cabins. We could only imagine horrors, listening to the terrifying sounds, fearing the worst, hoping to simply survive.

As mounted men rode through our little settlement, hunting down our family, my brother-in-law George – foolish man! - left his wife and children and the safety of the canebrake to dash home; I saw him slain just a few feet from door to the root cellar by his cabin.

After awhile, an uneasy peace descended. I whispered to the others to stay and remain quiet. Creeping to the edge of the canebrake, senses acutely attuned to the least movement or sound, I peeked through the curtain of vegetation. Mama, Narcissa, and Sarah Jane came into view, with my darling Kias holding baby Billie. For a moment, all seemed to be well, then in the distance, another chilling war cry rang clear. I watched in horror, petrified, as Kias handed the wiggling one-year-old to Narcissa and took off running. Within moments, Indians on horseback swept past the women and were upon him, and he fell, without making a sound. All I could hear were their rifles. It was all I could do to fight off a rising nausea, willing myself not to cry out and give away my hiding place.

I witnessed the murder of my own husband-to-be, and the wretched villains may as well have murdered me.

8

I almost cried out in terror as the tall stalks behind me brushed against one another. "Izzie –" came an urgent whisper. Molly reached for my hand. "What has happened? Can you see any....Oh, Dear!" Her grip tightened on my hand as we watched three raiders approach Mama and the others who remained standing near a grove of oaks. There was a brief exchange of words, none of which we could hear clearly, but the tones reverberated with anger from both sides. The Indians turned and galloped away, and Mama spat in their direction.

As soon as the warriors were out of range, the ladies gathered up their long skirts, Narcissa shifted the child on her hip and they hurried away into the woods with Jack, the fice dog that was Papa's pet, running after them.

"What should we do?" Molly whispered.

"We must go back to the others."

Backtracking through the tall cane, we could not discern if we had lost our way or if Janie, Allen, Bessie and the children had simply disappeared, either taking off on their own, or meeting up with other family members, or worst of all, captured by the foe. Regardless, they were nowhere to be found, and neither of us had the courage to call out to them.

Dejected, we sat down in the midst of the tall stalks and simply stared at one another. Silence blanketed the landscape; not even a bird dared voice a note. Soon, the sounds of savage rejoicing filled the air, and a thick dark cloud of the blackest smoke I have ever seen wafted overhead. "They must be burning the cabins," Molly whispered.

I nodded. "And looting." I thought of the hidden brooch and earrings. Beneath the hearthstone they should be safe. I was surprised to find I still grasped the Bowie knife tightly in my hand; my knuckles were white and I could hardly feel the hilt nestled in my palm. "Do you remember how Papa said the wood for the cabins was too green when we built? They probably will not be a complete loss. After sunset, we can go back and find what is left."

"Do you really want to?"

"What other choice do we have? If anyone else has survived, they will come back too, I am sure of it. Besides, there will be food there." Hunger was distant from our minds, but we both knew we would need to eat before much longer. Already, it seemed like months had passed, instead of hours, since the family had sat around the dinner table, anticipating a return trip to Nacogdoches in the coming week and my wedding party. I shook my head violently, trying to get the thought to fall into place that Kias and I would never be married, that I was a widow before ever becoming a wife.

"What if the Indians come back?"

"They have done all the damage they can do already. There's no reason for them to return."

After waiting for what seemed like an eternity, the sun finally began to move across the sky to the west and the black smoke to dissipate. Thirst made us brave enough to inch through the canebrake toward the crystal clear creek. At the edge of the cane, we looked carefully in all directions, even spying into the treetops for traces of friends and foes. A bushy tailed squirrel darted toward a sweet gum tree, pausing for a moment to look at them querulously, then scampered up the trunk to a far away limb.

I nudged Molly. "You go first. I will keep watch." I held the knife as firmly as ever, to calm my nerves and show Molly that she would be protected. Molly nodded, fear in her eyes. "Keep low to the ground," I added, frightened they would be discovered by a savage.

Molly propelled herself on hands and knees to the stream bed, head up, alert for any sign of human life. She barely bothered to rinse the dirt from her hands before cupping them and drinking. At her third scoop of water, she turned her head to the left and clapped her hands over her mouth, stifling a scream. I followed her sudden movement with my eyes and regretted it immediately. A half dozen yards downstream lay Junior, still and white, flies buzzing about his open eyes and the bullet holes that had drained the life blood from his body.

Heedless of danger, Molly stood and ran back to the canebrake, and we plunged into the thickness of its protection once again.

Finally, the sun set. I gently extracted Molly from the

frenzied embrace we had locked into as she burst into the cane upon retreating from the creek-bed. "We need to go," I whispered firmly. An owl hooted in a nearby tree. Frogs croaked and splashed in the creek. A cricket chirruped. Nature was resuming its rhythm.

9

As much as we would prefer not to, there just was not any other choice. Molly and I went straight to my parent's house. The brigands had set it afire, but the flames had not taken hold. In the dim light, we could see where the feather beds had been hauled into the yard and shredded; feathers and down covered the ground like new fallen snow. A pile of quilts lay in the front yard; a brief, sickening inspection revealed they covered Papa's body. Unsettled, we considered walking to the next house, but the unknown things in the distance and darkness dissuaded us. Inching into the cabin, we could see little. We felt around, trying to identify shadowy overturned furnishings and household goods by touch, seeking any food that might have been overlooked by the looters, and praying we would not find any other bodies.

I climbed the ladder into the loft and discovered three quilts tossed against the wall. I spread them out at the far end of the loft and softly called for Molly to join me. If nothing else, we could be warm and sleep through the night, and perhaps, when morning came, the light would help us find provisions and maybe a horse would return to seek fodder. Maybe, in the morning, we could begin the long trek to either Fort Lacey or Nacogdoches. Maybe, in the morning, this would have all been a bad dream. I thought we might should pull the ladder up into the loft for safety, but I was too tired to be bothered.

I awoke to the sound of a horse snuffling about outside the cabin door. At first, I could not figure out why I was next to Molly on a simple pallet of quilts in the loft instead of in my own soft bed, and then suddenly I recalled the terrors of the previous day. I wished with all my might that it had been a bad dream, but the reality of the hard floor of the loft beneath the quilts told me otherwise.

The horse whinnied and my heart leapt with joy. A four footed form of salvation!

A white man's voice, muffled by the log walls, came to my ears. At first, I thought it might be one of my brothers, and I sat up, preparing to call out a happy greeting. Before I could muster any cheer, another voice floated through the air, distinctly foreign in tone. I shrank back into the quilts in fear. Placing a hand over Molly's mouth too keep her from shrieking in alarm, I gently woke her. Through signs, I conveyed that she must be quiet. Together, we pressed their ears against small cracks between the chinked logs to better hear the conversation.

A mixture of English, Spanish, and Indian words peppered the exchange. Something in the white man's voice caught my attention. My eyes grew wide as I drew her finger to my to my lips to shush Molly's whispered inquiry. Turning my head, I peeped out the same crack where I had laid my ear. My nose flattened against the rough logs, obstructing my breathing as I struggled to view the men in the yard. A Mexican I did not recognize, an Indian I did – Tail, a Cherokee with a nasty reputation. A white man. Catching my breath, I froze in place, recognition confirmed, and sat back heavily on the quilts.

In the dim light, Molly realized by the look on my face that there was something terribly amiss. She took my hands in her own – they were ice cold - and held them to her warm cheeks. "Who?" she silently mouthed. I withdrew my hands. Clasping Molly's palm, I traced the letters H-A-W-K-I-N-S.

Molly puzzled over the letters until the epiphany broke through, flooding her brain. "Hawkins?" Her lips framed the words without sound.

I nodded solemnly. We looked at each other with more despair than when the Indians were attacking. Hawkins was a name we had long hoped to never hear again, and a man they would prefer the devil himself to seeing in person.

There was a long history between me and Buck Hawkins, none of it pleasant. His father was a wealthy man with large holdings of land, and wealth to keep it prosperous. Buck demonstrated an inflated sense of privilege and exercised it accordingly – especially where attractive young girls were concerned. His father was not amused, and tired of his son's antics. Rumor had it – and rumor in this case was probably right – that their pa had sent his boy off to Texas to seek his own fortune rather than laying in wait for an inheritance. My guess is the wilds of open country had only turned him further from ambition and industry to laziness and greed. There was plenty of fertile ground in the gang surrounding Vincente Cordova, specializing in kindling the emotions of the

Indians and defying local authorities where Indian and Mexican nationalist relations were concerned. Not to mention, Hawkins had a taste for whiskey and cards, and he excelled at neither. The whiskey went to his head and the cards robbed him of cash and anything else he was able to claim as his own - and sometimes things that owned by others. All in all, he never was going to claim a place as his father's favorite son.

As for the history between Buck and myself, it goes back to a winter evening in Alabama, when George and Nathaniel, after a long day of helping customers and bookkeeping for their dry goods store, stopped by a local saloon for a quick drink before going to their respective homes.

As they told it, in one corner of the saloon, a poker game was becoming lively, and the stakes were interesting. Curious, they wandered over to watch the next hand.

Hawkins sat at the table, feet tapping, his obscene speech slurred. Sam Gover folded, rose from his seat and said, "Boys, I have got to get home." He nodded to Nathaniel. "You are free to take my seat, if you feel lucky. It has not been that lucky for me, but I broke even and I am gettin' out while the gettin' is good."

By the end of the evening, Hawkins was three sheets to the wind and stone cold broke. Nathaniel and George had a decent pile of money between them, enough to purchase their wives' forgiveness for cold suppers and beds that had been empty for the better part of the night.

Sometime later the next day, after the winnings were safely deposited in the bank along with the store's earnings, Hawkins must have came to the fuzzy conclusion that he had been taken advantage of by the Killough's. The whole lot of them were out to get him, as best he could figure, and he had no intention of being cheated for another minute. Fortifying himself with another round of whiskey, he made his way to the mercantile, where he set to throwing rocks at the walls and windows, yelling, hollering, and making a general nuisance of himself with wild and obnoxious observations on the character of the proprietors and the quality of the goods.

The final straw was reached when I, at all of fifteen years of age, only recently deemed ready to put my hair up and lengthen my skirts to be the model of a budding young woman, leaving childhood to fond memory, appeared on the sidewalk, bearing a lunch basket for my uncles.

He strode toward me, blocking the doorway, grabbing my wrist, and twisting my arm behind my back, so the basket fell from my grasp. I cried out at the sharp pain; he shoved me unceremoniously against the façade of the building, laughing at my fear and outrage. "I think I will just take you, since them uncles of your'n took my money." His breath smelled sour and I nearly retched as he rubbed a day's growth of whiskers against my cheek. I shuddered with disgust. "Consider yourself bought and paid for, just like any of your Uncle James' darkies."

At that point, a rifle cocked behind us and Papa's calm, firm voice said "Let her go, boy, and I might not shoot."

Hawkins chuckled derisively. "You would never shoot anyway, old man, and risk hurting the little princess here."

Another gun cocked. I turned my eyes to see George holding the barrel of his Kentucky pistol against Hawkins' temple. Hawkins felt the cold intrusion upon his fun, and sensing that George meant business, released his hold on me. Backing away, Hawkins held up his hands in surrender, then broke into a run and disappeared behind the blacksmith's far down the street as I collapsed into Papa's arms.

Nathaniel, unseen by Papa and George, but well within in my view, briskly strode the opposite direction from Hawkins, then turned down an alleyway and merged into the shadows.

"You ought to have shot anyway," George said to Papa. "He is just going to make more trouble now. Would have done the whole world a favor, not to mention us."

Molly and I remembered those oft-repeated words as we sat in the cabin's loft, trying not to make a sound, not to even breathe, lest we be heard. True to form, Hawkins had caused much more trouble, terrorized every member of the our family, paying special attention to me and Molly. When Papa decided to pull up stakes and move to Texas, even knowing the Hawkins boy was somewhere in the new Republic, he vowed Texas was so big we'd never cross paths with them again.

I hate to say that my Papa was wrong, but he was wrong.

10

The chatter below faded as Hawkins and Tail wandered toward the next cabin. Molly whispered her need to use the outhouse. I shook my head violently. We could not take the risk of being caught by that particular Indian, or worse, by Hawkins. We looked around the loft; the sun was a little higher and more light came into the space. Apparently, the raiders had been in the loft, but had found little to amuse them, after absconding with my feather tick and sending the down to the four winds. Fortunately, the chamber pot had been overlooked in the looting, and sat in its assigned place. We took the opportunity to relive ourselves of night water, then went back to watching and waiting.

Huddled together in the loft, we alternated between whispering thoughts of what our next move should be and attentively listening for any sounds indicating the marauders had returned, or better yet, had left the premises entirely. I was in favor of making the trek to Fort Lacey, along the Saline trace, the last direction I had seen

Mama and Sarah Jane heading with Narcissa and the baby. Molly wavered and thought perhaps maybe we ought to stay in the cabins, in case any of the family had managed to escape and were making their return to the settlement.

Occasionally, we would hear shouts between the men, who seemed to be methodically searching the cabins. From what we could hear, there were at least four different voices, maybe as many as six. Hawkins' voice always carried clearly to our ears, if not the words, then at least the tone. He was rough, arrogant and explicitly obscene in his language. In addition to Hawkins and Tail, I could discern at least one Mexican voice and another that had the familiar cadence of my uncles' slaves back in Alabama, but with a distinctive foreign accent. I puzzled over the contradiction, distracting my mind from the memories of the day before and the uncertainty of the future.

We sat shoulder to shoulder, backs against the rough wall of the loft, somewhat hidden in the shadows cast by the exposed beams overhead. I closed my eyes, seeking refuge in the sweet memories of childhood. Before Uncle James, Papa's twin, died in 1833, I had spent many happy days wandering what was already known as 'the Killough place', a house that seemed to always be enlarging with one room or another, and outbuildings cropping up hither and yon. Uncle James and Aunt Sarah were intent on creating a plantation to support themselves and their fifteen children, and their children's children, "even unto the seventh generation", as Uncle was wont to say. For years, Creek Indians had visited the Killough residence; the youngest children of whites, Indians, and slaves played together without regard for race or language differences – somehow, children always find a way to communicate and enjoy one another's company. My siblings and I, with our cousins, had all grown up without a fear of our Indian neighbors. Even Mama and Papa displayed only limited concerns. I realized with a start that this was probably one of the reasons why we were in the fix we were in right now. Trusting souls, relying on past experience, the adults had not taken the precautions necessary to protect the lives of themselves or their loved ones. I remembered vague snippets of conversation over lunch, the day life went topsy-turvy. The men debated taking their guns to the cornfield when it was time to finish picking the corn. Pa urged the younger men to remember the warning of Yellow Beak, the old Cherokee they had met coming back from Nacogdoches. "He told us there is unrest in Kickapoo Town; Cordova is still set on driving out the white men and returning Texas to the Indians and Mexicans." But the younger men protested, Nathaniel being the most vocal. "Time and again we've taken our guns to the fields," he said, "and nothing has happened. Not a single sign of trouble. Carrying guns will only be a waste of time and energy; they will only slow us down. There's so little left to harvest; leave the guns here and we will be finished in no time." Then after lunch, he said "You all go on and I will meet you there – 'twas too busy to get the horses watered this morning, so I need to tend to them right quick."

I wondered if Nathaniel had lived or died. Then I wondered – no, that was a horrible thought. No matter how mean my brother could be, surely he could not be evil.

The cabin door opened, scratching a loud sigh against the rough-hewn frame. A footstep fell across the threshold, resounding with the heaviness of a man's boot.

Neither of us dared breathe.

We heard a trunk, which had escaped the pillage of the previous day, dragged across the floor, a click as it opened. The contents made a strange symphony as they were dashed against the puncheon floor. The family Bible, the remainder of a bolt of cloth, a handful of buttons –each made a unique sound.

With each new thump downstairs, my grip on Molly's hand loosened; I could sense my eyes growing vacant, sinking into passive surrender. The brave, courageous young woman I was yesterday was taking leave, transforming effortlessly into a vanquished soul. I could feel an opposite transition was taking place within Molly. Each new thump stiffened her backbone, the invasion of our homes, the violence against our family, all working together to strengthen her resolve to survive. "We must be prepared to fight our way to freedom," she whispered.

I shook my head. "They will kill us," I replied, a dull finality and acceptance in my barely there voice.

"We must try. We owe it to our parents to try."

The thumps ceased. It seemed to the us as though our hearts would beat so loudly as to give us away. A muttered oath floated up the stairs, the sound of the trunk being kicked and skittering across the room to bang against a wall soon followed.

A tentative step fell on the first rung of the loft ladder with a decided creak. It stopped. The creak came again in a blundering, bouncing rhythm, as if he was testing to see if it would hold his weight. How I wished I had pulled that ladder up the night before!

Molly shoved a quilt into my hands. "If he sticks his

head up here, I will get him first, and then you must throw this over his head to confuse him. Follow me – we will fly back to the canebrake, unless there is a horse nearby ready to ride."

I nodded dumbly. It was the only thing I could do, other than simply sit and wait to be taken.

The creaking stopped again. Whoever had been there descended the ladder and gone outside the cabin. Voices came clearly, almost as if the light mist of rain was amplifying the baritones and infusing them with a singular sort of impudence.

Curses and angry, vitriolic proclamations issued forth from the Hawkins man. Then came an unexpected tenor. We exchanged a look of surprise, then open-mouthed joy as we clasped one another, relief flooding our bedraggled spirits. "Nathaniel!" Molly called out, then clapped her hand across her mouth, realizing the what a dreadful mistake she had made.

Like a convict ready to dance at the end of a rope, silence fell with an abrupt jolt. The tenor voiced an oath, and a horse galloped away.

The hateful Hawkins began to laugh, and the laughter grew louder as he stepped back into the cabin.

I held the quilt in my hands. Molly shoved me aside. "Remember our plans!"

Buck Hawkins shoved his ebullient countenance in the opening to the loft, threw his head back and howled uproariously, delighted with his turn of fortune.

In one swift, fluid motion, Molly threw the slop-jar, contents and all, straight into his face.

The full force of the slop jar, contents and all, hit Hawkins square in the face. Balanced precariously on the loft ladder, he flailed about, trying simultaneously to find something steady to grab to regain his balance and at the same time, vault himself into the loft to exact his revenge on the conniving little upstarts we had become.

His destiny held neither outcome.

I whipped the quilt in the air, years of experience in bed-making paying off in a heretofore unimagined manner, and let it settle about his arms and head, further infuriating Hawkins, and effectively reversing his upward momentum. In addition, the folds of fabric muffled to a large degree his curses of protest and indignation.

Molly quickly jumped for the opening and half-fell, half-leaped from the loft to the cabin floor, and I instantly followed. We landed, rather unceremoniously, upon the quilt covered form of Hawkins, jerking furiously amid broken crockery, and jumped to our feet without hesitation. For a moment, it crossed my mind to bolt the door and windows and take the Bowie knife, secured in the waistband of the duster I wore over my calico dress, to Hawkins' throat. One look out the door at the pile of quilts covering Pa's body chased the thought from my mind. To cause more bloodshed was not within me. I stood, frozen in time, unable to move, barely able to breathe.

The door stood open. A clear path to the blessed canebrake was in view. The morning's misty rain had left a distinct fresh smell in the air that seemed to be the scent of hope.

Molly grabbed my arm, pulled me through the door and toward the promised safety of the tall cane.

Two, perhaps three, steps outside the cabin walls, a massive black arm arrested our flight. A monster of solid mass reined us in with arms the size of mature tree limbs and the strength of a black bear. He lifted us off the ground with ease, deftly avoiding the feet that kicked helplessly in the general direction of his shins and kneecaps. In her fury, Molly sank her teeth deeply into the sweaty sinew of his forearm. He did not flinch nor did he utter a word, though she drew blood.

The unwashed scent of our ebony captor and the firmness of his grip, combined with our fear, quickly trounced what little ambition we entertained for freedom.

Buck Hawkins had recovered himself and stood in the doorway of the cabin, wiping his face with a clean corner of the quilt, although it did little to improve his appearance. He was a scroungy creature by nature, unkempt and unclean, lean of build, with peculiarly penetrating blue eyes, which were at odds with long oily hanks of blue-black hair. "So, Raphael, you caught yourself a couple of spitfires. Whatever shall we do with them?" He strolled lazily, circling around the formation of man holding girls. He stopped in front of my face and lifted my chin with a coarse finger. "Well. Miss Killough." He stepped backward and made a mocking bow. "So good to see you again." He turned to Molly and his manner changed ever so slightly. He scrutinized her features coldly and dispassionately, seeking heaven knew what. "You must be Polly's girl," he remarked casually. "You've grown up a bit since I saw you last."

Molly spit in his face. He slapped her. She spit again, this time with blood from a cut lip. He wiped the spittle from his face and turned to deter her from taking aim again.

He turned his attention once again to me. I hung my head, silently commending my soul to God and praying for a quick, merciful death rather than suffer the indignities such captives were wont to endure.

Tail and a Mexican man came around the corner of the cabin. The Indian elbowed the Mexican, and pointed toward the girls, a lascivious grin spreading from one man to the other, like a contagion.

"Manuel, Tail," Hawkins called. "You two hog-tie these wild animals and toss them in the back of that wagon yonder. Raphael and me's going after that big stallion that bolted towards the creek." His fingers brushed my cheek again. "You touch either one of them just yet and you will pay with your lives," he warned. "The pleasure will be mine." He murmured the last in my ear as the bulky Negro passed me to the Mexican.

The Mexican replied in Spanish, and though neither I nor Molly understood the language well, his tone made it clear that he would respect, albeit begrudgingly, Hawkins' wishes. Tail deigned reply.

Lying face down in the bed of the rough buckboard wagon, I strained to hear the conversation of our captors. My stomach was churning from the ordeal. The Indian who bound me with leather thongs had caressed me in the most despicable fashion during the process, and the thought of what surely was to come made me nauseous.

Soon, it became clear we were considered spoils of the raid, the same as any common trinkets. From the rough language, we discerned their greatest value was as an Indian captive, profitable for any band that might chose to allow her family to redeem her for money, guns, ammunition, and other goods. "Perhaps since Nathaniel knows we survived, he will offer a reward quickly, and this will be long past in no time at all," I suggested in a whisper. "I am certain he only left because he was outnumbered, and perhaps he may yet return with more men to free us."

Molly made an ugly sound in the back of her throat. I knew what she was thinking. Nathaniel was cut from the same bolt of cloth as her father when he was on a drinking binge, only Nathaniel came by his hatefulness honestly, without the need for liquid courage. I am sure she sincerely doubted Nathaniel was likely to come to our rescue. If he did, he would have to explain why he sought out the company of Hawkins' group after the massacre, and why he left two innocent girls to their mercy. Besides, if Nathaniel was rounding up reinforcements to help save us, why did Hawkins loiter about the site, as if he had all the time in the world? My opinion of my brother was not one of high regard, laid upon a dual foundation of my own experiences and overheard private commentary between my parents as to his character where money was concerned, not to mention what I had been privy to in talks with his wife Orleana.

After what seemed to be an eternity, we heard the voices of Nathaniel and Hawkins, quarreling. Hawkins loudly and vehemently demanded payment, in gold, for the "getting your little problem solved – there's not a soul left to stand in your way of taking full title to this here land, and making a tidy profit off of it. And I want my cut, as agreed, right here and now!"

Nathaniel protested "I don't have the gold! I don't know where Isaac and George hid what was left! You're just going to have to wait until I get things fixed up with Hotchkiss and Opothleyahola. Here, take these as good faith!"

Hawkins laughed. "Kelsey Douglas bills? Those are worthless to me!"

Molly and I peeked over the side of the buckboard. Nathaniel's eye caught the motion and followed the movement. His face went blank, emotionless. He cocked his head in the direction of the wagon. "You could take the girls," he said. "They should be worth something."

"I thought you had other plans for them."

He shrugged. "Plans change. Take them to Coffee's Station and trade them off to someone."

"For what? A little white flour, a blanket or two? Not worth the trouble." Hawkins seemed to know he had the upper hand; we were already his property as far as he was concerned. He was just having fun to see how low Nathaniel would go to weasel out of a debt.

"Downriver to New Orleans then."

"Do I look like a madam of a sporting house?" Hawkins laughed. "Fine, I'll take them. But you still owe me, and don't you forget it!"

Thus, an accord was reached. Nathaniel mounted his horse and rode away. The remaining men gathered around the wagon, laughing and making lewd suggestions.

I saw Molly bite her lips to keep from lashing out at the motley crew. Beside her, tears came unbidden to my eyes, and formed rivulets upon my cheeks.

Suddenly, the men ceased their carousing, and we were once again filled with the odd combination of fear of what was to come and hope for some salvation.

Another Indian, this one known to us as Terrapin, had ridden calmly and soundlessly into our midst. He was old enough to command great respect, not so young as to be dismissed on account of youth, nor so old as to be dismissed on account of feeble body. I hoped his words would carry weight, if not with Hawkins, at least with the Cherokee warrior. Papa had characterized Terrapin as a simple man, dedicated to living in peace, among whites, Mexicans, and Indians who were constantly at odds with one another.

He spoke to Hawkins in the Cherokee language, of which we knew little more than a casual smattering. Between words and signs, the situation was explained, excuses were made and lies were told – mostly by Hawkins. He claimed he was just trying to reunite us with our family; that we were restrained only because our grief had made us hysterical.

Molly and I felt we could breathe when we realized it was Terrapin's intent to take us to his own home to the east, near Striker Village, and keep us safe there until we could be restored to our families. He played to Hawkins' lie, astutely observing that the warrior, Tail, and others, were headed to Kickapoo Town, just a few miles to the west, to meet with other Mexicans and Indians in the service of Vincente Cordova. The further we could be from Kickapoo Town, the safer we would be, he reasoned. He pointed out that Hawkins and his men could use the knowledge of where we were to barter for their own safety, should they meet any white settlers bent on revenge. To further sweeten the deal, Terrapin offered a coin purse, suggesting Hawkins could use the money to assist any other stragglers from the melee he might encounter along the way, yet knowing full well that Hawkins would keep any money for himself.

Hawkins agreed, rapidly taking the money, but suggested the best action would be to separate us. Terrapin was only one man; keeping one hysterical girl under control and safe would be difficult enough without having to worry about a second. He suggested Terrapin take Molly and declared he would be responsible for my welfare, stating his intent to return promptly to Alabama where both Hawkins and I have relatives.

Hearing this exchange, Tail, the Cherokee warrior, became angry. His eyes were dark with a thirst for violence. He had clearly planned on having Molly for his own use. From what I knew of him, he had lived alone on the edge of his own civilization, making enemies within his own people, allying himself with those who sought to drive away settlers of any origin. For the moment, he collaborated with the revolutionary Mexicans who promised a dedicated Indian land, free of Mexican, American, or Texian intrusions. I am sure he knew in his heart that the Mexicans would not honor their agreements any more than the Texians had, and that once the Texian rule was overthrown, his people would have to rise up against the Mexicans, while continuing to battle American expansion. Every settler he killed, he rejoiced in knowing it was one less to fight the next day. I think he believed that by banding together, the Indians could retake their lands, drive away or simply kill the Americans, push the Mexicans far to the south, and take women and children as they pleased, to repopulate their diminishing numbers. The black slaves of the white men, he had no use for, but since many of them had no use for the white men – the enemy of my enemy is my friend. At least until the enemy is vanquished. In the meantime, Molly was a firebrand he could enjoy conquering. Handing her over to this newcomer was an insult to him as a warrior and a virile male. Yet he had no choice. With a scowl, he shoved Molly toward Terrapin, then turned, mounted his horse and rode away, toward Kickapoo Town.

Manuel, the Mexican who had accompanied Tail, clicked to his mount and rode off after his comrade. Terrapin, Raphael and Hawkins watched them disappear across the creek and through the ruined cornfields. Hawkins shrugged. Raphael hoisted Molly so she could ride astride, behind Terrapin.

Terrapin inclined his head toward me. "You will not part with her? It would be to your benefit to travel unencumbered by a woman." His voice was well modulated, persuasive. He had lived far too long and experienced far too much to have not learned something of the ways of dealing with men of all races and morals. He knew that if left with Hawkins, I would not fare well, and that the retribution for the loss of this family would fall squarely and unfairly on the shoulders of the local Indians rather than the motley crew of troublemakers. I suspected he wanted to deflect as much of the Texians' anger as possible, without incurring the enmity of Cordova's allies. Indians could be just as brutal to other Indians, if not more so, as they were reputed to be toward whites.

Hawkins would not be swayed. Raphael moved to hitch the wagon to the stallion they had retrieved from grazing in what remained of the cornfields. My heart hurt so badly I thought it would burst. My only comfort was the thought that Molly would be cared for by someone she knew to be kind and fair, as I heard the hoofbeats of the horse carrying them fade into the distance.

When I could hear no more, a cold fear settled into my soul. My prayers for a quick and merciful death had been denied, and what awaited, I feared, would be a fate worse than death.

Hawkins climbed into the buckboard's seat and flicked the reins. "So, tell me again, Raphael – if I tire of this one, where did you say I could get a good price for her?"

Raphael, mounted on a horse as black as his own skin, rode beside the wagon. "Monsieur," he replied in his odd accent, "there are many in New Orleans who would pay well for such a young thing. I have seen ladies with fairer hair and brighter eyes sold at auction for the fancy trade for several thousand dollars. All they need is the word of a gentleman that she is his property – who is to say she is white? Many octoroons have tried to deny their color, many have failed. The word of a slave woman against the word of a gentleman? You know who will be trusted. Take her to the Exchange and put her on the block. But if you do not wish to sell her publicly and arouse suspicion, you should visit the Murray brother's café and ask for Madame Veronique. She is le femme le plus très beau; you will have no trouble recognizing her. She will pay you well, and no one will be the wiser, for no man will take the word of a woman procured. The café is on Levee Street, numéro neuf. Le nom du café est "La Maison du Soleil Levant".

We headed northeast in the buckboard. I heard Hawkins telling Raphael his plan to get to Shreve Town, where he would secure passage to New Orleans. No one, he figured, would be looking for a supposed Texas 'Indian captive' on a steamboat, much less in New Orleans.

He mused that he preferred to regain the money he had lost in that old poker game, or at least gotten paid for his more recent services, but there would be time for that later. Right now, he figured had the sweetest revenge imaginable: Izzie Killough, the unmarried, unblemished daughter of his enemy, at his disposal, to do with as he liked. He grinned, telling Raphael I had been a feisty little thing back in Alabama. He said he hoped I would still put up a fight when they reached the stateroom of the steamboat to New Orleans, because it would make taking me just that much more pleasurable.

I turned my head to the side and wept. I wished Papa had shot him years ago, even if the bullet had to go through me first.

11

I awoke, realizing I was in one of Papa's wagons, drawn by his horse, but recalling with horror that Papa was dead and I was in the custody of Buck Hawkins. We trundled over the bumpy wagon trail day after day, watching the sun slowly wend its way east to west, scavenging for food and fuel at the day's end and constantly replaying in my mind the terrors of that Friday afternoon, I became a mute automaton.

Approaching a trail leading to the Trinity River, Raphael turned his black steed from us, determined to regroup with Cordova. Hawkins tried to get the burly black man to stay and journey all the way to New Orleans, but he declined, avowing the slave-holding South was not for him; he had made himself a free man, and a free man he would remain, even unto death. "Eet ees not such a bad thing, ees eet, for to die a free men?"

I stared coldly at him, for he had already described earlier atrocities in which he had taken part – not the least of which was how he 'earned' his freedom, by the murder of his master, mistress, and their entire family. He vowed that if he was ever returned to slavery, he would repeat his deeds, finding his freedom in bloodshed. Having so intimately seen the brutal deaths of my own family, I was well glad to see him depart, as much as I despaired of being alone with Hawkins. Besides which, his presence and repulsive comments only served to encourage Hawkins' degenerate ways. I lived each day in dread of Hawkins and slept fitfully though the nights, nightmares of Kias, soaked in blood, soundless screams as he died, again and again and again, encroaching upon what little relief I might have found.

As we drew near the Louisiana border and the river traffic of the bustling port of Shreve Town, other travelers began to pull alongside and make conversation. Hawkins warned me against saying anything of her situation, or the late massacre of my family, threatening all sorts of evil and vile punishments for the least transgression, whether it be attempted escape or a slip of the tongue. The threats were no bother to me, however, as I remained close-mouthed with a far-away look, to the point where he told the inquisitive strangers that I was his sister who had lost her mind in the wilds of Texas.

Once at the docks, Hawkins sold the horse and wagon to a fellow whose own had all but collapsed from an exceptionally heavy lading. The act of taking on a load of fine furniture, arriving aboard a steamboat from the East via New Orleans, proved too great a burden for the wagon. The furniture mover was irked at the inflated price Willie required of him, but needing to expedite the home goods to his client, a prospering Shreve Town merchant with a wife known for her volatile temper, he begrudgingly handed over a handsome sum.

With the proceeds, Hawkins booked passage on the

steamboat. The vessel was barely wider than the log cabin I had called home in Texas, but nearly ten times longer. A sidewheeler, it made the best of limited space by packing in cargo – mostly cotton, but some animal hides, tallow and beeswax were on the loading dock as well. As accommodations went, it was certainly an improvement over exposure to sun and storm in an uncovered wagon.

The steamboat would be pulling out the next afternoon, Hawkins informed me. His words failed to register with me; he might as well have been speaking to a stone, for I was lost, and could not summon a word to my lips, had I even endeavored to reply. I stood mute beside him, a dispirited shadow, adrift in a world of inhumanity.

He looked me over, from my dust-caked blonde hair, the disheveled blue and white calico farm dress stained with mud and sporting more than one rip along the hemline to the battered brogans that were more appropriate to the campfire than the delicate flower of young womanhood he intended to bring to market. He growled to himself, realizing he was going to have to spend some of his cash in order to make me presentable to the madams of New Orleans. He grabbed my arm unceremoniously and half-led, half-dragged me along the rough streets of the young town.

We turned off the Texas Trail onto Commerce Street, and somewhere between Milam and Crockett Streets, near the western shore of the Red River, he pulled me into a hastily erected, rough hewn residence, enticed by a woman, who was about my height and shape, standing on what passed for a front porch. He thrust me into an incongruously delicate parlor chair, drawing the woman aside and rapidly speaking in barely muted tones. Money changed hands, from his to hers, and she approached me with a wary but kind smile.

"Honey," she said, taking my arm and tugging gently, "we are going to get you cleaned up and looking presentable. You come on with me, now."

I glanced fearfully at Hawkins, the first emotion I had truly felt in days.

"You will be fine," the soothing feminine voice intoned. "The gentleman's going to be right here waiting for you."

I hung my head and followed obediently.

In a small, slightly chilly room, the woman helped me undress, making quiet clucking sounds as she did so. Tears began to stream down my cheeks, the heartbroken, soundless crying that had filled my nights ever since Nathaniel sold me off. Sold me off! The realization hit home again and the tears poured with renewed fervor. The kind stranger brushed a few tears of her own away, then smoothed her hands over my damp cheeks, unknotting what was left of my hair roll, and combing out the tousled tresses. "My name is Annie Mae," she said, conversationally. "What is your name?"

I stared dumbly at a blank space on the wall, past the water pitcher and basin, the bar of lye soap, and other accompaniments to bathing, as if watching a play. My eyes welled up with fresh tears. I blinked, the salty drops breaking free and releasing my tongue in the process. "Elizabeth," I whispered, as if it were a great secret that must be taken to the grave. "Elizabeth Isabelle Killough."

Annie Mae saw to my toilette, washing my hair and getting me bathed in warm water, before giving me a fresh chemise. She had me try on a dress from one of her trunks, placed a pin here and there, and had me take it off again. She encouraged me to rest on the narrow but comfortable feather bed in the little room. Within moments of reclining, I finally slept, soundly, for the first time since before the massacre. When I awoke several hours later, my frayed and torn calico had been washed and mended, and left to dry in front of a warm fireplace. She had the dress from her trunk ready for me to try on again; she had made some very minor alterations while I slumbered and it now fit perfectly. The fabric was a printed muslin, the bodice nearly off the shoulders, gathered tidily at the waist, with long, cuffed sleeves with just enough puffiness to allow some freedom of movement. The fabric was lovely; gold and russet blossoms nestled against leaves in varying shades of green and brown. It must have been expensive material at one time, but the dress had been remade so often that it had lost some of its original glory. All the same, it was clean, comfortable and fit well. Properly dressed and refreshed, I eagerly consumed a bowl of buttermilk-soaked cornbread which soothed my stomach, irritated from days without proper nourishment.

Hawkins, Annie Mae informed me, had been persuaded to take a room for himself at the Catfish Hotel, a somewhat rough but respectable establishment built of logs, built soundly enough for shelter but rarely well-chinked against the weather. "He'll get a meal of salt pork that's mostly fat, and a spoonful of greasy turnip greens that were only half-washed, if he's lucky," Annie Mae confided with a satisfied smile. "Not the best fare, but he looks like he could use a comeuppance. Mark my words, if a meal like that doesn't come up, it is going to blast out." She chuckled at the thought. I smiled back, the first smile in days to cross my face. My new-found friend's mien turned serious abruptly.

"I know he is not any sort of gentleman and I know

you are in some sort of trouble. You don't have to tell me what it is, just know that if you want to get away from him and get back to your family and friends, all you have to do is say so. I will help you." Annie Mae was matter of fact, without a trace of pity or judgment.

I wondered what Annie Mae had been through herself to be able to size up the situation so succinctly. I considered the offer for a moment. Perhaps I could get back to Alabama – but, no, that's where Hawkins was headed himself. There was no way of knowing what he would do – or say – once he got into town and met up with my kinfolk. And if I was there, with my own tale of woe – it would be bad blood all around. Someone would surely get hurt – probably Hawkins, but he wouldn't go down without a fight, and the menfolk who are kin to me are just as likely to be killed just like Kias and Papa and my brothers. Except Nathaniel, who I had begun to suspect planned the whole vile business. And to go back to Texas to him was unthinkable. I shook my head 'no'. "I have nowhere to go," I replied flatly.

"I can see perfectly well that you're a decent white woman. I used to be one myself. He says he's gonna take you downriver to New Orleans. My bet is, that rogue plans to sell you as a high yaller colored gal into a boarding house, to be used by men in any way they like, and you will never see a cent of the money they pay for your services. Is that what you want?"

"No, of course not. But when I get to New Orleans, I will think of something. I will find a way. I will run away if I have to, find work as a seamstress or governess or school teacher or something." My words sounded sincere, but my voice lacked conviction.

"They will say you are a runaway slave and come after you."

"They would have to prove I am colored, would they not?"

"That is not hard. All it takes it the word of a few 'good' men in court and you are colored. You are property. There are plenty of quadroons and octoroons with just as pale skin as yours or mine."

I had not considered this possibility.

Hawkins arrived the following afternoon to retrieve me. My old calico shift was clean and dry, packed in a small carpet bag; Annie Mae had gifted me the bag, along with the printed muslin dress and underthings.

"A woman's word doesn't carry much weight," Annie Mae said in our last private moments in the bedroom, "especially a woman in my line of work. But all the same, take this. It is a little misleading," she added, a thin, smug smile overriding just a slight twinge of sadness, "but a woman without a man or family to protect her has to rely on being sharp witted and sometimes a bit sly. There are a lot of bad men in this old world who will take advantage of you faster than a jackrabbit can hop into a briar patch." She gave me a secretive wink. "That knife you had on you – it is at the bottom of your bag. If sharp wits fail, a sharp blade just might do the trick."

She shoved a folded paper into my hand, along with a drawstring reticule with what few coins she could spare. The paper read: 'I, A. M. McGowan, know the bearer of this paper, Elizabeth Isabelle Killough, to be a free born white woman of Jefferson County, Alabama, lately of Nacogdoches County, Texas. Inquiries as to her circumstances and character may be made by writing me in Shreve Town, Louisiana.'

She kissed my cheek. "Good luck and God bless."

12

The boat to New Orleans was overcrowded, smelly, and loud. Hawkins thrust me into a stateroom, little more than a closet with a bed, tossing my carpet bag after me. His figure filled the doorway, a lascivious grin relishing my palpable fear. "You just make yourself comfortable, honey, and I will be back to play with you real soon."

Somehow, he managed to bar the door from the outside. I shrank onto the bed, defeated.

When he returned, some hours later, disheveled and drunk, he was in no condition to make good on his intentions. I had a momentary reprieve, for which I was grateful. If only I had some way to escape the boat, or dispatch my captor! I was too fearful to jump into the water, not out of fear of death, for I would welcome that, but fear that I would not perish, but only be returned to his 'care'. And there was naught in the room to bring his existence to a swift end, save my knife which would surely leave me with blood on my hands, dress and shoes.

I would not be able to escape unseen, otherwise I would have gladly taken action. My brief flirtation with initiative gave way to deep melancholy.

Our journey was blessedly brief. Upon his sobriety, he considered the benefit of delivering me intact to the procuress. He convinced himself he would be well rewarded for his 'gentlemanly restraint'. For my part, I retreated into myself, not speaking unless necessary, eating and drinking little, restricting my movement to within the confines of the cabin. To see others, to hear voices, to speak, to eat and drink seemed too much of life, and I wanted nothing more to do with life. I simply wanted to be with Kias.

Upon docking in New Orleans, we disembarked and I viewed for the first time massive blocks of buildings, in a rainbow of colors – white, red, orange, brown, green, blue, gray – of immense height and girth. In the distance, a gleaming columned dome held court over lesser tributaries. It was toward this landmark we proceeded.

Grecian columns rose proudly to support a wide portico, a marble staircase granting admittance to the Exchange, equally known as the Saint Charles Hotel. I had never before seen such grandeur in my life, and I doubt I shall ever see its rival.

We descended the staircase to the saloon, and I marveled at the grand staircase spiraling upwards to the crowning dome, a viewing gallery winding around its circumference. Within the rotunda, a slave auction was being conducted. I froze in fear, recalling Annie Mae's warning that I could be marketed as an octoroon and no one would stand in Hawkins' way.

A bird-like, raven-haired woman, olive skinned, with an aquiline nose, high cheekbones and brown eyes was causing nearly every man to turn his gaze upon her as she effortlessly glided through the saloon. Her dress was neither opulent, nor plain. I supposed it was the height of fashion, but I had not seen a fashion plate in so long I could not be certain. The fabric and cut, however, bespoke wealth and class. She was heedless of the attention of her admirers; her glance caught my carpetbag and Annie Mae's remade gown. She bestowed a smile and beelined for me. Her expression was inscrutable. I wondered if she had mistaken me for another.

She fairly lit at my side, touching my arm. She bestowed upon me the faire la bise greeting common to the French Quarter populace, and whispered quickly "Elizabeth Isabelle?"

I nodded, confused. I had never met this woman before, yet she knew my name. Again, I began to wonder if this was all some fever dream, or if I had indeed died back in the canebrake and this was simply some strange twist of afterlife.

She took firm hold of my hand. "Come" she said.

"Here now," Hawkins interjected. "She is mine – she is with me. I will not have her going anywhere without me."

Her gaze bored into his face with willful determination. "I am the woman you are seeking. I am Madame Veronique de Soleil Levant. You have business to conduct with me, do you not?"

Hawkins was taken aback, then quickly regained his composure. "Yes, I believe I do."

Madame wended her way through the throng of businessmen, idlers, socialites and assorted spectators, leading us to a secluded arrangement of settees and tables in an open parlor. "Let us sit and come to an arrangement." A light brown-skinned boy of about twelve appeared to stand by her side. I had not noticed him before, but he must have been behind her skirts the whole time. "My son," she explained, with a dismissive wave of her hand.

He handed her a simple reticule, the drawstring tied securely. She fastened her large brown eyes on Hawkins. "And now," she said, in a low, smooth voice, "Shall we just sit here and rest for a moment." She turned to me. "Sitting and resting is lovely, is it not? I only want you to feel comfortable and rested. Would you like to have a glass of water or wine?"

"Water will be fine," I replied. She made a motion with her fingers and the boy disappeared.

"Whiskey for me," interjected Hawkins.

"Do you find intoxicating beverages and business transactions mix well?" The inquiry was outwardly polite but tinged with cutting mockery. Hawkins shifted uncomfortably in his seat. "Perhaps you would prefer your drink after we've concluded our transaction."

"Perhaps," he allowed.

The boy returned with a crystal water goblet for me. The liquid was clear, cool and refreshing. I had not realized until it touched my lips how thirsty I was.

She continued meeting Hawkins' eyes with her steady gaze. "There is no need to hurry. We can just take our time and sit here and we can come to an agreement, I understand you have come a long way and gone to a lot of trouble and expense. You are eager to continue your journey, are you not? Would you like me to simply give you a fair price or would you prefer to bargain for awhile?"

Hawkins blinked. He was in a hurry. He wanted the

money, he wanted whiskey and he wanted to be on his way. "What do you consider your fair price?"

She smiled enigmatically, untying the purse strings. She withdrew a handful of silver coins. "Fresh from our very own, brand new Mint." She paused, cocking her head to one side, addressing the boy and myself. "Son, why not you take this nice young lady outside and see if there is a carriage for hire?" Hawkins started to sputter but she shushed him. "Is it not easier to conclude our business without the object of our transaction attending us?" I moved uncertainly at first, feeling sick at being sold once again, but the desire to get away from Hawkins overtook my fear of venturing into an unknown city with strangers.

The boy and I had hardly reached the street before Madame joined us. What had transpired with Hawkins, or the amount of money that had changed hands, she kept to herself, but I feel certain he did not get the better end of the deal. A hired hack was at hand, and we proceeded to wend through a maze of streets teeming with people of all sorts, most of which were as foreign to me as I am sure I was to them.

Once we arrived at the establishment of Mme. Veronique on Treme Street, my senses began to return. I was given a bowl of gumbo, thick with rice, and a watered down cup of brandy to help me sleep. As if I needed encouragement to fall into slumber after such ordeals! A small bedstead and washstand occupied a small room off the back parlor; I was assigned to this quilted and feathered retreat for the evening. I believe I slept for nearly a full day before awakening fully.

After I awoke and had a good breakfast with a bracing round of dark and bitter coffee, Mme. Veronique called me into her tiny office, discretely tucked into a cupboard beneath the staircase. There was barely room for a writing desk and pair of chairs, illuminated by oil lamps. We sat facing one another; she looked deeply into my eyes and took my hand in hers.

Her words came in measured tones, calm and forthright.

"I received word to expect you from a former employee, Annie Mae."

My breath caught and my jaw dropped in wonder.

"Sometimes the post is swifter than the boats." She smiled. "Annie was privy to your 'gentleman's' plans, including where he planned to – " she paused, searching for the right word "seek an arrangement to his benefit. Annie placed you in the same dress she wore when departing New Orleans, one I had made for her by Mrs. Page, so I would be sure to recognize you." She paused, lost in reminiscing. "Mrs. Page was a treasured seamstress in the city and her skill with a needle was exceptional." Her tone changed. "Her husband trucked her off to Texas a couple of years ago; there has been no word from her since." Concern crossed her brow. "Have you happened to have met Harriet Page in your travels?"

I shook my head no, still dazed by the turn of events.

Madame's fingers traced the fancy work along the cuff of my sleeve. "See? She worked her initials into the embroidery. It was her calling card, and her best advertisement."

I looked where her forefinger rested. An embellishment I had only glanced over without scrutiny, I could now clearly perceive the letters H and P intertwined. I ran my own finger along the threads, appreciating again the attention to detail the dressmaker had dedicated to her vocation.

Madame coughed delicately, changing the subject

slightly. "Annie said you are a young woman of a decent family, with an education and morals. This is as far from your sphere as the moon is from the earth. Annie was much the same way, at least until she thought a man loved her. She kept my ledgers for me, watched the ladies and gentlemen, and was quick to settle any differences or expel anyone disturbing the peace of the house, among other duties. She begged me to care for you as I did her, and to let her mistakes be a lesson to you. If you have no other safe repose, you are welcome to employment.

There is nothing to fear here; a house of ill repute is the safest house in New Orleans for an inexperienced girl without friends or family. You will not be harmed here; nothing is taken that is not willingly offered.

Here is the one place a woman has full authority over her own body. No guardian, father, brother, uncle, clergy, or other man can demand your compliance. If you wish to remain chaste in this house, you are welcome to accept employment as my hostess; if you prefer to earn greater income, you may claim a room upstairs. Your wages as a hostess will be fifteen dollars a month, your room and board included, which you may supplement with wages from the upstairs ladies for running errands, changing linens, bringing up refreshments, sewing or mending and so forth in addition to your duties for the household. As an upstairs resident, you are free to establish your own rates for services, and will owe the house fifteen dollars per month for room and board, plus charges for refreshments sent to your room. If you need to consider the choices, you are welcome to speak with the ladies of the house.

I run an honest house – I do not tolerate stealing or cheating between my employees or from our clients. Anyone who wants to conduct themselves in such a manner can just go on down the street to Whittaker's and be one of his girls – if they think they can tolerate the drunken rages of his lovely Suzannah and her jealous fits over his "fresh meat"."

With that she smiled, and suggested I might want to take some time to walk about the house and gardens, talk with the ladies, and weigh my decision.

I spent most of the afternoon on a seat beneath a shady tree in the courtyard of the parlor house. I saw little of the gardens; my mind's eye was focused on what might have been, what should have been, what was supposed to be, and this soul-numbing reality. For awhile, I felt my dear Kias was beside me, fighting to return from beyond the veil. Tears dampened my cheeks, dried, and returned unbidden.

We had such dreams, Kias and I. In less than a month, we would have been married. He had wanted to stay in Nacogdoches, take a job as a clerk, become a Freemason, and read law until he was ready for a practice of his own, maybe even run for office in a few years. We were going to have a house, a nice house, with a woman to help cook and clean and sew, and a pretty flower garden all around. We were going to have children, lots of children to love and raise up with good morals and exceptional character. We were going to grow old together. Have grandchildren. Sit in rocking chairs and watch the moon move across the night sky. And now he is gone and there is nothing left. Nothing of us. Nothing of our dreams. Nothing at all. I am nothing – nothing at all without him, without us. So what does it really matter what becomes of me now? What does it matter what I do or do not? There is nothing but emptiness inside of me. Emptiness and memories that never had a chance to be made. Life that never got to be lived. His life is over, and mine may as well be. Nothing really matters anymore.

At sunset, I arose from the shadows and retreated into the house. I was staying. I would accept the offer of employment as her hostess. To be honest, there was nothing else to do but stay.

13

My duties at the Treme Street house were numerous, but simple. Mornings came late for our residents; I helped Cook get breakfast served, and assisted the upstairs ladies as needed. By afternoon, I was positioned in the front parlor, to answer the door and admit the gentlemen. Nothing could have prepared me, however, to admit one particular gentleman early one November evening in 1841.

"I do believe we've met before – Nell, isn't it? Oh, no, you only look like Nelly. You corrected me once before, some time ago, in front of my billiard parlor in Nacogdoches. Killough, isn't it? Elizabeth Killough? Whatever are you doing in a house like this? No, wait, let me think a moment. I know, I know, the usual story. Let me see – in your hour of need, your gentleman deserted you, your family abandoned you, and you were left alone and friendless, blameless in the matter, yet with no where to turn but the sad city streets. Am I correct?"

"All too correct," I assured him coolly.

He reached toward me with his right hand; I noted it was malformed, where in earlier years, had been an extension of normal, even graceful, proportions. He caught how my eye had wandered, glancing at the appendage ruefully. He held it out for my closer inspection. I shrank away.

"A daily reminder of my sacrifice for your honor," he reflected, putting an emphasis on 'your'. "A wound suffered in battling the Indians to avenge your family, although I sincerely doubt the Indians were responsible for that atrocity. Indeed, I have heard otherwise many times." Richard Parmalee's eyes began to gleam. "As I recall, the last I saw you, you were preparing to wed the noble Mr. Williams. Pray tell," he purred, "what became of him?"

'He is dead," I flatly stated.

'Hmm," he mused. "And your dear father and brothers?"

'Also deceased," I admitted.

"And yet you found your way to a gaudy bawdy house several hundred miles away from your humble home." He moved his face closer to mine until I could smell the odor of bourbon on his breath. I did not flinch. Pure evil emanated from those wicked irises! "Perhaps you were unhappy with your lot in life," he charged. "Perhaps you incited others to wantonly massacre your kith and kin, leaving you free to live in sinful splendor! Perhaps you even fired the first shot! Yes! I see it now! Their demise was your desire, your doing!" He withdrew, smirking. "That, after all, is what I have heard, in the strictest of confidence." He paused briefly, then in a confidential undertone added "Perhaps you don't know, your brother Nathaniel lives."

I regarded him coldly.

"I saw him just last month; he was in my saloon." Parmalee chuckled. "You failed to kill them all, I'm afraid."

"I did not kill anyone," I refuted, fists clenched by my sides.

'I'm sure you did not," he agreed, reasonably, "but then, whose word do you think a jury would believe? Your dear, grieving brother who is a pillar of church and community or you – a woman who provides, shall we say, services, in a sporting house?" He laughed. "They would let you tell your tale in court, and then the judge would instruct the jurors to dismiss the testimony, on the grounds that not only are you a woman, but a woman of bad character, who associates with women of bad character. I have that on good authority. You would be found guilty of murder before you could snap your fingers."

I turned and walked away, my head held high. I would not give him the satisfaction of seeing how his words tormented me. Yet, torment me they did. So far from home, I had no way of knowing what to believe. Given how Nathaniel had treated Molly and me, who knows what evil lies he is capable of spreading? How badly I miss my mother – how dearly I want to go home to her – and how desperately I fear what fate might await me if I dare venture near her arms!

I slept fitfully that night. My dreams would begin with Kias, happy and whole, taking my hands and leading me in a dance on the puncheon floors of our own cabin, then as we turned round and about, skin and blood would melt from his bones as his skeletal fingers gripped me ever tighter, whirling faster in a dervish frenzy, until I screamed myself awake.

Aside from sporadic, though thankfully infrequent,

interruptions by Parmalee, my life was astoundingly settled and surprisingly pleasant. I turned my hands to numerous tasks in the parlor house: marketing, sewing, gardening and nursing as the occasion warranted. I did my best to stay busy and sleep as little as possible, for my dreams still brought little save torment and terror.

On an errand one early winter evening, the seventh of December, 1842, I hurried past an abandoned mansion toward the corner of Royal Street. A fleeting movement in the shadows caught my eye. I felt as though time stopped – not for the first time in my life; I had felt that way the day of the terror. It came with seeing the precipice of Death. Yet this moment was decidedly different.

A Negro man, darker than the night itself, naked from shoulders to waist, seemed to step from the garden gate. What remained of his clothing was tattered and shackles were clamped to his neck, wrists and ankles, but their chains made no sound as he approached, nor did I hear his footstep. His eyes were empty orbs; I felt he was staring right through me.

I felt no fear. Instead, a great sorrowful agony swept upon my soul in ever increasing waves of dismay and bewilderment. Transfixed, I could do little more than barely draw breath. I have no idea how long I stood this way before I felt a warmth by my elbow. Without turning, I knew another flesh and blood being was beside me, and the being in front of me was only a memory of this world.

A woman's low voice sing-songed an indistinct stanza; a cloud of ash and dust flung from a copper hand engulfed the apparition and a scream rent the air as a whirlwind descended betwixt myself and the shade.

I turned. The turbaned troubadour regarded me with a probing yet calm gaze. I met her eyes and appraised her with equal curiosity. "You have a gift", she said matter-of-factly.

"Or a curse", said I.

"No." Again, she took measure of my countenance. "You only feel cursed. You have been betrayed, seen too much tragedy, and felt too much sorrow for such a young life. That is not a curse. It is instruction in strength and faith."

I nearly laughed. "Faith? God abandoned me long ago, why should I have faith?"

"God has not abandoned you, but it is not faith in Him of which I speak. You must have faith in yourself and your own strength."

"I'm not strong", I retorted bitterly. "If I were strong, I would make him who betrayed me disappear even as you made that ghost evaporate. I would banish him from haunting my nights and remove him from this very earth, if only I were strong!"

She smiled a little. "The man who dealt you so much pain is not a ghost. Yet." She smiled a little more. "What made that man disappear – you must be curious – is that I helped him get justice, so his soul could rest." She paused and scrutinized my reaction. "That you can see the other side is part of your gift. You can sense more than most. And when you can sense more than most, you can use it to your advantage. You can learn to help fate and faith along, if you want. I can teach you."

So, in shadows of the LaLaurie ruins, I became a student of Marie Leveau.

14

Between my studies with Mme. Leveau and my employment with Mme. Veronique, my life went from pleasant to enjoyable. Learning from Mme. Leveau proved interesting and useful. I was particularly drawn to herbs and healing; it seems I had a natural gift for not only distilling the oils and essences of plants and flowers, but also of channeling that ineffable quality of life energy into my efforts and into others. I occasionally caught a glimpse of otherworldly apparitions, and chanced to hear a word or two wafting my direction, but my instructress assured me I had nothing to fear, and I learned to accept these beings as nothing more than a part of our world that I was blessed to see.

Under the tutelage of Mme. Véronique, I acquired the skills of conversing with men and women from all walks of life, albeit leaning more towards the better classes of gentlemen. One of my tasks was to admit callers into the house, and occasionally, to make conversation should their intended companion be indisposed. I was not a servant in the house, yet not a server of delights, and trusted to keep my place in that limbo residing between respectability and Bacchanalian delights. There was a night in particular, in the summer of 1847, when the front parlor was especially brilliant with guests, spirits, music, and laughter, that again changed the course of my life.

Many of the ladies were occupied in their rooms above, and I found myself in discourse with a man – not quite a gentleman, but not a rake or rogue – who, despite consuming prodigious amounts of drink, spoke as soberly as a Sunday sermon. Oh, he had moments of flights of fancy, but he was never rude of speech, only entertaining with tales of travels betwixt New York and Texas. I thought it curious he abstained from engaging services; few crossed the threshold whose only intent was to liberally quench their thirst and converse. But perhaps this was only natural to his kind; he was a scribe, a reporter of crimes and criminals, an inquirer after tales of bravery and cowardice, a penman persuading a voyeuristic public to see the world through his eyes, and draw conclusions in accordance with his own. I found his English accent most charming, and the scar just under his left eye, alongside his nose, added character and intrigue to his face.

He – William H. Attree – regaled me with an account of the glorious heroes of the Alamo, and whispered of the inhumanity of Santa Anna in ordering the outright murder of five valiant survivors found by General Castrillón. My visage must have altered exceedingly upon this confidence, for he immediately apologized for having broached such a violent topic. "I see I have touched a nerve – I beg your forgiveness! It was imprudent of me to offer such vulgarities as amusement." He peered into my eyes, searching – for what, I know not, but I think perhaps he saw into my very soul. Heretofore, I had noticed he paid particular attention to my appearance, and seemed to be put in a reflective state of mind, but upon this arousal, his attention was fully focused on the present. "You have witnessed murder", he pronounced quietly.

Before I could utter a word, the doorknocker rapped sharply, and I hastened to my duties. I spied the camblet cloak through the window before the visitor's face; combined with the shock of the recent exchange, I felt myself grow faint, even as I admitted the profligate. He accosted me in syrupy tones, "My dear Nelly!", grasping my hand with a firm grip and squeezing to the point of pain, even as he bent to press his impudent lips to my palm.

I seethed. Swallowing indignation, remembering my place, I replied with a frosty politeness "Good evening, sir. Welcome back to New Orleans. Perhaps you do not recall – my name is Elizabeth. Will you be seeing Miss Clara this evening?" It was bad enough that this man knew my true origins; it was worse I knew he associated with my brother Nathaniel.

"Miss Clara holds the most delightful charms, indeed, but I would much prefer discovering the warmth of your companionship."

"My companionship is not available, sir. What name shall I give Miss Clara?"

"You know my name," he retorted shortly.

"By all means, Mr. Parmalee, I certainly do."

"I go by Frank Rivers here," he growled.

"As you wish, sir." I tried to extricate myself from further communication with the mercurial man, and slip into the back parlor, with the intent of sending an errand girl upstairs with a hastily written note announcing the binomial visitor.

"That's not what I wish," he snapped. In two swift strides, he was upon me, grasping my wrists. "I wish to have you, my sweet Nell – I have wished for you for a long time and I will do with you as I want – as you want!"

"You shall do nothing at all with me," I declared.

In a thrice, he pinned me against the wall, his good left hand upon my throat, his twisted right hand grotesquely brushing the hair from my forehead. "A common strumpet like you does not defy me," he snarled. "I shall have my way, and if you are very, very good, you might see the light of day tomorrow!"

My attention was captured by a movement behind Parmalee's shoulder. A resounding crack rent the air and sent Parmalee to the floor in a stupor.

When I looked up, Mr. Attree was standing close, a finger to his lips. I inclined my head to one side, silently suggesting an expeditious exit to the rear courtyard.

Once ensconced in relative privacy, he took my hands with unexpected gentleness and led me to a little ironwork settee, and bid me sit. He looked at me a long moment; I became flustered. "Dear child," he began tenderly, "long ago, I fell in love with a young lady who looked very similar to you. She was in this", he raised his eyes to the upper floor of the house, "unfortunate profession. Sadly, she slipped from my grasp."

I was confused. Did he mean to make me a stand in for a lost love? Or save me from a fate far worse than death?

"Do you know the man who was pressing himself upon you?"

"Yes." What a strange twist, I thought. Surely, after a single conversation, he is not taken with jealousy!

"As do I. Who do you know him as?"

"He is Richard Parmalee of Nacogdoches." I was quite certain upon this account.

Attree shook his head gravely. "Not quite. He is Richard Parmalee Robinson, formerly of Connecticut, once of New York." He allowed the words to register, but I was at a disadvantage. The name sounded familiar, but I could not place it offhand. "And you, my dear, are a ringer for Helen Jewett, sometimes known as Ellen, sometimes as Nell. Let us pray you do not become a dead ringer!"

At that I gasped. The pieces fell into place. I had become good friends with Clara Hazard, an upstairs girl, and she, in turn, had been friends with Helen Jewett during a sojourn in Philadelphia. Clara had once remarked upon our resemblance. I realized quickly this accounted for Parmalee's insistence on calling me by this sobriquet. Though she had never met Robinson herself while back east, Clara had recounted the tale of the notorious murder of Helen Jewett and ill-fated trial many times. I shuddered. She might not have known him then, but perhaps he knew of her – or at least, her friendship with Helen. What might he do to her, I wondered.

My voice wavered as I sought verity. "Richard Robinson? The one they acquitted because the judge instructed the jury to dismiss the testimony of the women who witnessed the crime, just because of their profession?"

"The 'Innocent Boy'? Yes." He grimaced. "I prefer 'The Great Unhung'!"

"And Helen", I said, assessing his features, "you loved her."

"Until death", he replied. The drink was beginning to catch hold of him. "Where is the proprietress of the house? She must know the danger that is presented here

– especially to you. That monster is capable of the most inhumane deeds known to man; he is depraved, without a conscience or a soul!"

"She should be in the front parlor. I will go fetch her."

"We will go together. Hurry, and through a different doorway than whence we came, before he recovers and makes a scene again."

As we hurried across the shadows, I ruminated briefly on the acquaintance between Parmalee and my brother Nathaniel. Nathaniel had never been a pleasant person, but I had never judged him evil until after the raid. Did Parmalee's depravity infect my brother, or simply encourage a long buried seed to blossom? How much has Parmalee reported to Nathaniel of my life here? And is he reveling in my shame? Or is he sending Parmalee here to ensure I do not return to Texas? How much of Parmalee's taunting of Nathaniel blaming me for the great tragedy is true – or did Parmalee concoct the story himself to manipulate me?

That very evening, Mme. Veronique sent me, with Clara, to a suite in the Saint Charles Hotel, the inaugural edifice of my sojourn in New Orleans. We played the part of a a lady traveling with her companion – Clara, of course, was the lady, as her wardrobe could more easily fit the role, and I, with plainer and more modest clothing, the lady's companion.

For six weeks, we resided in the hotel, secluded, professing a need to take shelter from an outbreak of fever near our usual residence in the country. It was a ruse that would not arouse much suspicion; the fever had already claimed several in the country as well as the city. By the time the fever ran its course, over two thousand succumbed, including Clara.

15

I tended to Clara as best I knew, with the aid of Mme. Leveau, yet our efforts were in vain. She succumbed quickly, and as I watched, her spirit arose from her body, like a person rising from their bed. She smiled, stepping forward on naught save air, to clasp me in a ethereal embrace. The specter gently shrank into itself, becoming nothing but a simple pinpoint of violet-white before disappearing from this realm. The moment was brief, but the memory of that gossamer touch and the lilac scent of her soul-light lingered for days afterward.

I moved on from the hotel, no longer comfortable taking room and board from Mme. Veronique, as nearly the whole of her house had been decimated by the epidemic. Many of the young ladies had either died or had moved to healthier climates; many of the gentleman callers had ceased to call, due to illness or emigration, I knew not.

While a resident of the Saint Charles, I had made the acquaintance of Margaret Haughery, a ruddy broad-faced

Irish woman of about my own age, employed as a washer woman at the hotel. She, in turn, introduced me to Sister Regis of the Female Orphan Asylum. Sister kindly allowed me to board, provided I could assist in the care and education of the little ones entrusted to their supervision.

Margaret and I each had rooms within the institution, a enormous building a full four stories tall, set high off the ground to protect it from flooding. Tall windows lined each wall of the first three levels; the upper floor was cheated somewhat with only diminutive dormers. Our quarters were modest, practical, and serviceable, well suited to the sisterhood who cherished service, faith, and simplicity. I must admit I rather missed the whirlwind of hotel life. There had been concerts, masquerade balls, traveling salesmen pitching their wares – a flurry of activity in every nook and cranny. I tried to fill that longing for adventure with educating the children and exploring the faith that bound these consecrated souls to their God, but I fell short time and again.

I turned my efforts outward, with the approval of Sister Regis. Together, Margaret and I scoured the neighborhoods of the city, seeking out those in need, offering solace and comfort to the dying, and assuring fearful mothers the welfare of their children would be well provided by the Sisters, should they be called to their heavenly home. The home's rosters multiplied, from a scant handful of tiny inhabitants to well over a hundred. I was granted permission to earn a wage outside the institution; I joyfully embraced the opportunity.

In the more affluent neighborhoods, I made a concerted effort to be more pleasant and agreeable, with the intention of making inroads to a better social standing for myself. Margaret was more inclined to be businesslike; her goals were financial rather than personal. Our differences made us an excellent team for the time we were together; she was a good soul who feared neither God nor man. God had allowed such tragedy in her life, much as mine – we were both orphans, deprived of our ordained marriages, deprived of children – and she put the love and devotion she would have given a husband and children into the Sisters and the orphans. I still did not know where I would put my love, but I knew my path would not run parallel to hers for long.

I endeavored to be useful as a nurse during the yellow fever ravage, followed by an epidemic of cholera. Many of the families in the better neighborhoods had taken me on as a sitter for the sick, or a lady's companion, for genteel women. When the sicknesses afflicting the city waned, I held several letters of recommendation for responsible positions in respectable households. I settled upon entering the newly established home of Charles de Choiseul, a young attorney recently arrived from Charleston.

He was gentle in appearance, broad of brow, dark haired with a mature demeanor, far beyond his limited years. I saw little of him; business and family matters consumed his waking hours. A distant relation – an uncle, I believe – was due from abroad. The visitor arrived in the dimness of an evening, in a closed carriage, a creature constrained by some unseen demon. His stature was not imposing; his form was slender. Blond hair fell in disheveled waves across an aristocratic brow. His eyes intrigued me – drowsy one moment, alert and attentive the next. A second-floor bedchamber awaited his inspection, well aired, with a wide gallery accessible from the room to enjoy the sights and sounds of the inner courtyard. Furnishings in the finest French style, silk bed linens, a gaslight chandelier and every conceivable luxury lay waiting for the esteemed guest. By my estimation, he was not impressed.

I also awaited his inspection, outside the bedchamber door, as the master of the house introduced his kinsman to the quarters. Mssr. de Choiseul bade me enter. "Elizabeth shall be your nurse, or companion, should you prefer." I curtseyed. "She arrived with the finest letters of reference."

This annunciation appeared to agitate the newcomer. He began to pace the floor, glancing to and fro as if to ascertain an escape route. Mssr. de Choiseul's eyes grew wide, as though he feared his kinsman might take some rash action. "Monsieur," I interjected, addressing the gentlemen I now considered my charge, "might I bring you some refreshment? A glass of wine, perhaps, to ease your mind after a long day's journey?"

The nervous lips trembled for a moment, as though grasping for speech. Finally, "Oui, oui, mam'selle. Wine would be most appreciated."

I hurried downstairs.

A hoary headed sentinel guarded the lower landing. Sharp, ancient eyes surveyed my form and figure. "Mam'selle," he intoned. I stared at him – rudely, I fear – for he had the manner of an apparition, a revenant from another world. "Je m'appelle Pierre." He inclined formally in my direction.

I bowed my head slightly, and hastened away to find a decanter of port, tray and wine glasses. The necessary items adequately assembled, I discovered the housekeeper, Marie, engrossed in conversation with the patriarchal phantasm. I knew naught of the French language; aside from the tenor of inflection, their words were meaningless to my ears. The dialogue ceased upon my appearance. Marie took the tray from my hands, giving the task over to the wizened wraith, who ascended the stairs wordlessly.

Quizzically, I raised an eyebrow to Marie. We drew aside, into an ante-chamber, and she answered my unspoken query. "Pierre arrived with Monsieur. He will attend as his valet, and you will remain as a sitter and nurse." Her voice dropped to an almost inaudible whisper. "Monsieur must be watched carefully. He suffered a great tragedy; he lost all his family and his mind is ill at ease."

My heart contracted with compassion. How keenly I was acquainted with the terrors begotten by such tragedy! I silently vowed to assist him in regaining a sound mindset.

The days passed easily; the nights were another matter. As the sun dipped below the horizon, the gentle guest grew nervous and tense; anxiety and apprehension lined his face. Some evenings, Pierre could, using the native language, assuage the fears that plagued our patient. Other evenings, I would sit and read to him, essays, poetry, serials and novels. The master of the house had given me leave to choose as I would from the library of the house. Emerson, Poe, Thackery – all were well-received by my listener. Then came the immensely popular work of Currer Bell, a tale of an orphan governess in love with her young pupil's guardian, who is secretly and regretfully wed to a mad woman.

I concluded one evening's recitation with the fateful flames of Thornfield Hall. Monsieur had been paying careful attention to the tale. "Mam'selle," he asked, "what do you think of this Rochester fellow? Was he wicked to wish himself a new life, with a sane and loving wife?"

"It is only natural, Monsieur, to wish for a mate compatible with oneself. How can it be wicked to wish for what is natural?"

"Indeed, how?" he mused. "Mam'selle, you have a kind and compassionate heart. I hope you will find a compatible mate for yourself, for there is nothing so lonely, so agonizing, as to be with one who has no understanding of the other."

We fell into a companionable silence as the autumn leaves drifted by the shadowed windows. "Mam'selle, I fear I may pass a restless night. Would you be so kind as sit as my nurse, to come to my aid should the night terrors lay hold my soul?"

"Of course, Monsieur."

He shook his head, a half smile lighting his doleful features. "Non, Mam'selle. Not Monsieur. Tonight, I am simply Théo."

And so I sat near his bedside that long, fitful night. In the wee hours of the morning, close to three o'clock, I was quite close to dozing myself when I heard the stair-treads creak. The rustling of a woman's skirt sounded near the chamber door. My patient nearly awoke; he turned, crying out "Partir!"

I thought I heard a paper being pressed under the doorway, followed by that of slippered feet shuffling away and eerie, muffled sobs. My mind may have tricked me, or I might have been asleep myself, for by the light of day, there was no paper to be found, and no woman of the household admitted to walking the stairs in the night.

In the morning, I confided in Marie what I felt was a

dream, and the odd coincidence of Monsieur's simultaneous nightmare. A troubled look creased her brow; she excused herself quickly without comment. By afternoon, a vial of laudanum, by doctor's orders, sat upon my patient's tea table, with directions to avail himself of the restful properties at eventide. He refused. The sight of the draught seemed to inspire more terror in his breast than the violent nightmare he had endured.

Again, I sat as a night-nurse; again, his slumber was troubled. And, again, the sense of a woman's tread outside the bedchamber door. I arose, curiosity overcoming concern, and pressed close to the door jamb, hoping to spy the elusive sprite. My efforts were to no avail; the moonlight cast only the usual shadows. Yet, I perceived sound – a sob, a moan, a heartfelt sigh of desperation? I could not be certain, but the sense of a soul in pain troubled me greatly.

The third night, Pierre sat watch over his master. I prepared to pass the hours in my own bed, but sleep eluded me. Arising, I drew my wrapper close and ventured forth, thinking perhaps to retrieve some volume which I could then peruse by lamp-light. As I approached the library doors, a deep chill unsettled my nerves. Some unnatural shadow swallowed my being; I could not see to move forward nor back. The sensation persisted a moment, or an hour; I cannot reliably say which. I do not know what occurred from that point; the next event I recall clearly is Marie helping me to sit up from the floor, pressing a cup of water to my lips, her features filled with fright.

I was ill for several days. I did not see Monsieur again. Mssr. de Choiseul arranged with a colleague to send me away with one Mr. Jesse Duren, a client in several legal matters involving the purchase of lands in Texas. I was provided with a trunk, furnished with an ample wardrobe fit for a lady of good standing, and a reticule generously filled with coins, silver and gold. Mssr. de Choiseul, aware of my fondness for the written word, kindly added to my treasure trove a collection of favored tomes.

16

I went home. How odd those simple words! Mr. Jesse Duren, formerly of Talladega, Alabama, escorted me to Texas. We booked passage upon a stage from New Orleans to Houston, thence to a mail coach headed to Nacogdoches, changing again to venture northward, where the route would terminate in the new town of Tyler, although our journey would end a bit before that locale. The first coach was a delight; the gold trim shone brightly, the woodwork had been polished until it gleamed, the leather seats were smooth as silk. A team of six strong horses impelled the coach, with a full complement of twelve passengers. As we commenced the journey, I marveled at the comfort afforded by the to and fro rocking of the carriage – what a tremendous difference from that buckboard ride to Shreve Town so long ago!

In Houston, we were maneuvered into a smaller conveyance, although still comfortable. Only a team of four was necessary; the interior of the coach accommodated nine travelers. In Nacogdoches, our transportation diminished further, to a mule team and room for six itinerants.

Passing from that fair city where I had memories of happier days, tears sprang from bottomless wells, and I turned my face to the window, embarrassed by the sudden surge of sorrow and longing. How I missed in those moments my mother and father, my brothers and sisters, nieces and nephews, and in equal parts, Kias and my dearest Molly! How deeply I felt their absence!

More than a decade had passed since that awful day, and so much can change so quickly, that for all I knew, none of my relations might be in residence. After confiding in him the horrors of the slaughter and the aftermath – omitting any references to my procurement by Madame Veronique and substituting a history of living among the Sisters of the Female Orphan Asylum after escaping Hawkins' grasp as we arrived in New Orleans – I informed Mr. Duren as we traveled should it came to pass that only Nathaniel remained, I had no desire to meet him nor to remain in the area. Mr. Duren assured me I would be welcome to accompany him back to his household in Houston, where he and his wife would endeavor to assist me in establishing myself.

At length, I composed myself. Our expedition took us to Douglass, then one new community after another – Alto, near Mr. Lacey's fort, then Rusk, Gum Creek – for the most part, following the same trace we did in the spring of thirty-seven, alongside that cheerful creek with so many shade trees.

In due time, we arrived in a little spot christened Larissa, near our original settlement. I was astonished to find a town square, surrounded on all sides by bustling businesses. Wood working shops, a blacksmiths, dry goods, mercantile, even a two story edifice with a tall pole bearing a sign inscribed "INN". It was here our modest carriage came to a halt; the residence served as a way station for the stage, feeding and housing weary travelers before they rumbled off to their next destination.

One shop bore the name "Reierson"; another, "Johnson and Dewberry; a third, the hotel, "S.L. McKee". Mr. Duren arranged for appropriate lodgings – as a single woman traveling under his guardianship, the innkeeper suggested I take a boarding room from a local woman not far from the town center. The lady in question, a Mrs. Sullivan, had been widowed at a young age, remarried quickly, but had never been blessed with children. She and her husband were older, of good moral character and standing in the community. Mr. Duren would have accommodations at the inn. The wife of the proprietor of the inn, Lockey McKee, a mother of four, kindly allowed me to use their private quarters to wash my face and refresh my clothing before presenting myself to Mrs. Sullivan.

The question of our evening's shelter settled, Mr. Duren made inquiries as to the residence of any of the original Killough family settlers. Mr. McKee proudly shared the information that Mr. Nathaniel Killough, the sole Killough survivor of the massacre, was currently in town, and regaled him with tales of Nathaniel's benevolence and magnanimity in establishing their community, as well as subscribing to establishing the foundation for an educational institution of grand proportions. His morals, Mr. McKee stressed, were beyond reproach; he was a Mason in good standing and justice of the peace for the community. In his elegant rhapsody, one would think Nathaniel no less than a saint on earth.

Mr. Duren, having heard my tales, was quietly amused. McKee wasted little time propelling Mr. Duren to the blacksmith shop, where Nathaniel was awaiting repairs to his carriage. I was not there to see the introduction; I only have Mr. Duren's account to rely upon, but I am certain of his veracity. To whit, Mr. Duren sized up the men before him and found his own conclusions as to their character. Mr. McKee, he felt, was a man who could only see virtue. Nathaniel, he declared, was a two-faced scoundrel, adept at presenting a gentlemanly façade while manipulating others for his own advancement. I did not disagree with Mr. Duren's assessment.

Nathaniel made an attempt to inquire discreetly as to Mr. Duren's interest in his sad family history. Mr. Duren parried that he had read of the attack in the newspapers long ago, and compiling histories of depredations had become a hobby of his, something he felt should be preserved for future generations. He assured Nathaniel he would be happy to take down his account, and if there were other survivors willing to recount that event, he would listen to their tales with compassion and circumspection.

Nathaniel replied rather shortly that the only other survivors were women and infants; and the women, by the very nature of their sex, could not be relied upon to give a coherent and intelligent report, as their recollections were tainted by the emotion of the moment and could not be trusted. Without giving any names, he intimated that nearly all of them had become mentally deficient due to the distress of experience. Mr. Duren gravely assented that such doings could indeed have an effect on a person, and took his leave.

All this was conveyed to me as we embarked to find Mrs. Sullivan's residence. I was disappointed but not surprised to find Nathaniel claimed to be the sole survivor. I held my head high, knowing I had survived far greater, and I felt for the moment, as a triumphant queen returning to her kingdom. I had obtained directions to the burying place of Kias, my father and brothers, and planned to pay my respects before resigning myself to returning to Houston with Mr. Duren, beginning life anew, yet again. I wore a new dress designed with my favorite colors of pink, brown and cream, with matching slippers and bonnet. I felt, for the first time in a very long time, proud and confident.

The hired carriage came to a halt. Mr. Duren knocked upon the front door of a the clapboard covered walls of what had once been a simple log cabin. The homestead seemed eerily familiar. A woman answered the knock; I stepped forth from the carriage, ready to make a new friend.

Her hand flew to her mouth. "Izzie!" she exclaimed, stumbling forward. Mr. Duren caught her up as she began to fall.

17

I was quite befuddled. How was it this lady knew my name? I hastened up the steps to the weatherbeaten front porch as Mr. Duren guided the stricken form gently in a rocking chair near the doorway. Her eyes were closed as she mumbled what seemed to be a prayer under her breath. I took her hand, spotted with age and creased with labor. Her fingernails were short, though neatly rounded, clean yet yellowing. My examination turned to her face, hair generously gray with only the barest remnants of auburn color, parted in the center and pulled back fiercely into a thick knot at the nape of her neck. Her face held traces of what her youthful features had been; her eyelids fluttered and opened.

Our eyes met, recognition transversing time and space; so much was said without a word spoken. I sank to my knees at her feet, my hands holding hers in her lap, quivering with emotion.

Mr. Duren broke the silence. "I take it you are acquainted?"

I nodded. "Allow me to introduce my sister-in-law, Mrs. Sarah Jane Killough."

Sarah Jane managed a feeble smile. "Sullivan, Sarah Sullivan. I am married to John Sullivan. We will have our tenth anniversary next spring." Composing herself as she regained her strength, she bade us stay a spell, meet her husband and share their evening meal. I was all too glad to find my place in her kind heart had not been relinquished in the intervening years.

Mr. John N. Sullivan cut an imposing figure. Nearly six feet tall, broad-shouldered, thick tousled hair in every shade of grey from lightest to darkest and soulful dark brown eyes were a combination to created take a woman's breath away, and I saw the gentle gleam of pride in Sarah Jane with every glance she gave him. As deeply as I missed my protective big brother Isaac, I could see that she had found someone who was his equal as an invincible champion and guardian.

The discourse of the evening meandered easily from one topic to the next, before finally settling upon the subject of the newly established town. John offered up a concise recitation: McKee had laid off Larissa, bringing in not only a large contingent of his family and friends from Tennessee, but also encouraging Johan Reierson in settling a group of his Norwegian countrymen. Christian Halvorsen was one who fit into the community well, having recently joined the Masons. The Olsen and Hansen men were talented woodworkers who had set up shop near the Reierson store on the town square. The McKees, in alliance with Nathaniel and others, set about building a Presbyterian church headed by Reverend McKee and a rudely-constructed log schoolhouse with the impressive moniker of "Larissa Academy", which they grandly planned to expand to a full fledged

University. Their desire was to emulate a romanticized vision of Ancient Greece, replete with philosophers and scientists, mathematicians and linguists, musicians and thespians, all scholars and sophists. The town's founders prided themselves on being men of exemplary virtues, John concluded with chuckling incredulity.

"Sounds to me as if what this county needs is some good old fashioned vice to balance out all that virtue," Mr. Duren mused.

"I reckon so," John replied. "About the only vice around here is old man Roddy selling whiskey next door to the Baptist preacher's place."

"Maybe you need another little town, with more 'interesting' entertainment, just within a stones throw." Mr. Duren mused, scrutinizing the Sullivans. "I have heard first hand how vile Miss Killough's brother can be, and after meeting him today, I am of the opinion that he could benefit from a bit of rain this little Larissa parade." He paused, considering his next words. "Do you suppose anyone in the neighborhood would be willing to sell enough acreage to build a few shops and houses?"

Sarah Jane and John exchanged a look. John nodded her direction. "As far as I am concerned, the land we have is all hers. She fought Nathaniel for her inheritance from her first husband, and the house and land are hers to do with as she pleases. If she wants to sell, then sell we will. We might even get the Sammons to sell as well. It is a shame Polly and Jeff Wallace sold out last year and moved away; that would have added a good deal of land."

I raised an eyebrow, puzzled.

She paused for a moment. "I reckon you need to get caught up on the family news. Orleana passed about a year after Julia was born in November of thirty-nine. Nathaniel wasted no time marrying Bethena Fisher; he started courting her before the flowers had withered on the grave. They married barely year after Orleana was buried." I could tell there was more to the story, but she was quick to move to the next tidbit.

"Owen died awhile back. Polly married Jefferson Wallace so the boys would have a daddy. They lived here for a bit, then sold their place, packed everything up and moved to Brownsboro." As far as Sarah Jane was concerned, Polly was out of sight and out of mind. She continued with those who were in sight and very much on her mind. "Narcissa and her new husband," she explained, "had to fight for her share just as I did for mine. We did not have to go as far as Eli Wood did for his brother George's share by taking Nathaniel to court, but it almost came to it. Your mother intervening was our saving grace."

My heart swelled at the mention of Mama. Nigh on the first thing Sarah Jane had told me was that Mama was still living, and more importantly, living with Nathaniel. I was already impatient to fly to her side and embrace her once more, although my unabashed desire was tempered with concern of how seeing her daughter, long believed dead, might affect her. Furthermore, I worried how Nathaniel would react to my resurrection. I wavered between needing to see my Mama and needing to stay away from my brother. Maybe sleeping on it would make things clearer.

We resolved to visit the Sammons family on the morrow; Mr. Duren retreated to the hotel whilst I found blessed repose beneath the roof of my own kith and kin.

18

Narcissa paled when I crossed her threshold. Four children swarmed underfoot, two boys and two girls. She was conspicuously expecting a fifth. Sarah Jane caught her firmly by the elbow and led her to a chair. I recalled the two had opposing personalities, but Sarah Jane had always been willing to let Narcissa take the lead. It seemed the tide had turned in the intervening years.

Mr. Sammons, Narcissa's husband and father of her growing brood, stomped heavily on the front steps, dislodging great chunks of red dirt from his shoes. He surveyed the scene with an air of resigned displeasure. I wondered if he simply did not like having company, or if was our particular company he found disagreeable.

Sarah Jane made herself at home in the Sammons' cabin and put a kettle on to boil. I still thought of it as Samuel's place; it was the one built for him and Narcissa before little Billie was born – and there was little Billie, no longer little. He must have been about twelve or thirteen, nearly full grown. He just needed a bit of filling out; he had grown up tall enough already. He bore no outward scars of that fateful day, but then neither did I nor Narcissa nor Sarah Jane. Our scars were all deep within our souls.

Over hot tea, strong and steeped with herbs, Sarah Jane recounted the charges she held against Nathaniel. For the first time, I heard her speak of Molly. I found my cheeks damp with tears, whether from joy or sorrow, relief or fear, I knew not.

Her recitation exhausted, Mr. Duren smoothly stepped into a salesman's patter. I saw Narcissa nodding and her husband dipped his head in agreement. By noon, an agreement was reached to the satisfaction of all parties. The Sammons family, who had already been considering a move away from such a troubled past and uncomfortable present, readily transferred their homestead to Sarah Jane and John. Sarah Jane and John, in turn, handed over their section of land to Mr. Duren for the establishment of a new town to compete with Larissa. He called it Talladega, in reference to the Alabama origins of our Killough family, as well as his own.

Mr. Duren set about making a proclamation in Larissa's square as the public gathered Saturday morning. He offered a free city lot to any man who would build a house upon it and live there. A large number of men took him up on the offer, including William Taylor, a man of proven political aspirations and good connections. Mr. Duren matched Larissa's educational institution with a saloon, the churches with a racetrack and gambling hall, and the Masonic lodge with a brothel. Other businesses, more mundane, sprang up as well, giving the dry goods and mercantiles of Larissa a taste of competition.

As Talladega grew, so did my waistline. I was dismayed to find myself in that condition unique to women. My first impulse was to remove myself from the community, but I had no idea where I might go. Sarah Jane and John insisted I remain. I had no argument with which to counter; I stayed, miserable and sick in body and soul.

Already, neighbors knew me as Sarah Jane's niece from Alabama; now I became an unexpected widow, my improvised husband tragically felled when traveling to meet me at the Sullivan home. I chose the surname McGowan; I was content with this fallacy and no one asked any further questions. We had decided early on the most prudent course was to not have my path cross Nathaniel's – at least, not yet. I ached to see my mother, but I satisfied my yearning with a glimpse from beneath my widow's veil as we drove past the Cumberland Presbyterian church she attended with Nathaniel, his new wife Bethena, and his daughters Eliza and Julia. Fortunately, John Sullivan was of the Methodist faith, and Sarah Jane and I accompanied him to services in their sanctuary.

Knowing how I keenly I missed the expanse of family, John took off one morning headed south-east. Sarah Jane was mum about where he was going, but she went around the house humming happily to herself all day. The following day, John returned with a woman and boy riding beside him. I nearly tripped over my skirts racing down the front steps. My own dear Molly was here! She stayed with us for three glorious days and two blessed nights. With her by my side, I felt more myself than I had in years. It was as if all the pain and sorrow just melted away, warmed by the love we shared.

I felt happiness for the life growing beneath my heart. Assured of being surrounded by a loving family – the Sullivan's and now Molly and her kin - I became excited to have a child to care for and watch grow into adulthood.

If it is a girl, I will give her the name Annabelle Mae, for the woman who cared for me in my darkest hours. If I bear a son, I shall call him William, for my old friend Mr. Attree, who most assuredly saved me from horrors beyond imagination.

Sarah Jane inquired as to the paternity of the child. I told her it was the result of an assault by a madman, and implored her to press me no further. To Molly, however, I confessed. In the house de Choiseul, my dearly adored patient – Théo - he became all my world, and I became his. At least, to whatever extent his afflicted heart would allow. One night, when the terrors were grasping at him, he called out and I hastened to his bedside. He seemed to know me, and be comforted, but soon was beset by confusion again. I struggled to soothe him, to pull him away from the tall windows, to entice him to sit by the fireside if he would not return to the bed. He took my hand, and his eyes changed – they boiled over with fiery passion – he embraced me, a stream of incomprehensible words murmured in my ear. "Henriette" was all I discerned, but the appellation did not prevent me from returning the fervent affection he lavished upon my face and lips. He needed me, and I needed him.

19

My time as a lady in waiting was not unpleasant, physically. The toll was emotional, and I feared, mental. Many times I wished to run to Madame Leveau and consult her wisdom; my nights, and eventually my days, grew increasingly disturbed by apparitions, and later, voices. Sarah Jane was of no help; she had never been able to conceive again following the raid and the loss of the child she carried, so had little recollection or experiences with the curious turns of body and mind when with child. Not only did I see Kias, sometimes healthy and whole, sometimes in bloody rags on a ravaged body, but also Papa, followed by my long buried brothers, the last of which to appear was Isaac. I refrained from sharing this final vision with Sarah Jane; I feared she might become as unhinged as I felt I was. Madame Leveau had counseled me well in warding off such things when dealing with victims of fevers and disease, but violent death, she allowed, was more difficult for both the living and the dead to accept.

Sometimes, it takes longer for them to leave this world, even though they are no longer of this world. She taught me some ways they could be helped, or at least, deterred from the living. I sought out the right plants to pick, dry and burn; I collected flowers to distill and anoint the windows and doors. None of the wisdom I thought I had absorbed was useful in my endeavors to lay the dead to rest and bring peace to my mind.

Some nights, I saw Kias over my bed rails, looking at me with such sadness that I was moved to tears. My growing belly was evidence of my betrayal of our love, of all our grand plans, and the children that should have been ours. I had never intended to be unfaithful to him, even in death, but life...oh, life! I cannot hold a specter in my arms, I cannot feel his lips on mine, I cannot carry a child of our own making! I never expected to find myself facing motherhood without Kias as my husband, and I wanted anyone else to be my husband, especially after all the wickedness I had seen men inflict upon the fairer sex!

I managed as best I could; some days were better than others, some were simply not worth living through but I did anyway. I was relieved when my son came quickly into this world, as if he were as desperate to escape my womb as I was to escape my life. Sarah Jane did not begrudge me my disinterest in the child. She brought him to me to nurse, and fulfilled all other motherly duties, for which I am eternally grateful.

The appearances of these phantasms all but ceased in the weeks following William's birth, until one afternoon. Papa appeared. He was aglow, shining with anticipation. "Izzie!" His voice was clear as a church bell on Sunday morning. I thought for certain he was here to finally take me with him, to wherever the hereafter might be. "Go see your mama." I hesitated. "Now! I will meet you there!"

Hastily I pulled on a sunbonnet and set off, leaping upon Sarah Jane's little mare, foregoing a saddle and riding astride. I had no idea what I was going to do or say once I arrived; I trusted Providence to provide.

Mama was sitting under an oak tree in a rush-bottomed rocker. I did not see Nathaniel or anyone else around; nothing could be heard aside from the rushing water of the creek below and the birds above in the trees. I slid down from my mount, painfully aware that I had not ridden in quite some time and was unaccustomed to using those muscles – and that perhaps, it was too soon after childbirth to be riding astride a horse.

I held back a moment, considering, then Mama looked straight at me and I ran to sink my face into her lap. Her gnarled hands stroked my hair, just as they had when I was a scared and frightened child. "Oh, baby girl. Mama's here and Papa's here and everything is just fine."

I looked up and through tear-filled eyes saw Papa standing beside her. She turned to look at him too, and I swallowed hard. She could see him just as easily as I could! I wanted to laugh with delight, but I could only gape, looking from one to the other.

"It is my time to go, Izzie. I just wanted to see you one more time. Papa made sure I could. We love you. I love you."

"I love you too," I choked hoarsely. "Please Mama, please forgive me for not seeing you sooner!"

"You do not need forgiveness for acting out of love," she whispered. "I know what Nathaniel did and what he is. You did the right thing. You are my sweet baby girl."

Her breath was coming slowly and she spoke with great difficulty. I held her hands as her chest rattled.

A ball of light came from somewhere near her chest – I was never quite sure where it originated, but it was there, pulsing with what I can only describe as life. It was there for a moment, and in the next, she stood next to Papa. They both were shimmering, glowing like a sunrise and sunset all rolled together with a rainbow of colors surrounding them. They embraced, and I saw them as they must have first seen each other, when they first met, before they married. I beheld Beauty and Love as one.

Mama's earthly body, an empty vessel, was all that was left before me.

I arranged her hands on her lap, kissed the top of her loosely wound bun of grey hair, and turned to leave. Then, I thought better of it. Papa had arranged for Nathaniel's house – our house, to be accurate, the one Mama and Papa and I had lived in - to be empty for a spell, and I would take good advantage. I walked into the house and went to the fireplace. The hearthstone wiggled free with just a little encouragement and there lay the earrings and brooch. "Thank you," I said, hoping Mama and Papa could hear. I wandered about for a few moments, recalling happier days, putting the horrors out of my mind as best I could, then turned homeward to Sarah Jane, John, and little William.

20

The visit with Mama did me good. I had no need to attend her funeral; Sarah Jane and John went and I stayed home playing with William. I am sure Sarah Jane deflected any nosy busy-bodies by letting them know it was far too soon since William's arrival for me to be going out in public. If Nathaniel ever had any inkling that I was the niece in the Sullivan household, or that I had been to visit Mama on her last day, he never let on. But it would not surprise me if he did suspect. Nathaniel had a preternatural ability to ferret out secrets and hold them close, until they could serve his purposes.

I do know he treated Sarah Jane and John with aloof indifference when he spied them among the mourners, knowing full well Sarah Jane still considered Mama her mother-in-law. Nathaniel carried a deep grudge, incensed by not only having to give Sarah Jane and Narcissa their shares of the land, including what their husbands would have inherited from Papa, but also by the fact that they had the temerity to continue to hold title and not sell at a fraction of their value to him, as he fancied himself the patriarch of the Killough clan. Adding insult to injury, they had gone so far as to transact land deals without his blessing, and even involved "that Duren man" who brought all manner of vice to his virtuous enclave. It mattered naught to the Sullivans.

Our lives went along quite nicely without Nathaniel Killough.

I had just passed the occasion of my thirty-second birthday, purportedly a widow with a small child, sharing the household duties of the Sullivan farm, living in a cabin built in good part by the hands of my departed Papa and brothers, generally content with my lot in life when excitement came to our little community in the form of Ebenezer Leighton Harvey. Eben.

He cut a dashing figure, tall but not too tall, broad shouldered with unmistakable strength in his upper arms and forearms, dark brown hair and the most arresting blue eyes I had ever seen, before or since. He wore a neat mustache when most of the gentlemen in our area were clean-shaven, and I found myself wondering what it would be to be kissed by those smiling lips topped by that delightfully debonair attachment. I blushed just thinking of him, and contrived to be introduced to this exquisite form of a man.

My wardrobe was not as stylishly abundant as it had been upon my arrival from New Orleans. I spent some time regarding what items could be adjusted quickly and to good effect, for William's arrival coincided with a distinct change in my dimensions. I settled upon a choice of ensembles, the first one a demure but eye-catching day dress. The taffeta of emerald green and black plaid matched to a fitted bodice with an extended peplum and wide pagoda sleeves, all trimmed in bars of wide black velvet, edged all around in white bobbin lace. A cameo brooch hung from my neck on a black velvet ribbon, and jet ear bobs dangled from my earlobes, brightening my appearance, and hopefully, my prospects. This I would wear to town, relying upon fortuitous happenstance as well as Mr. William Taylor, an attorney-at-law who was the most influential gentleman in Talladega and rather fond of playing matchmaker for widows, myself included.

Had Narcissa been in residence, she would have been scandalized. Sarah Jane was patient with me, perhaps thinking this was just a fleeting fancy, as she helped me dress and arrange my hair. Keeping company with a man had not appealed to me since Kias, aside from that brief encounter resulting in my son. This was an entirely new feeling for me; my heart sung and my spirit trilled in response. And I had yet to meet him!

I felt both foolish and hopeful, boldly approaching Mr. Taylor. I dared not display the eager anticipation I felt in my breast, but he saw through my subterfuge. I inquired if he had the acquaintance of the new gentleman in town, the showman who was a traveling ventriloquist. Mr. Taylor looked me up and down, and smiled paternally. "Men like him," he lectured, "are not the type for settling down. Anywhere."

"The Sullivans and I thought perhaps he might enjoy a meal somewhere other than the hotel," I suggested.

Mr. Taylor shook his head. "I am sure he has had any number of invitations already, and he will only be here for a few days, a week or two at most."

I was crestfallen. Mr. Taylor took my hand and patted it. "Mrs. McGowan, I will make the inquiry. I can make no promises."

Taking my leave of the esteemed gentleman's offices, I passed the object of my attentions on the sidewalk. I brazenly looked him in the eye and smiled, then cast my eyes downward, embarrassed by my forward behavior. I noted with satisfaction he smiled in return, a flirtatious twinkle in his eyes. My heart all but stopped in a rush of self-conscious panic as he was admitted to Mr. Taylor's office.

Mr. Taylor sent a note around to our place that evening, saying that if it would be alright with us, he and Mr. Harvey would be happy to join us for dinner the following noon, before the performance at the opera house at seven that evening. In recompense, Mr. Harvey would provide us with front row tickets to his show.

21

I fussed all morning over what to wear, but later, Sarah Jane told me it would not have made a bit of difference if I had worn the finest gown or a burlap bag – Mr. Harvey was taken with me. For the next week, I walked on air, roses bloomed in my cheeks, and laughter filled my soul. This was pure joy! I was in love, unlike anything I had ever experienced before; instead of sleeping, I would sit in bed, utterly amazed and astonished that I could feel this way and that someone so special could feel the same about me! The time flew by, and too soon, he was making preparations to leave for his next engagement, in Nacogdoches. I thought my heart might break, and I could see he felt the pain of separation as well.

Distraught as I was, I bravely bade him farewell with a quivering lip. My spirits sank, thinking I might never see him again or feel the wild tides of emotion he had roused within me. I took to my bed, and Sarah Jane tiptoed around the cabin, keeping William entertained with a picture book, coarse linen with stitched letters and embroidered pictures I had sewn together for him. Hours passed, the sun set and the moon was full overhead. I had no more tears, yet sleep evaded me.

When dawn broke, Eben was at our doorstep. He had gotten as far as Gum Creek, taken a room, and unhitched his horse from the wagon. He could not sleep either, so he rode back to Talladega for me. We left William in the guardianship of Sarah Jane and John; it was the only decent thing to do for the boy since they had been his parents more than I had ever even attempted to be.

We were married by Judge Jesse Watkins in Douglass, on the way to Nacogdoches. The judge remembered me from when Mama and Papa first came to Texas. His father had had us out to the church meeting to meet Reverend Bacon, from whom George and Allen bought our land. That seemed like a century ago; I hardly had any memory of that church meeting, aside from the building being such an odd shape and having to keep a lookout for Indians.

Suddenly, as Mrs. Elizabeth Harvey, formerly Elizabeth Killough (and the fabricated Mrs. McGowan), I realized I was on my way to Nacogdoches, and a chill quelled my exuberance. Nacogdoches only meant one thing to me anymore: Richard Parmalee Robinson.

The show Eben presented in Nacogdoches was well attended. The highest society matrons, their well-connected husbands and young ladies and gentlemen of all walks of life welcomed the opportunity to be entertained by my talented husband. I scanned the crowd from a discreet vantage point, seeing a few faces with a hint of the familiar, but to my great relief, I did not see Parmalee. But who – or what – I did see that evening was to set Eben and myself upon a path neither of us could have foreseen.

I was accustomed to seeing spirits, although when living with Sarah Jane, it was my brothers, Papa, and Kias that I mainly saw. Every now and again, there would be a shadow in the woods, maybe what remained of a traveler who met an untimely end, and sometimes, in town, I would notice a glimmer of a man or woman, even an occasional child, tagging along beside a living loved one as they went about their tasks. Rarely did these beings acknowledge me, focused as they were on their more solid kinfolks. But every great once in awhile, one would catch me looking their direction and seem to realize I saw them as plainly as they saw me. Occasionally, one would venture to speak, but I always pretended not to hear. Marie Leveau had taught me that it was my choice whether or not to converse with the spirits. I chose not to, and she granted that might be wise. She did caution me that someday, there might come a time when it would be equally wise to listen to what spirits might say. I figured I had passed that time when I listened to Papa about going to see Mama, but following the events of that night in Nacogdoches, I saw my gift in an entirely different light. But I am getting ahead of myself.

I recognized Atala Hotchkiss in the crowd – I had made her acquaintance when we first came to Texas; we were about the same age, her father Archibald was quite prominent in town. She looked almost exactly as she did when I last saw her, more than a decade ago. She had a young girl, quite pretty, of about ten years of age with her, who looked so much like her that she must be a daughter. Most women our age had been married quite awhile and had several children. I had considered her a friend in those early days. She had always welcomed me and Molly into her circle of friends, and we got along well in the way young girls like to giggle and gossip. She had flirted a bit back then with Parmalee, but he had put her off and she had turned her attention to other young men. I supposed she had settled down with one of the more outstanding fellows, for she had only been interested in the ones from a good family, with ambition, and, of course, good looks. She said she would just die if she had to have children with an ugly man, and risk having ugly children!

I longed to renew our friendship, to make myself known to her. I hesitated, knowing all too well Nathaniel had let it be known far and wide that Molly and I were long since deceased, and although I did not worry about exposing his lies, I was not inclined to explain publicly where I had been and what I had been doing with myself all these many years. In truth, I declined to explain privately those experiences to anyone, not even Molly or my new husband. Especially my new husband. The gentle, evasive half-truths I had told for the last few years satisfied many, but the full truth still niggled at my conscience. I had not always behaved as a well-brought-up Christian woman, although some might find certain extenuating circumstances to excuse my missteps in life, not everyone would be understanding, much less forgiving.

Atala was deep in conversation with a long-faced fellow with a perpetually perturbed expression. I searched my memory and connected him as Mr. Bennett Blake, a widower with a very young son back in thirty-eight, who owned a mercantile in town. I wondered if perhaps Atala had set aside her prejudices, not only against ugly men, but also widowers with children. I could see Atala was becoming quite agitated, teetering between distress and anger, while attempting to divert the child's attention from the adult discussion. Mr. Blake bowed and removed himself from the vicinity. Atala made a valiant effort to compose her emotions. I could no longer restrain my tender feelings for the friend of my youth, and wended my way towards her.

22

"Lord have mercy!!" Atala's eyes widened in surprise.

I hugged her.

She was flustered and delighted; we chattered aimlessly for a few minutes and she introduced me to her daughter, Catherine Phillips.

"So nice to meet you, Catherine," I said. "My husband is the ventriloquist you have come to see. I am Mrs. Harvey."

"I am Kate," the child corrected me.

"We call her Katie," Atala interjected with a tender smile. Kate, or Katie, returned her attention to scanning the crowd for friends her own age.

"Is her father here with you?" I inquired, curiosity needling at my mind.

"Ben Phillips was Katie's father. We were married only a few years; he died when she was quite young."

"I am so sorry."

"So am I," she confided. "My husband is not with us tonight. I remarried, rather too quickly, I am afraid."

"Not a good decision?" I postulated.

"In some ways, yes, but in other ways...I am not sure some days." Kate asked if she could join a playmate closer to the stage, and Atala gratefully gave her leave. "I hate to say anything in front of her. She is so fond of Richard, and he dotes on her."

"Richard?" A knot began to twist in my stomach.

She sighed. "Yes. That is what Mr. Blake was all about just now, pestering me again with his 'concerns' for our welfare. He is absolutely convinced that my Richard is an infamous murderer, and has done his best to loudly proclaim his past sins to the whole town."

"Richard Parmalee?" I already knew the answer, but I wanted to hear it from her.

"We married in forty-five." She fell silent, her expression lost in thought. "Father thought it was a good match. He was quite adamant that Katie and I be well situated. Father was right that we would be well provided for, and the marriage has given Richard every appearance of being a good family man, which reflects well upon him in society and among his fellow Masons. I think our marriage improved his standing and his opportunities. He is doing well; along with his interest in the store and saloon, he owns a stable and smithy, and he just started a stagecoach line last year. He is making quite a tidy fortune, and he is always the first to donate whenever there is a need. We have a lovely home, plenty of servants, and want for nothing." Her words were hollow. I heard the echo of loneliness in the timbre of her voice.

"And yet?" I probed gently.

"It is a marriage in name only." She whispered this confession. "I do not understand him at all. There will be no more children for me, not from him. He will not..." she paused delicately "consummate our union. He swears it is not my fault, that it is his – but I find that difficult to believe."

Now I was shocked. This brazen rouge who I knew to be a profligate debaucher would not claim his marital rights? I shook my head in amazement.

Atala continued. "There must be something wrong with me, because I have seen the way he looks at other women. But the ones without good morals are the ones he usually finds interesting. Which is why I am not unconvinced of Mr. Blake's accusations. I simply have no desire for my name – and Catherine's! – to be drug into such sordid gossip. Between you and I, I am quite convinced my Richard is that same Richard Robinson who stood trial for murder all those years ago and was acquitted. Richard, however, will not say yay or nay to the charges, and taunts those who ask with penny pamphlets about the sordid tale of Robinson and Jewett! He keeps a supply in the house, even leaving them on the table by the front door! I have no idea what frustrates me more – his unwillingness to admit to the truth of his identity, or the thought that he did indeed murder that poor unfortunate creature and continues to hide his guilt. Mr. Blake is convinced he is not reformed, persisting in consorting with women of ill repute, and might even be violent with them. I just cannot fathom what leads him to such deeds!" She wrung her hands, twisting her wedding ring round about as she did. "Oh, Izzie, I am so sorry to burden you with my sorrows, when we should be rejoicing in each other's company, and you should be telling me of all your adventures! I cannot begin to express how overjoyed I am to know you are alive and well! I can hardly wait to tell Richard – for though we do little else together, we do talk!"

I felt the blood drain from my face. "Perhaps," I suggested, "telling your husband might not be wise. He and my brother Nathaniel were great friends at one time; Nathaniel, like Mr. Parmalee, has secrets he wishes to keep – for his own reasons, I am sure. And my life – and Molly's – will be the better for Nathaniel's friends not knowing any more about our lives than necessary."

Her brow furrowed. "Why are men such..." she searched for the right word, and could not find an appropriate one.

"Devils?" I offered.

"That, and worse!"

"Not all are," I avowed, remembering my husband, and recalling others like John Sullivan who were good, just and decent.

"True." She smiled. "Ben was wonderful. I wish we could have had the life we dreamed of together. I wish we could have had more children, and he could have watched them grow up and become the good people I know they would be."

I patted her hand. "I understand. I felt that way so many times, after Kias was killed. Life takes terrible turns, it seems, with sorrow and heartbreak at every corner. I cannot tell you how many times I wished I had died with him that day. I cannot understand why I did not die. I cannot fathom how I managed to continue living without him, but I did. I just kept waking up every morning alive. I hated waking up every morning. I hated being alive. I hated going though every single day without him, without anyone to love me or for me to love, without any purpose in life. But then, God must have taken pity on me, because He brought me Eben. Therein is the only explanation I have for how that blessing happened." I squeezed her hand. "Perhaps God will bring you some measure of joy too, someday."

Her eyes glistened with unshed tears. "At least, I have Catherine. She is a daily reminder that there is joy in the world."

I felt a twinge in my breast. How I wished I had such maternal devotion to my little William! I had thought, perhaps, once he was born, I would be blessed with an outpouring of pride, that I would be enthralled, enchanted by this tiny person. Yes, he was a good baby, and yes, he was a delightful toddler, but no, I never felt that mystical – or is it mythical? – bond between a mother and child. Sarah Jane felt it, and I am glad of it, since he is all the better for having her and John as surrogate parents. These thoughts, and more, swept through my mind in great torrents, upsetting my soul, and I felt it best to excuse myself. I parted company with Atala with a tender embrace and her promise to keep our meeting a treasured secret for the two of us.

Eben rented a room at an inn for the duration of his engagement. We had agreed we would not be in town long; he expected to give three shows at most, and then we would move onto the next town, probably into San Augustine. It was a working honeymoon, but I was delighted to simply have any sort of honeymoon.

I entered our modest accommodations alone, leaving Eben to conclude his performance while I prepared for our first night as man and wife. The grand trousseau I would have had for marrying Kias was no longer mine, but I did have a respectable selection of clothing. The housemaid at the inn, a lithe mulatto girl who looked to be not yet twenty, brought up fresh water for the ewer and basin, along with a rough block of soap and clean strips of flannel to use as towels. She carefully lit the lamps in the room, creating a romantic glow. "Missus Harvey, kin I gitchu anythin' else?"

I thrilled to being called "Mrs. Harvey"; it brought a smile to my face and joy to my heart. "No," I replied, "I do believe everything is quite in order." She gave a little curtsey and closed the door softly behind her.

I hummed a happy tune as I slipped out of my things, until I stood before the washstand in my white chemise. Glancing in the mirror, I barely recognized myself. Is this what love has wrought – a miracle? I had considered myself pretty as a girl, vain creature that I was, but never beautiful. All those years from New Orleans to Talladega, every glimpse I had of my reflection, I only saw a sad, plain, disinterested woman with not even the tiniest hint of life. But now – now I saw beauty in my features, a glow to my complexion, a sparkle to my eyes, a quivering fullness to my lips, radiance in the strands of my hair – I was made anew! I hugged myself and twirled around, giddy with anticipation.

The brass knob rattled, a precursor to the oak door opening. I took a step toward the threshold, ready to greet my beloved with all my affections.

Instead, Richard Parmalee loomed in the doorway, eyes narrowed, his breath heavy with exertion and bourbon.

I shrank back, moving toward the window, "Get out of my room," I commanded as firmly as I could muster.

"Nelly, you little…" He mumbled some words, the only thing I was certain of was the language was not nice.

"I am not Helen." I thought at worst, I might could overturn the oil lamp and escape, at best, I could break the window – how much good that might do, I could not imagine, but it was all I could think of doing.

"I thought I got rid of you and your conniving..." He lurched into the room, unsteady. His withered right hand hung useless at his side, but his left hand – he had become adept with that new favorite – held a folded straight razor.

I thought to appeal to his vanity. "Mr. Parmalee, remember yourself and your position in this town!"

"I saw you with my wife tonight. What did you tell her about us?"

"There is nothing about us to tell!" I was beside myself, confused, wondering if he truly recognized me as myself or if he remained fixated upon the thought I was somehow Helen Jewett. As which person should I address him, to best deter his advances?

"I told you I could not marry you. I told you I had to marry someone Father approved of, someone of a good family, with money..."

My mind whirled. I had never had any such conversation with this madman! Surely he has lost his mind, or is he simply drunk and mistaken, reliving his past. Reliving his past, if he sincerely believed me to be Helen Jewett, my life was in imminent danger. My breath came in short, fearful gasps.

"Nelly..." he took another off balance step sideways and forward. "I did as Father wished. I married well. You will not interfere..."

I backed up against the window and fumbled to raise the sash behind me. I felt a cool waft of night air.

"This time, you will not be coming back, ever again. I learned from my mistakes last time. This time, you'll go away for good..."

He flipped open the razor, the blade glinting sharply. Taking the deepest breath I could manage, I screamed.

I heard footsteps racing through the hallway. Eben burst into the room just as I saw a spirit form materialize and wrench the weapon from Parmalee's hand. My dear husband turned on the dastardly intruder, his fist connecting roundly with Parmalee's jawbone. I heard a distinctive crack, and hoped it was Parmalee's jaw and not my husband's hand. The razor clattered to the floor, breaking the blade from the sheath, sending the two pieces scattering beneath the bed and dresser.

Eben readied another assault on Parmalee's visage, connecting with his proboscis and effecting a flood of crimson. Parmalee flailed about, as the housemaid and innkeeper arrived at the door. Eben looked the innkeeper coolly in the eye. "Get this trash out of here," he demanded. The innkeeper, recognizing Parmalee, hesitated momentarily, surveying the scene.

I moved to the bed, pulling up the top quilt to cover myself for modesty's sake, and embarrassed, the innkeeper took Parmalee's arm, saying "Here now, sir, you've had a bit of drink, perhaps a bit much? Let me help you find your way home." The wide eyed maid looked at me questioningly, and I replied with a tremulous smile and quick nod. I would be fine; I was just shaken. She closed the door for us, and I was certain the word of what had occurred would be all over town by morning. I felt such sorrow for Atala; she had done nothing to deserve such a wretch nor the gossip that would ensue.

Eben took me in his arms. I breathed in the scent of him, deeply, memorizing the smell of cherry tobacco and brandy, feeling the contours of his body against mine, my cheek nestled between his chin and shoulder, his lips brushing against my hair as he murmured soothing words of love and trust.

I opened my eyes for a moment. Where Parmalee had made his lunge, there was a the ghostly figure of a woman, almost a mirror image of myself. I knew without doubt this was Helen – Nelly – and she had been responsible for the loss of his straight razor. She smiled radiantly, then faded into darkness.

23

We left Nacogdoches the following afternoon. I sent a note to Atala, by way of the maid, explaining what had transpired. I could only hope she trusted me and could someday free herself from communion with that man.

As winter waned, we reached New Orleans. Eben's performances were well attended. He was developing new material, trying different approaches, and gaining a following. Still, he felt there was more he could do. Perhaps, he opined, there was more we could do. He broached the idea of bringing me onto the stage with him. I was flustered. I could not imagine myself getting up in front of such crowds, being an object of scrutiny and curiosity. Besides, what could I do?

We attended the performances of other entertainers. We saw musicians, thespians, magicians and mesmerists. Eben and I were invited to participate in a spirit circle. Henry Rey, a creole freeman of color I had made the acquaintance of many years ago, was starting to investigate the spirit world through séances and mediums. He knew of my apprenticeship with Madame Leveau, thought perhaps I might be talented in communicating with the world beyond. There was a fellow, a Reverend Harris from New York, at the Verandah Hotel on St. Charles Avenue, who was a Spiritualist of the 'rapping' variety. Henry suggested Eben and I have a private séance with this 'Reverend'. Eben readily agreed. I was dubious. Aside from seeing Helen's spirit that fateful night, I had not shared fully with my husband my experiences with the other side. I hoped this gentleman might be a charlatan; I feared he might be genuine. I feared he might expose me as a half-witted sibyl.

In my opinion, he was both charlatan and genuine. The séance followed the usual format. The rappings and table turning gave vague messages of love, peace, hope and the need for patience, that better days will come. Was my nature revealed while we were in his presence? Perhaps. To my knowledge, no one had informed him of my 'gift'.

As we prepared to take our leave from his rooms, he fixed his gaze squarely upon me, saying "If one has a disposition to ascend into the ethereal realms or is gifted with power to unlock the secrets of nature and unveil the mysteries of the heavens, one is presumed to be mentally diseased." He gauged my reaction, which I thought was of no discernible change, and continued. "Fear not, dear lady. To see through the veil is no disease of the mind, it is a blessing of the spirit. Expose the work of Heaven, and bring forth a new world, for this world shall soon be ripped asunder."

Eben closed his hand over mine and thanked the Reverend for his time.

· · ·

I contemplated those words, and decided I should tell Eben the whole of my 'blessing'. I spent the next several days explaining to my husband the nature of my visions, when they began, what I could – and could not – see, what I could hear, and whether or not I could clearly or reliably communicate with Spirit. He had more questions than I had answers. Sometimes, I was nearly to the point of tears, trying to explain that I simply did not know, that I did not want to know. He pressed to know if I could foretell the future – the near future or the distant. I swore I could not, but he kept coming back to Papa telling me to go see Mama. I protested, that was not my knowledge, that was Papa's on the other side. Eben wondered how much of the future the spirits could ascertain, and if they could be persuaded to share their knowledge. Again, I pled ignorance and apathy. I truly did not know nor want to know! I felt then, as I do now, that all shall be revealed when I arrive on that other shore, and I have no need for prescience.

But Eben was thinking, planning, devising a means of riding the rising wave of Spiritualism as performance.

We decided to seek more permanent lodging in the city, locating a small but charming home, fully furnished, with a front parlor suitable for private appointments. Eben undertook learning mesmerism. He was a quick study, and adept in the art. His subjects quickly succumbed to his instructions, and he found the work intriguing and profitable. The occasional difficult client, he would use his vocal ability to create otherworldly voices, which, if nothing else, convinced many he was in contact with the spirit world himself. Time and again, he asked if I would add offering my gifts to the seekers, and time and again, I demurred.

We began attending services in a new type of church, one which was generally (but not officially) identified as Unitarian, Universalist and Spiritualist, aptly described as 'The Stranger's Church'. Parson Clapp led the services; there were no Sunday school classes, no women's sewing circles, no men's Bible classes, no prayer meetings, no missionaries, and no donations – only the good reverend's sermons. Although he was a former Presbyterian minister, his ideas were far from the Presbyterian teachings of my youth, yet, in view of my experiences, a welcome sojourn. As time passed, other preachers took the podium. One in particular, a reverend from Tennessee named Ferguson, made quite a stir. He claimed his theology came from mediumistic messages in séances, with the general messaging being "One God, one race, one destiny." He declaimed "Eternal doom or damnation is a hideous fable of a barbaric age; a dream of the fanatic, a tool of the designing, and a curse to all who receive it." Between the sermons of Reverends Clapp and Ferguson, and the cajoling of my dear husband, I was finally persuaded to subject myself to Eben's mesmerism, to settle for myself my relationships with those beyond the veil and my duty to those on this side of that distant shore.

"Close your eyes, be one with the Spirit, be one with the Light. Seek and you shall find, ask and you shall receive, look and it shall be shown unto you."

I awakened from the somnambulist state with an inexplicable sense of well-being and purpose. I recalled clearly all that had exchanged between myself, my husband's gentle guidance and the spirit world. Both Reverends had attended our experiment and were joyfully convinced of my mediumship. I found myself no longer reluctant to take up that mantle, and basked in their congratulations on such clear and conscientious communication with the afterworld. Many had been brought forth from Spirit to deliver words of reassurance, wisdom and descriptions of the after-state, all upon the questioning of the theologians. The messages conveyed through my altered state aligned well with their own inclinations, and in some cases, gave them impetus to expand their convictions. As for myself, I found a quietness of my own spirit, content with my gifts and how I should go forward sharing messages of hope, love and faith from the far world to our own.

With great enthusiasm, the reverends shook Eben's hand in turn, bowing to me and taking their leave, proclaiming their mutual desire to continue having sessions in the future. As soon as the door had closed behind them, I turned to Eben, saying "We need to pack. Our future is not here."

He smiled.

At the end of July we boarded the Eclipse, one of the fastest and most luxurious steamboats, for our journey up the Mississippi River to Louisville, Kentucky. I was following Spirit and Eben was happy to let me lead, as long as there was money to be made.

24

We took a comfortable stateroom on the boiler deck of the riverboat, with enough space to hold private audiences for those seeking to consult the spirit world. Politicians, businessmen, widows, newlyweds – there was no end to the parade of humanity desiring to see the future, consult with the departed, or experience for themselves the somnambulistic state. We did our best to accommodate them all.

Most of our clients engaged i the usual inquiries of wishing to hear "I love you" one more time from the dearly departed, advice on speculative investments, or moving a household to a new locale, but within those communications, a singular disturbing trend began to emerge from the other world. Time and again, Spirit urged caution, speaking of a great price to be paid. Spirit asked – nay, begged - the living to embrace compassion and kindness to all beings; even venturing to speak of the evils of greed across the country, both North and South, and the peculiar institution which at least, needed reform, and some declared, dissolution. We repeatedly heard dire predictions of wrath and perdition, damnation and destruction, and the Valley of the Shadow of Death incarnate upon the land. Such foreboding gave pause to only a few.

Our third day, we dined on stuffed shoulder of lamb with mint sauce and broiled oysters, with beets, spinach and tomatoes, followed by English cream with strawberries and pound cake. The cake and cream complemented the perfectly ripe, sweet strawberries, a blissful finale to dinner. I was content, though tired. We tarried over the last of the dessert, making small talk about the weather, the latest letter from Sarah Jane, and what we might encounter upon docking in Louisville. Our progress on the river was punctuated by regular stops. It seemed every town and almost every plantation had a dock where passengers departed and others boarded, cargo was hauled aboard, and provisions replenished. As interesting as the rhythm of ingress and egress was, I was eager to disembark. I heard whispers among the waiters and maids of illness spreading among the crew and travelers alike and I knew of at least two deaths, for I had seen spirit forms wandering in confusion about the decks.

The afternoon passed in the usual way. We strolled the hurricane deck, enjoying the breeze, then repaired to our quarters. I read for a bit and Eben busied himself with whatever newspaper was available. That evening, we partook of a cold supper – breads, meats, cheeses, sugared fruits, nuts, custards – enjoying a cool breeze and a crisp wine. As the last light faded from the horizon, I bid my dear husband goodnight and retired to our room. He planned to join some gentlemen for brandy and cigars, which would keep him occupied until the wee hours of the morning. I bolted the door and changed into my dressing gown, prepared to continue reading Thoreau's 'Life in the Woods' by lamplight until I felt the call of Morpheus.

The stateroom adjoining ours had been empty the previous evening. Tonight, it was occupied and there was much coming and going, to judge from the sound of the door opening and closing, and footsteps from people of varying gaits and weights. I heard men's voices, low and worried, just outside our door. The commotion prevented me from properly focusing on my book. I set it down in annoyed frustration.

I dimmed the lamp and listened in the semi-darkness, catching snatches of conversation. "Rinaldo, I do not think he can last much longer."

"I thought he was looking better."

"What will your sister say if her husband dies and you procrastinated summoning a doctor?"

"She will probably say 'good riddance'"

Hurried footsteps approached them. "Excuse me, Mr. Hotchkiss."

Mr. Hotchkiss – Rinaldo – your sister – her husband. Those words formed an ominous picture in my mind. I went to the door and opened it. The gentlemen bowed, apologizing for having disturbed me. I looked at each in turn, searching for a vaguely remembered face. There. It had been years since I had seen him; he was no longer the skinny boy I had known, but it was him. Rinaldo Hotchkiss. Atala's brother. Richard Parmalee's brother-in-law.

I smiled wanly, abruptly and acutely aware of my appearance, although the dressing gown over my chemise was perfectly within the bounds of modesty, it was not how a proper matron should appear to a group of gentlemen in the saloon of a riverboat. I retreated, bolting the door as quietly as possible, hearing the solemn reverberation of their footsteps receding into the distance. My heartbeat pounded fear into every vein of my body. Knowing Parmalee was on board, quite possibly in the room adjacent, terrified me. I needed to get to safety. I needed to get to Eben.

25

The following afternoon, the fourth of August, I had recovered my senses somewhat. Eben promised to remain by my side for the remainder of the journey. I put on my newest frock, a jacquard weave in Prussian blue trimmed with embroidered grosgrain ribbon dripping with blue and gold fringe, the capelet bodice and tiered sleeves accented by a matching set of white lace modestie and engageantes. A pretty dress always bolsters my courage!

We took our usual stroll on the hurricane deck. Rinaldo Hotchkiss and his companion approached us from the opposite direction. I discretely nudged Eben, nodding towards them.

The gentlemen tipped their hats to us, and Eben responded in kind. I mustered a warm smile. Rinaldo spoke first. "Begging your pardon, ma'am, you look familiar to me. Have we met?"

I was prepared for this. I gave a little laugh and let a twinkle come into my eye. "It has been many, many years. Your sister and I were friends back in the early days of the Republic. I do not expect you to remember me; Atala had so many lovely friends, and many quite prettier than I. I am Elizabeth, and this is my husband, Mr. Eben Harvey."

He nodded, with a broad grin. "Of course! But surely you were the prettiest of them all! I simply could not keep straight all the young ladies that Papa called the "giggling gaggle"! What a delight to make your acquaintance again!" A shadow crossed his face, and I realized he must have been privy to whatever gossip was spawned in our wake after Parmalee's inebriated visit to our lodgings in Nacogdoches.

Eben took charge of the conversation. "Where are you gentlemen headed?"

Relieved at this redirection, Rinaldo introduced his companion, Mr. Daniel Coe, a brother-in-law to Parmalee by marriage to his sister, Cynthia, and his partner in the livery and stagecoach businesses. Mr. Coe explained they were journeying to Washington DC to meet with officials of the post service, with the intention of expanding their mail service routes. Unfortunately, Mr. Parmalee had taken ill with a fever. He feared the prognosis was not favorable.

Eben lowered his voice, confiding in the pair. "My dear wife has exceptional skills as a nurse. Before we met, she saw many patients through yellow fever and other maladies. Perhaps she could be of some assistance to your friend?"

If Rinaldo had connected us to the incident in Nacogdoches, it was now forgotten. He looked at me hopefully.

I nodded assent. "I carry some medicines with me that might help." I did my utmost to appear concerned and compassionate, even as my mind turned to the tincture of jimson weed in my carpetbag. In the right amounts, it can heal. In the wrong amounts, it can be be poisonous – even deadly.

"Any assistance would be greatly appreciated," Rinaldo tried to sound hopeful but failed. "One of the boat's washer-women has been tending him. The captain says she is a excellent healer; he relies on her whenever a passenger or crewman falls ill. She has been giving Richard all sorts of things, poultices of black snake root, infusions of sarsaparilla, and ground up roots from blackberry briar bushes. Some days he is better, and some days he is worse. He has had spells of delirium, and other times, he is as lucid as you or I."

"Is you Miz Helen? He be a-callin fo' you."

I could not lie to the old woman. But I could not tell her the truth, either. "May I have a few minutes alone with him?"

"Yas'm." She took a moment to rinse out the rag she had used to sponge off his forehead, in hopes of lowering the fever. Her eyes were large and sad. "Ah's done all Ah knows. Hit's up to de Lawd now." She closed the door softly behind her.

He roused, murmuring "Helen."

"I am not Helen. My name is Elizabeth."

"Helen," he repeated.

"You look terribly familiar. Let me see – is it Rivers? No...Robbins...Robinson? No. Let me think! Parmalee, is it not?"

He raised his head slightly, and caught sight of me. He stared, expressionless for a time, then his eyes met mine. I saw the fog lift from his mind, and he spoke with clarity. "You. You never figured it out, did you?"

"Whatever do you mean?"

"I did it. I killed him. Hawkins, Nathaniel and I – we planned the whole thing. Van Sickle was in on it too. Nathaniel and Hawkins wanted the land and the money. I wanted you. Nathaniel was supposed to bring you to me, after it was all over, but Hawkins bullied him and he reneged on the deal. I made sure your fiancé was out of the way so you could be mine. I am the one who shot him, the coward – running away from me instead of standing and facing me like a man. I shot him in the back. I had no other choice. Barakias Williams, he was the only thing that stood between us – until your brother betrayed my trust."

I was speechless. Numb with shock, I could not move. I could not think. I could not even breathe until he spoke again.

His mind clouded again. "Forgive me, Helen." He looked beyond where I stood. Was he asking my forgiveness? Or hers?

I filled his glass with whiskey and added the tincture of jimson weed, and a dash of rue for good measure. He would never hurt anyone again.

We docked at Louisville on Monday the sixth of August, as rioters filled the streets of that fair city. A stretcher bore Parmalee to a carriage and thence to the Galt House where he lingered for two days. From there, he was laid in a vault at Cave Hill Cemetery.

Eben and I decided to continue our journey. St Louis held much promise. We headed west.

26

Steeples and smokestacks. Row upon row of tall buildings, stepping forward uniformly from the land, adhering to the gentle curve of the river-way, politely separated from one another by narrow passageways. It seemed to stretch on for miles and the steamboats docked in a neat line were too numerous to count. Such was my first sight of St. Louis.

I knew no one in this city; in many ways, I felt as if I were once again being led into uncharted territory, thrust friendless into an abyss of humanity which cared neither if I lived nor died. In weaker moments, my soul trembled. I relied heavily upon my faith in Spirit and my trust in Eben, taking comfort in his effortlessly masculine charm as he navigated our next steps.

He engaged a room for us at the Barnum Hotel, close to the river. The establishment was new, outfitted with the most elegant furnishings. I was entranced by the minute details of perfection, and made note of how I might create such an atmosphere in our own home, once we found a suitable property. For some time now, Eben has delighted in planning for us to give public demonstrations of mediumship, semi-private spirit circles, and private sittings, perhaps even establishing a Spiritualist church of our own, with him at the helm. I simply wished to use my gifts as best I could, have a cottage of our own, some books to read, and allow him to manage everything else.

I had resolved before leaving New Orleans that Eben and I should having matching attire for our public appearances. Eben used the term costumes, but I felt strongly such wording was inappropriate. More akin to vestments, I insisted. We were offering a spiritual service, not a performance. Wisely, he acceded to my reasoning.

I chose a light brown silk moire for my 'sitting gown'. I debated between an off the shoulder neckline with cap sleeves or a more modest neckline with short pagoda sleeves. I settled on the former, reasoning I could easily add a capelet for modesty, should the need arise, and the gown would be well suited for evening wear. The neckline and sleeves were trimmed with runched silk in a fine claret color delineating between the gown and the Brussels lace embroidery edging the sleeves and neckline. The lace was scalloped along the edge, with an abundance of crescents of delicate fronds, accented with a variety of florals. I chose two pairs of undersleeves, one rather plain, and the other with double cuffs, ruffles, embroidery and lace to match the trim of the gown. There was, of course, a crinoline, lace trimmed petticoats, chemise and other undergarments, which I need not detail, unlike the lady who made such a fuss over flannel petticoats.

For Eben, I chose a frock coat in the same claret as the trim of my gown, lined in the light brown silk moire with a matching cravat. His waistcoat was of a chocolate brown and claret paisley; his trousers were simple black woolen broadcloth. He cut quite a dashing figure.

To acquaint ourselves with the city, we began attending services at a Unitarian church, taking in lectures at the Mercantile Library, and acquainting ourselves with the opera houses and theaters, from the noblest edifices to the rudest barns. Within those halls, our immediate future lay.

Eben proved an excellent promoter of our services, for entertainment and elucidation. As distasteful as I found the description, I will admit it was an accurate one. He presented himself as an accomplished student of mesmerism, and myself, as a talented trance medium, available to the scientific scrutiny of one and all. For a price, of course.

Each venue had their own structure of contracts. Eben's preferred method was to sell tickets at a nominal charge, the proceeds of which would be ours for the most part, and then split any other proceeds from our engagement with the proprietor. This generally was understood to mean the sale of spirits - the liquid variety, not the incorporeal. I was unhappy with the sale of alcohol during our presentations and implored Eben to seek situations where such vice would not be tolerated. When I realized he had no intention of honoring my requests, I sought the aid of Spirit.

We were steadily employed throughout the months of September and October. In mid-October, Spirit spoke through me a way which would greatly change the course of our professional lives.

Each presentation would begin in a similar manner. Eben would give a general lecture, brief, on mesmerism, and perhaps even give a demonstration using a volunteer from the audience. Once the attendees were satisfied with his ability to create the trance state in a subject, he would then introduce the topic of communication beyond the veil. Elaborating upon the familial tragedy I had witnessed as a child (his interpretation, not mine), he went on to weave a story wherein I developed the ability to speak with the departed. His words were not explicitly untruthful, yet he shaped my life story to fit his ambitions. Such prevarications meant little to me, except for the occasional twinge of conscience and unease that perhaps my dear husband was not seeing me for who I was, but only for what I was – an economic asset to himself. After my life story was presented in its abbreviated and inventive form, he would then conduct me to the stage.

The first time he escorted me to the platform, I felt a knot in the pit of my stomach. My mouth went dry; I felt faint. Thankfully, he had anticipated my discomfiture, dressing the stage in advance with a settee, footstool and a small table upon which a decanter of fresh water and a crystal glass reposed. (At this point, I must interject that the public water of St. Louis, coming from the river as it does, is not always the most enticing to observe, but has the most satisfying, sweet and pleasant taste of any water I have ever enjoyed!)

Seated, I focus my attention upon my dear husband, and under his direction, I am soon in a trance. What proceeds from there, I cannot tell. I only know what has been related to me by others. In that October demonstration, I am told I gave quite a dictation from the trance state.

The question was put to me – and, again, I recall none of the phenomenon – "How shall a man live?".

Spirit, speaking through me, gave the usual answers and platitudes, enjoining mankind to live by the Golden Rule, reminding the assemblage that all have free will. Man may choose to do good, to be kind, generous and thoughtful, to be temperate in habits, to eschew that which might make him disagreeable company to others, whether that might be in the use of alcohol, the habit of gambling, or the misrepresentation of himself or others. Likewise, man may choose to do evil, to make slaves of other men, to live licentiously, a profligate who brings shame and embarrassment upon his family.

Then, Spirit turned to prophecy. There were the oft-repeated warnings of a coming judgment upon the land, which did not move anyone, regardless of their allegiance to North or South in the growing rift across the country. Spirit closed with an unusual statement. "Pride goeth before destruction, and a haughty spirit before a fall. You are prideful, and haughty in your ambitions. The bridge you build to the future will not hold; you must restrain your eagerness. Be humble, take care, assume nothing, otherwise women will weep and children will be orphaned, and Progress shall be stilled."

I was as puzzled as anyone when these words were related to me. The meaning became apparent late in the evening, Thursday, November first. The joyful occasion of the morning, when a multitude of leading men of the city set out to celebrate the rail connection between St. Louis and Jefferson City, turned somber as the Gasconade bridge collapsed, taking train car upon train car into the riverbed where injury and death awaited the ill-fated passengers. The bridge, incomplete, with only temporary supports, was presumed safe for passage for political expediency, heedless of human cost. Over forty men's souls were lost as a result; more than three times that number maimed or wounded.

27

The communal tragedy was a bittersweet blessing for us. We, with the city, mourned the great loss, but word of my prediction from the trance state established a reputation for legitimacy. We were pressed to obligate ourselves to further presentations; for awhile, I complied but soon wearied physically and emotionally. I admitted my despair to my dear husband one afternoon as he booked yet another engagement for us.

"What would you have us do, then? I am too old to return to traveling as a ventriloquist, and I doubt you would relish the prospect of constant motion."

If he thought to incur feelings of guilt in my breast for depriving our household of its daily bread, he had underestimated my resourcefulness. "Several of the widows from the train disaster have approached me with requests for private consultations, desiring to communicate with their loved ones. More than a few are approaching the dénouement of their own lives; just this week, Mrs. Chouteau and Mrs. O'Flaherty sent notes asking if I would call on them."

Eben ran a forefinger across his mustache, as he was wont to do when considering a new thought.

I continued, "As for you, dear husband, did you not mention just the other day that you have been approached to assist with the operations of the new Grand Opera House? I suspect you might enjoy such an endeavor."

Thus, the framework of our lives was established for the next few years. With the proceeds from the sale of our little cottage in New Orleans and feeling assured of continued income with Eben employed by the opera house, he allowed me select a home for us in St. Louis. I was delighted at the prospect.

We settled upon a narrow row house, designed with a French influence, facing a pretty park. The front parlor became a business office of sorts, where I received paying visitors. Most were widows, a few elderly ladies brought their husbands, hoping for some word from beyond of a lost child, but they all sought the same reassurances: that their loved ones did not suffer, that they were happy and awaiting reunion beyond the veil. Occasionally, I was asked to advise on the future. I declined more often than not, not due to inability (for Spirit can convey direction, be it forewarning or encouragement) but because when queried, Spirit showed me such great sorrow upon the horizon that it pained me to convey the messages.

Spirit, of course, was not the only bearer of tidings. In the summer of 1859, I received a letter from Sarah Jane, relating the latest news of Larissa and what little remained of Talladega, with a few choice remarks about the increasing number of yellow babies from the slave women owned by Nathaniel, and the news she had gotten from friends back in Alabama that a certain Mr. Hawkins had departed this earth. I must admit, my heart rejoiced a bit upon reading those words.

The sorrow and sadness Spirit showed me came to fruition in the form of a great and terrible war. Eben and I refused to take sides, which was a difficult position to maintain. Emotions ran high, and the city was divided. We had good friends who were staunch Unionists, and many who were equally in favor of the Confederacy. Some of our circle were abolitionists and some were slave owners. We did not own slaves ourselves; we engaged a free woman of color as our cook and housekeeper. The story that Sarah Jane once told had stuck in my mind, a cook in Nacogdoches had poisoned – although not to death, only to the point of dire illness – the family who owned her.

Spirit relayed, time and again, that people must treat one another as equals, for our soul-spirits are all the same and of the same Source, the same Creator. Furthermore, Spirit bid we use our free will to choose unconditional love for one another, to set aside instruments of destruction and come together with open hearts, forgiving one another with heartfelt compassion. In my opinion, Spirit asked far more of humanity than humanity was willing to consider giving.

The war continued, incessant bloodshed, loss upon loss. All around us, division and anger and even outright hatred spewed forth from every threshold and into the streets, community and businesses, making life nearly unbearable. I received one family after another, seeking comfort in the loss of sons, husbands, brothers, fathers, blue coats, gray coats, redlegs, bushwhackers, jayhawkers, and innocents caught in the crossfire. I did my utmost to comfort the bereaved, but at last the toll proved too great for my constitution. I desperately desired an end to the suffering and an end to being called upon day and night to seek lost loved ones beyond the veil. I confided in my dear husband the depths of my distress.

"Suspend giving readings," was his simple and forthright advice. "We have enough set aside; there's no need for you to make yourself ill with other's troubles." He thought for a moment. "The Bauer fellow at work – he has a relation, a cousin of some degree, I think, over in Jefferson City, who has been writing him about setting up for a theater once this blasted war is over. Bauer has asked if I would go with him to visit and look over his plans. Maybe you and Frau Bauer could make the trip with us, and we could all have a regular outing." He paused, and I could tell his mind was already thinking of the pleasure he would take in sharing his knowledge of the entertainment business with a new crowd.

28

We arrived at the Jefferson City Bauer residence as news of devastating losses at that little spot in Pennsylvania, a place called Gettysburg, filled the newspapers. I felt physically ill, although nothing bodily was afflicted. A sickness of spirit, a deep sorrow and dread of what was yet to come overwhelmed me; I saw my reflection in the looking-glass, but it did not reveal the truth within, the tears I wanted to shed and could not, the pain I felt from invisible wounds, the grief that permeated my lungs until I thought I would suffocate.

I did my utmost to make pleasant conversation with the Bauer wives. Frau Bauer spoke with a heavy German accent and had difficulty with the English language, much to her own amusement as well as others. Mrs. Bauer of Jefferson City had less difficulty, and her pronunciation of our language was further advanced than her St. Louis counterpart. During the afternoons, we sat in the parlor. I brought some needlework and books to occupy my hands and mind; when I was thus engaged, they would fall to speaking in their native tongue. I did not take notice, as I knew their conversations centered on only two things: their husbands and their children. Both women had produced a multitude of offspring, much as my own mother. By my count, there were at least eight children in the Jefferson City household, with more to come. I had little to contribute to conversations of child rearing and was thankful for the quiet time to tend to my own tasks, which in some small way, calmed the storms in my spirit.

I surmised from Eben's evening reports that the gentlemen's discussions and tours of the city were interesting but held little promise for him. He enjoyed the sojourn, but was eager to return home. The day before we were scheduled to depart for our familiar walls, he suggested we take a drive around the city and even into the countryside, so I could see some of the sights which had impressed him. I ignored my gnawing sense of foreboding and readily agreed, delighted to see him enthusiastic and wanting to share his experiences with me.

Mr. Bauer graciously allowed us the use of a trap and horse, and we set out in the morning to tour the capital city. I wore one of my favorite dresses, a bright rose colored wool trimmed with dark blue velvet and gold braiding. Eben's eyes lit up when he saw me well-dressed and smiling; a nice dress always did wonders for my disposition. I had great hopes this would be a lovely outing.

The city, of course, was under Union control, and the atmosphere was colored by division and acrimony, but I could see what a lovely, well-designed community lay beneath the contentious surface. At length, we turned to the countryside, and I again brushed aside the ill ease, attributing it to the presence of so many reminders that our county was at war with itself.

We had not gone far, but we had gone too far. The bucolic scene was assaulted by hoofbeats. My heart stopped, my mind recalled the same sound, the same pounding of horses racing, bringing death and destruction on the day Poppa and Kias were killed. Fear gripped me in an icy embrace.

The riders surround us. All men, all ragged, all with a hungry, angry look to their eyes. Some were barely men, one was merely a boy. All were deadly.

"Where y'all from?"

"We are visiting friends in the city. Our home is St. Louis," Eben answered calmly and clearly. For all his years in the South, he had never fully relinquished his flat New England Yankee tones.

"You doan sound like you are from around here," came the challenge. "You doan sound like one of them Germans neither."

Eben must have realized at that moment the difficult position we were in. He shifted almost imperceptibly, casting his eyes for a brief moment my direction. I caught his meaning, and in my Alabama born and bred drawl, replied "My husband and I have moved around a lot over the years, gentlemen. I was born in Alabama, near Talladega, and we met and wed just outside of Nacogdoches, Texas. We lived in New Orleans for a spell, then came to St. Louis about ten years ago." I took a breath and waited, hoping that would be explanation enough.

"What you doing out this a-ways?" There was suspicion in the question.

Again, I answered. "I wanted to take a drive and see the countryside, before we have to head back to the St.

Louis tomorrow. I am just a country girl at heart, and I miss seeing real land."

That seemed to satisfy the man who appeared to be in charge. "Reckon you have seen enough?"

I nodded. "Quite enough," I replied submissively. Eben tipped his hat, picking up the reins and turning the carriage to return to the city. The horse took off at a reasonable pace; Eben was cautious not to appear intimidated by the gang. They remained behind us, in the middle of the road, talking amongst themselves. I could hear voices rising with anger, and it frightened me. "Faster," I whispered to Eben, slipping my arm through his.

"No, not yet. They must not think we are scared. They will come after us for sure if they do." He reached inside his coat and pulled out his gun, placing it between us, hidden by the folds of my skirt. "You may need to take the reins if they come at us." His clear blue eyes, shining like the sky above, held mine. "I love you," he said earnestly, taking my hand and squeezing it as if by holding onto me, we could hold onto each other forever.

Tears filed my eyes. Blinking them back, I glanced over his shoulder. The younger two seemed to be arguing; the youngest one was almost dancing on his mount. I heard him hollering "You are just gonna let that Yankee go?"

Eben flicked the reins and the horse picked up speed.

Gunfire.

.   .   .

Eben collapsed against me, blood coming from his back, from his head, from everywhere, splattering and gushing onto my hair, my face, my clothes.

The boy whirled around the front of the trap, his pony prancing wildly. He waved a gun recklessly my direction. I closed my fingers around the pistol by my side, keeping my eyes on the child. He could not have been much older than my own William, back home with Sarah Jane and John. Blood bubbled out of Eben's mouth, the death rattle I recalled all too well escaping his body.

Another young boy came up, this one a bit older, but still not a man. "Frank!" the younger boy called out, "I got him! I got the Yankee!" Then he looked like he was going to be sick, seeing me drenched in Eben's life blood.

Frank – I suppose – answered him sullenly. "That is the stupidest thing I have ever seen you do!" He turned to me. "Ma'am, I sure am sorry about my brother. I tried my best to stop him."

I kept my gaze on the child who killed my husband. After what seemed to be an eternity, I found my voice, cool, clear, convicted. "May you die the same way, in cold blood, unaware of the danger at your back." I loosed my grip on the hidden pistol and picked up the reins from where they had fallen from Eben's hands, turning to the other boy. "Get your brother out of here before I decide to shoot him myself."

The trap lurched forward. Eben's body lolled against me. I did not look back.

I heard a quiet "Come on, Jesse. Time to go."

29

I took Eben's body home to St. Louis and buried him.

I had his will probated and paid bills accordingly.

I was lost without him.

After about a month of my alternating between roaming aimlessly thorough the house and staying in bed for days on end, Bettina, our maid – my maid – sat me down with a strong cup of tea and firm words. "Miss Elizabeth, it not mah place to say dis, but iffin I doan, ain't nobody gwine to, so's you jest as well lissen at me." She then proceeded to give me the talking to that I desperately needed, strong words, but kind, encouragement and promise. She held me as I wept, weeping for what had been, what might have been, and what might yet be. I was beaten by life, afraid of moving forward, afraid of remaining still, afraid of living another day, another hour, another moment.

"I am going home." I announced. "I am going back to my boy in Texas." Over the hours that turned into days as Bettina and I talked, I had broken all propriety and told her my entire life story. She had listened, with wonder and amazement, sharing my past sorrows, sharing my past joys, and gently guiding me to this decision, whether she knew it or not.

"Miss Elizabeth, it be too dangerous fo' you to go all dat way by yo'self."

"My son is there. And what family I have left. And my brother..." I paused, considering. "I have questions that need answers, and he must settle with me. He owes me that much. That much, and more."

Bettina cocked her head, as if she was trying to recall something. "Where you say he be?"

"Larissa," I answered. "Just a tiny place, not near any town of any importance."

"Lemme study on it," she mused. "Jus' might hep yo' a bit."

A few days later, a large Negro man, sturdily built, with muscular arms, perhaps all of thirty years old, appeared at the back door. Bettina brought him into the parlor where I was sitting with some needlework, making minimal but satisfactory progress. I looked up with some apprehension. What new trial might this be?

"Miss Elizabeth, dis here Daniel. He belong to Mist' Paul, but he be from Larissa."

I blinked in wonderment, then nodded. "Bettina, I would like to speak with Daniel alone, please."

"Yas'm."

A half hour later, I set out to buy the first and only slave I ever owned. Daniel.

In the days that followed, I arranged for the sale of my home and most of its contents, packed sparingly, bought a good wagon and team for traveling, helped Bettina with preparing food and drink for the journey, and gave her many household goods in appreciation for her service and what had come to be friendship. I would not allow her to come with me, even though she had wanted to, for the South was still a place of uncertainty for free people of color. Daniel, on the other hand, was now legally my property, and I had the papers to prove it should anyone try to remove him from my service. It was the only way I could protect him as we traveled to Larissa. He had reason to want to return, as did I, and our arrangement worked well as an means to an end for both of us. I promised him that once we arrived safely, I would provide him with manumission papers if he so desired. It seemed to me to be a fair arrangement, and he was satisfied as well.

We headed for the northeast corner of Arkansas and followed the trail southwest, to where it became Trammel's Trace leading into Texas. From there, we found more roads than I had known of ten years prior. Finding our way to Larissa was easy, compared to the route Papa had taken nearly thirty years ago.

· · ·

Only once did I have to show the papers declaring me to be the legal owner of Daniel. That one time was when we arrived in Larissa.

30

I found Larissa to be a fading shadow of its former self. The bustling businesses on the square were dusty and quiet, most were shuttered, although their shelves were not completely barren. Daniel had descended the wagon seat to lead the horses to a public trough, as I took in the scene with wide-eyed wonder. There was a three story building, which I recognized from Sarah Jane's descriptions to be the famed Larissa College, and two dormitories, deserted, that had housed the male and female populations of that lauded institution.

Slightly disoriented by the changes to the landscape, I asked an old Negro woman if she knew where John and Sarah Sullivan lived. She nodded, and gave directions with a wave of her hand and a nod to the west.

Daniel resumed the reins, lifting himself lightly to the weathered board with its scant back rest. A stern looking figure approached, a dour man dressed in black with a fussy tuft of beard jutting from his chin to his chest, but not extending to his cheeks or sideburns. He stared at

Daniel, and Daniel looked him square in the eye. I felt as if lightening would strike any moment, although the sky was clear and blue.

I addressed the gentleman. "Good afternoon. Is there a problem?"

He motioned toward Daniel "Is that yours?"

I smiled. This was what I had prepared for, producing the documents from my reticule. I would not hand them to him; I knew better than to trust a stranger with such important information on such fragile paper. I brandished the bill of sale with as much finesse as I could muster. "Yes. He is my property. And I am on my way to my aunt's home, so if there are not any further questions, we will be on our way."

His eyes shot daggers at me. "No, ma'am. No questions. Just a warning. Be careful with that one."

When we were out of earshot, I asked Daniel if he knew the man.

"Yes'm. He be Reverend Yoakum. He owned me afore, he sole me off on account of Mist' Killough."

"You told me in St. Louis that they sold you to buy equipment for the school, and to get you away from your wife, because a white man wanted her. Was Mr. Killough that white man?"

"Yes'm."

"And you wanted to return here?"

"Ah want my wife."

I thought for a moment. "Daniel, I will give you your papers, but I cannot do anything about your wife. What if she has been sold as well? What if she cannot leave her – situation?" I wanted to ask 'what if she has children' but I refrained.

"Ah'll fine her, Miz Lizbet. Doan mattah iffin she here nor dere. Here is whar ah start lookin'. All de res' come later."

Sarah Jane and John were delighted to see me. I was equally delighted to see them, and distressed to find William away at war. The first thing I did was take out Daniel's papers, pen and ink, and write out his manumission order on the back of my ownership papers. John signed as witness, and Daniel took off, on foot, his proof of freedom in hand, to seek out his wife. Silently, in the deepest part of my heart, I wished him all the luck in the world.

After a healthy if sparse meal and some hours of convivial conversation, I turned to Sarah Jane and said "I am ready to see Nathaniel. It is time."

"He is not well," she stated. "The shock of seeing you might kill him."

"As is my intention," I replied. Her eyes grew wide; John simply looked on solemnly.

"Let me go see him first," he offered. "I will not say a word about you; I will only be checking on his well-being."

I agreed. "Tomorrow, then. And then, it shall be my turn."

John reported Nathaniel was failing, that he was writing his last will and testament. He seemed forgetful, John added blandly, as if remarking on the weather. I resolved to pay my visit the next morning. I was still tired from the trip, and needed rest and nourishment before this final foray.

. . .

The cabin door was ajar; Lockey and the children were nowhere in sight. None of the colored women or their children were on the property. I wondered if Daniel had found his wife and spirited her away. I stood in front of the door and squared my shoulders, drawing in a deep breath, checking to ensure the poppet and gris-gris bag at my waist was still secure. I entered. Nathaniel struggled to stand from his chair by the hearth. The look on his face when he recognized me was that of a man facing the Grim Reaper.

"Brother, you sought to make me as Ishmael; I have become as Ahab. To the last I grapple with thee; from hell's heart I stab at thee; for hate's sake I spit my last breath at thee."

My dear brother Nathaniel, standing there in his comfortable home, beside a warm hearth, well-dressed even in his illness, was taken aback by my outburst.

"Twenty-six long years I have waited; ten in brothels in New Orleans. I learned things there, not the sort of things you think I learned either! You made me among the lowest of the low, but you have no idea of the power the lowly wield! Then the years afterward, plotting, planning, preparing. Yes, I have prepared for this day! I was taught well back in that sultry city, and I was taught to take my time, for time is the greatest asset when avenging a wrong. And you, dear brother, have done so many, many wrongs! Great Neptune's ocean!!"

Brother regained his composure. "Pray tell," he crooned. "Just what wrongdoing do you accuse me of? I am delighted to see you – if you truly are my long-lost sister. I have yet to be convinced of your identity." He smiled benignly, seated himself, and continued. "The last anyone told me they had seen of my sister Izzie was as she fled to hide in the canebrake with several others, who, like my dearly beloved sister, were never heard from again."

"That may well be the last many saw of me, but it was not the last you saw of me. You and that despicable Hawkins returned the next day, and Molly and I were here, in this very cabin. As for my being beloved, you never loved anyone except yourself. Do I need to remind you what transpired that day? What you, Parmalee, and Hawkins conspired?"

He paused, considering. I could almost read his mind: to say anything more might implicate him; to remain silent, he could at least deny my ravings as that of a mad woman.

"You sold me downriver, quite literally! All the way down the Red River to New Orleans! You handed me over to that man, knowing what he planned for me! And you would have done the same to Molly, had that Indian not taken her away!"

"Oh, yes, I did hear something of my dear little niece being found among the savages. A Reverend Parker wrote to me of it, long ago. I forwarded that communication onto her loving and devoted parents, but alas, they did not have the wherewithal to attempt to redeem the poor captive, and then, what if the good Reverend had been wrong about her identity? He made mistakes before with his own kinfolks." The feigned concern was marked by boredom, as though a trite matter of little import.

I could not tell if he was truthful or not about the letters. Perhaps they were written and forwarded; I knew Molly was content with her lot in life, and to my memory, Polly and Owen had no more been loving and devoted parents to her than Abraham Lincoln was a good Confederate.

"I remain unconvinced of our kinship." He paused, regarding my figure and form. I am sure I looked quite the spectacle. Weeks of travel, blistering sunlight and foul weather had all but ruined my skin, hair and nails.

"So if you really are my sister Elizabeth, why are you here?"

"I am here for the same reason I was there for Richard Parmalee. To see that justice is done."

"What have you to do with my friend Richard? He has been dead nearly ten years now."

"Yes and I was there for his death just as I will be here for yours."

"Richard was a good man! What did you have against him?"

"He was a murderer and you know it. Just as you have been a murderer."

"I have never hurt anyone - I never murdered anyone."

"You may not have pulled the trigger but you were as much of the reason why Papa and Allen and Samuel and Isaac and George and Kias are all dead. You killed them just as surely as if you had pulled the trigger yourself. Just as Parmalee murdered Helen Jewett."

Nathaniel laughed softly. "He was acquitted of that charge."

"I know acquitted of the charge and guilty of the murder are two very different things. He was freed only because he had lawyers with enough money behind him to make sure that he was acquitted."

"Richard died of a fever."

"Richard died because I treated his fever. And now you have an illness, and I am here to treat you." I smiled, recalling the moment Parmalee realized he was slipping from this world, his fear of what lay beyond, his fear of punishment, recognizing at that moment his gross misdeeds. I could see that cognizance beginning to dawn on Nathaniel. "You and Richard both went around spewing your benevolent generosity to this good cause and that good charity to cover up for your evil ways, but that will not save you in the end! Not on this earth and not in the next!"

Nathaniel attempted to affect a threatening stance. He bade me consider God's judgment on my actions. Wicked, he called me, to seek revenge – for a crime he did not personally commit!

"I read somewhere that revenge may be wicked, but it's natural."

"You are drunk with your novels! You have pushed away the Bible and forgotten His truth!" He growled. "Do you not recall: Vengeance is mine, saith the Lord!"

"Vengeance is his in the afterlife, and mine in this life", I claimed. I drew a poppet from my apron pocket. The hours I had spent creating this vessel of pain and sorrow! Each scrap of cloth that went into it's making, surreptitiously gleaned over years of feigned innocence, carried the memory of bloodshed and tears. The gris gris tied securely to the little doll was a labor of love and longing – love for my dear, dead Kias, longing for the life we would have had, should have had, the children and grandchildren that would never be.

"What is that abomination?"

"That 'abomination' is you. I have captured your soul, and I shall destroy it in the flames as your God destroyed Sodom and Gomorrah! The evil you have wrought is no less!"

I broke open the gris gris and with a mighty breath,

blew the dust of yesteryear into his face, so when he drew breath, he must choke upon the graves themselves. I drew from my pocket that very Bowie knife I had secreted away that long ago day, plunged it into the heart of the poppet, then threw the cursed thing, knife and all, into the depths of the fire. It exploded into glorious flames. As my brother coughed up blood and retched upon the settling cloud, I took no mind of him; I simply turned and walked out into the fresh air and sunshine.

And so it was I became the instrument of Nathaniel's death. Two weeks passed from that scene and he was laid in the burying ground, near and yet apart from our father, brothers and my own dear Kias. Was there a satisfaction in my heart? Yes. I knew he would never hurt anyone again. At least, not in this world.

I am sick as well. I have no strength to fight anymore; Sarah Jane and Molly have promised to see their husbands bury me, privately, next to my own dear Kias, in that same ground as Papa and my brothers – even Nathaniel, for he shall not intrude upon my eternal slumber.

I lost everything that October day, and I can rest now that I have seen justice on earth, not by a judge and jury, but by my own hand. Aside from a meager few, no one would ever have believed my story, much less convicted Nathaniel of having a hand in those atrocities. Parmalee's getting away with murder proved that much, that the law of men can be corrupt; the law of consequence however, cannot be evaded.

BOOK THREE

SARAH JANE

1

I have gone a lifetime biting my tongue and biding my time. Now it is time to let my tongue loose and tell a tale too strange to be imagined, too much truth for belief.

I was born in 1810 to John and Elizabeth Williams, their only daughter and second born child. Owen was my older brother; Barakias and Elbert came well after me, Kias in fifteen and Elbert in twenty-two. We were poor, but Pa was honest and worked hard. We only had enough land to get by on, a crop to sell, and a garden plot to feed us. We never took charity from anyone, at least not until Ma died. Elbert was still suckling and he would have died if James Killough had not sent over a wet nurse, Sallie, to stay with him until he was weaned. But it hurt Pa's pride to be beholden to anyone, even though it saved Elbert's life. Pa took to drinking afterwards, a little here and there, and then, as the years went by, a little more and a little more. Folks still thought highly of him though, on account of they understood he was still a good man, just broken from grief.

Of course, losing Ma was not the only sorrow and taking help from a neighbor was not the only embarrassment Pa suffered. There was Owen. My big brother had never been much of an asset, and he repaid the generosity of Mr. Killough by getting involved with the gentleman's niece, Polly. They got married right quick afterwards, and my niece Molly was born six months later, a chubby baby girl with a full head of hair and sharp eyes that never missed a thing. Owen took to drinking too, more out of enjoyment than heartache. Poor Polly was stuck with him, bless her heart; she did her best by him.

I was only twelve when Ma died, and the wet nurse taught me everything I needed to know about running a house and raising children. Once Sallie went back to the Killough plantation, I took over the household chores and taking care of Kias and Elbert. Life was not easy, and it did not get any easier with time. Just more routine. Every morning started with bringing fresh wood and water into the house, stirring up the fire, getting the boys up and dressed, food on the table, tending to the cow, the hens, our little vegetable patch, keeping the house clean, washing and mending clothes, and even mending shoes. I could handle a rifle as well as Pa and better than Owen, and I taught the boys how to fish and hunt, clean what they killed and cook it up over an open fire. I was determined I would never need a man to keep me from going hungry, and I think I did pretty well.

Polly and Owen moved in with her folks, Miss Urcey and Mr. Issac, right after the wedding. They stayed there too, except for the times Owen would take off on a drunk, and not be back for days on end. I have no idea where he would go off to, but off he would go and slink back half-sober when he got good and ready, or maybe when whoever he was shacked up with got their fill of him. Owen could be nice as you please when he wanted to be, but when he was in a drinking mood, he would start being ugly. He could say some of the most hateful things to Polly, and later on, Molly too. I cannot understand how Polly stood it, but I think her Ma made her stick with him more than Polly wanting to stay with him. It was bad enough, Molly coming so soon after the wedding, without going from the frying pan into the fire with a broken marriage.

Pa passed in thirty-five, and I was left with Kias, a strapping twenty year old, and thirteen year old Elbert. Kias did what he could to help out; he was clerking at George Wood's store and making a little money. I never had much schooling but I made sure Elbert got as much as possible. Molly was only a bit younger, and Izzie, Polly's youngest sister, was a bit older than him, and the girls tutored him as best they could. He managed to make passing grades in reading and composition because of them, and geography and history too. Luckily, he was naturally inclined to figuring, so numbers came easily to him and they did not have to teach him anything there. In fact, it seems to me, he helped them in that area himself, since neither of them were at the top of the class in mathematics.

Kias and I managed to keep body and soul together, and keep Elbert focused on book learning, but I realized I was going to have to reconsider needing a husband. I was twenty-six, a veritable spinster, but I was healthy, strong, and capable of running a household. I had raised two children well, I went to church regular, and the women of the county respected me. I might not have my pick of men, but I was not going to be alone all my life. It was just a matter of letting the right matrons know I was interested in matrimony.

A solution was closer at hand than I expected. While visiting with Polly, I took her and Miss Urcey into my confidence. They exchanged a knowing glance betwixt themselves. I was curious. To be sure, they had someone in mind, but I could not begin to figure who it might be. Of course, I had been so wrapped in homemaking since Ma died, and more so since Pa passed, that I had never paid much mind to which of the neighborhood boys were becoming men and which ones might become good husbands. Honestly, at this late date I expected my prospects to be limited to widowers with little ones who needed a mother.

I was astounded when they suggested Issac Junior.

2

Tall and thin, mousy hair with an off-center widow's peak, jug ears, an easy – but an overly toothy – grin, and green eyes summed up Issac Junior's appearance. We were evenly matched in age, and I was pleased to find in temperament as well. Placid and pragmatic, that was my Issac.

We stood to be married in the preacher's front parlor and went home to dinner where our families gathered to wish us well. Isaac gave me a locket as a wedding gift; I had a new pocketbook for him, with a ten dollar bill drawn on the State of Alabama enclosed. The money was a gift from my brother Kias, for the two of us. When I opened the locket, I found it was empty. Isaac saw my disappointment and took the locket from my hands. Looking into my eyes, he bestowed a kiss in the center of the locket, closed it and handed it back to me. "It is not empty," he assured me. "It has my love for you inside." I was never one for shows of romance, but my eyes swam with tears. He loved me, and it made my affection for him grow.

I am sure it was awkward for Isaac to have our wedding night in Ma and Pa's old bedroom, but Pa had left the house to me, not my brothers, wanting me to be secure and have a roof over my head without being beholden to anyone. The house would be ours as long as we wished to keep it.

We got on well, and the local gossips who had raised eyebrows at our swift engagement and marriage were sorely disappointed when a baby did not appear in due (or undue!) time. I smiled sweetly to the ladies in the shops and at church, and kept my own counsel on how my waistline remained trim. Truth is, I had gone to Sallie, Elbert's wet nurse, who midwifed at the Killough plantation and knew a thing or two about getting and not getting babies. She educated me in the ways of women who preferred to not be encumbered with a child, or who wanted to allow more time between births, without denying their husband's pleasures. I put that knowledge to good use.

We barely passed our first anniversary when Issac's pa, Issac Senior, announced his hankering to go to Texas, and bring as many of us with him as wanted to go. Issac's sister Patsy and her husband bowed out; his older brother James had no interest in making the trip. But all the rest were willing to pack up and move out, though Heaven only knows why we did. We had all heard, in one form or another, the claim that there is no place in the world where a living can be procured more easily than the Texas frontier. To make a good living with ease was intriguing, but for the most part, Issac and I just wanted to stay with family. We wanted to start our own brood far from the restrictions of the social structure of our community. Our idea was we would be on more equal footing in a place with fewer folks and where the folks around us shared our faith, politics, and family history. Seems we misjudged at least one member of the family, but that comes later on in my story.

Our trip to Texas was uneventful. There were the usual concerns of weather and road conditions, conveyances and costs, but overall, nothing out the of ordinary. From the coast of Texas to Nacogdoches, the heavy spring rains and mud was our greatest concern, and I lost count of how many times the wagons became stuck or nearly so.

Once we arrived in Nacogdoches, toward the end of March in thirty-seven, the reality of our situation struck us. We were indeed strangers in a strange land. Texas was everything and nothing like it had been described. In Alabama, we had been accustomed to plantations, slaves, merchants and laborers, and everyone was either white or black or a mixture thereof, and President Jackson had pretty much solved our Indian problem by sending them all off to Indian Territory. Not that I ever felt like we had an Indian problem, but if the President of the United States felt we did, then maybe we did. That was something for men to deal with, not me. All I ever wanted to deal with was having a simple home and a quiet life. And here I was in Texas, where nothing was simple or quiet! What had we gotten ourselves into?

3

When we arrived in Texas, each married man was allotted a headright grant of 1280 acres, with the stipulation they become citizens of the Republic and remain in residence for three years. Unmarried men were entitled to 640 acres. Seven married men, one unmarried - Elbert was too young to qualify - meant eight headrights, which would have been fine and dandy, but each of those headrights was in a different county, all far from any inklings of towns or cities. We would have been separated by miles and miles of inhospitable country, isolated not only from civilization but also from one another. To make matters worse, every single parcel of acreage was out on the open prairie, and, quite frankly, besieged by wild Indians. Of course, we did not realize this until we were firmly on Texas soil and had given up our former homes.

The menfolk made a good show of being willing to go forth and conquer the wild prairies, Indians and all, but the truth was, none of us, men or women, were eager to put our scalps on the line for a few acres of flat land that was foreign to the livestock and crops were were accustomed to relying on for sustenance. Isaac and I, the only childless couple, mulled over our options and saw very little to inspire confidence in the future we had envisioned. I counted myself fortunate in having a husband who considered my opinions and desires, rather than one like his brother Nathaniel, who simply made decisions and expected his wife to carry out his wishes with dutiful respect and even good cheer.

Isaac's ma, Miss Urcey, more spiritually inclined than any of the rest of us, set herself to prayer over this situation. She followed the admonition to "pray without ceasing", and for days, all we heard from her were petitions to the Lord. Narcissa, my brother-in-law Samuel's wife, reacted differently. She made herself sick with hysteria, and with her being in the family way, Samuel's concern for his unborn firstborn led him to seek out a doctor.

Which is how, between prayer and hysterics, we were led to what would become our settlement.

Doctor Jesse Watkins, late of Tennessee, came to examine Narcissa. Under his keen questioning, Samuel admitted he felt the cause was distress over what seemed to be a bleak and limited future, both socially and mortally, for Narcissa feared death at the hands of savages above all else. So, the gray haired doctor did what it seems all Texians are inclined to do with all newcomers; he inquired as to what church affiliation we held.

Finding our collective faith to be Presbyterian, he beamed with delight. Sunday was nigh upon us. We accepted his invitation to the services in the church that bore his name: Watkins Settlement Presbyterian Church.

One of his sons, Richard, I think the name was, would be preaching, and the Reverend Sumner Bacon could be relied upon to be in attendance. Between these good men and God, he assured Samuel, we would be blessed with a resolution to our predicament.

Located a few miles northwest of town, on what was called Hayter Road, the church was of unusual design, yet eminently practical. Like the homes around it, the construction material was rough hewn logs atop a foundation of stone native to the land, in this case a blue-gray marl, more gray than blue. The log walls were notched at the ends and daubed with a mixture of red clay mud and straw, and the roof was of logs cross-covered with straight boards. Unlike the homes, it was designed to serve as a fortress as well as a house of worship, physically embodying the hymn 'A Mighty Fortress Is Our God'. Six sides, each with port-holes for defense, gave the worshippers within a clear view from all sides of any approaching danger. Men with sharp eyesight were appointed to keep watch at the ports. Sometimes, we were told, neighboring Indians came to hear the services, and sometimes came to attack. Congregants arrived bearing arms, which were placed at the ready in each of the many corners of the room. Sitting on the split-oak pew, I was entranced by the charm and sensibility of the design of the church and the faithful yet fortified membership, however I am afraid I paid little heed to the message from the pulpit.

Fortunately, our reception was not impacted by my inattentiveness. The Reverend Bacon, in consultation with the men of the Watkins and Hayter families, took aside my father-in-law, husband and brothers-in-law after the services for a brief discussion before the dinner-on-the-grounds meal commenced. Whatever had been said must have met with unanimous approval, for there were smiles all around, and in the blessing for the meal, the Reverend gave thanks for God's guidance in bringing the Killough family to the Republic, and asked that in His graciousness, He bestow upon us abundance and fruitfulness in all our labors. Our heads bowed, I fluttered my eyelids open a slit to glance toward my husband. As usual, he was observing the prayer with his eyes wide open, perhaps more so after hearing the tales of wayward Indians, and he caught the tiny motion of my head as I turned ever so slightly his direction. He smiled and nodded. Satisfied I would hear the full account later, I rested my eyes again and gave my own silent, heartfelt, thanks.

4

The full account was brief. Isaac succinctly reported the Reverend Bacon owned a generous parcel of land several miles to the north-west, just south of the Neches-Saline river, which he was willing to sell. He assured the men the Cherokees living in the area were generally friendly, although he could not vouch for the Kickapoos who lived in a village across the river. George and Allen would be riding up that way directly to have a look. As it was already May, the men were anxious to get seeds in the ground so we could have some crops by fall. If the soil appeared as fertile as the reverend supposed it might be, with access to good water and lumber for building and without hostilities from the local Indians, then we would move forward to establish our homestead.

"And if not?" I needed to know what alternatives we had, or rather, if we had alternatives.

He shrugged. "We can always go back to Alabama." Seeing my reaction, he quickly amended "or, we could find another parcel. Maybe here, maybe not." Taking my hand and looking deeply into my eyes, he said "As long as we are together, as long as you are by my side, we will find our way in this world." He kissed me, and I felt all my worry and fear melt away in his arms. He was right. As long as we were together, this world would be our own glimpse of heaven.

The ten days George and Allen absented themselves for reconnaissance, we vacillated between being fraught with fear for their safety and giddy with anticipation. Isaac and his pa made themselves useful by getting to know the men who owned businesses and were involved in church and politics – in short, the men responsible for nurturing this new Republic of Texas. Isaac would run off a whole list of new names every evening, with a short description of each man, to help firm in his mind who he had met and what their positions they held. He had a terrible memory for putting names to faces, or faces to names. He could always recall one but not the other, and it frustrated him to no end. He had the idea that telling me what a person looked like, their profession and other tidbits and linking each statement back to their name might help him organize his thoughts and improve his recall. He did not say as much, but I know he was also hoping it might help him not be so awkward in public; he was very self conscious about not being able to call a fellow by name, or place where he had met a person earlier, or under what conditions. I did my best to reinforce his efforts by later asking things like "who did you say the gentleman was with the gray hair and carried a cane at the dry-goods shop?" If he caught onto what I was doing, he never mentioned it. I like to think it helped a bit, from time to time. At any rate, he seemed to finally be gaining some confidence.

Narcissa kept Samuel busy tending to her needs; she wanted him by her side constantly, having him do every little thing for her, or just sit and be in her sight. He wearily confided in Isaac that if she was going to be like this every time she was with child, that there just might not be any more children. Nathaniel frequented the courthouse; I had no idea what could have drawn him there, but he seemed to be meeting people at least. My brothers – well, at least Kias and Elbert – made themselves useful, picking up odd jobs around town and making sure our wagons and horses were well prepared for whatever journey lay ahead of us. Owen inspected the saloons, quite thoroughly. I expected no less of him. Molly and Elizabeth seemed to be having the time of their lives, as pretty young girls should when in a new city with handsome young men bustling about the square. It did my heart good to see them neatly dressed, light hearted with ready smiles. That would go by the wayside soon enough, I knew, once we moved on and set up housekeeping away from the shops and other entertainments.

When my brothers-in-law returned, pronouncing the property fit for farming, with abundant timber for building and wildlife for hunting, it was cause for celebration. Isaac and I were relieved by the decision to keep our extended family together, even though some family members could be challenging to live among at times, at least they were family and we were accustomed to their personalities. Perhaps, I thought, the time is near for Isaac and I to have a child of our own. The thought made me smile, and when I broached the subject to Isaac, he smiled too.

I became pregnant the following February.

5

Our little family compound was awash in newborns. Narcissa, Orleana, Bessie, and Jane each had a babe in arms by the time I found myself with child. I was secretly delighted to be the only woman in the family way; no one complained that her morning sickness was worse than mine on the days the bile rose in my throat, no one compared her thickening waistline to mine, no one had a child in the womb kicking harder or turning somersaults more often than mine. My pregnancy was my own, not a shared experience, and I reveled in each day's changes.

Isaac was just as enthralled as I was. At night, he would stretch out his palms over my belly, as if to measure the growing bubble beneath my skin. When our little one would shift positions within me, he would gently push back at whatever tiny limb was pressing outward to test the confines of its world. Often, it would become a game of Papa and Baby, back and forth, getting to know one another before ever meeting face to face.

He would ask "Do you think it will be a boy or a girl?"

I would reply that I had no idea; that sometimes his mother would say she thinks a boy because I am carrying high and mostly in front, but there are days when the baby seems lower and my weight more in my hips, so maybe a girl. Then he would sigh, and say "As long as you and the baby are healthy and whole, that is all which is important to me." I would reach out and stroke his face, loving the contours of his cheekbones and chin, brushing my fingertips across his lips to catch a memory of a kiss, and every time, I fell in love with him just a little bit more, which amazed me because I could not imagine I could love him any more than I already did.

Spring is a wild thing in East Texas. The grasslands are filled with wildflowers in brilliant blooms; many flowering trees dot the woods with bursts of color against the burgeoning greenery. But storms whip up quicker than you can turn around and spit. In the spring of 1838, more than just thunderstorms and cyclones threatened us. There was plenty of fuss about Mexicans living among us who were still loyal to Mexico and Santa Anna. It was not my place to question the wisdom of General Houston in allowing that scoundrel to go free after the Battle of San Jacinto, but still I wondered. All it seemed to me to do was make some folks of a mind to go back to the way things were instead of going forward with the way things are.

One of those folks was a fellow living down around Nacogdoches, Vincente Cordova, who used to be pretty important before Texas got its independence. I reckoned he missed being important, and maybe he figured he was missing out on making himself a pile of money under the old ways of doing things. But, again, it is not my place and it was not any of my business, at least not until the people around him started talking up overthrowing the Republic, getting the Indians involved in helping them, and trying to run off settlers like us.

George and Allen, the most level headed men I have ever known aside from my own Isaac, were bothered enough to insist that we all pack up and go to Nacogdoches, where they figured there would be a better degree of safety should a revolt occur. Certainly it was considerably safer there than our own homes and a good bit safer than Mr. Lacey's fort. All the same, I was loathe to leave our home.

Packing up our trunks brought me to tears. Try as I might, I could not control my emotions. I placed our clothing in one trunk, adding in the few tiny gowns I had prepared for our little one, along with blankets and quilts. Another trunk held our household goods. It was a meager collection, mostly some simple drabware and pewter. I packed our oil lamps carefully, ensuring the globes were well protected from breakage. Our cookware, comprised of a frying pan, spider skillet and a pair of stew pots with sturdy legs, would be packed separately in the wagon, for easy access while traveling. I did not leave anything behind if I could help it, for I worried our homes would be robbed at best, or worse, burned to the ground by the insurrectionists. Last to be loaded was the cradle Isaac and his pa had just finished making for our babe. My heart thumped when it bumped against the backboard of the wagon, and I had a wild thought that our child might never feel the smooth sides sanded down by his grandfather or the warm coverlet crafted by his grandmother. I stopped a quick cry that rose in my throat, and pushed it down, firmly telling myself to cease from such foolish thoughts.

And so we removed ourselves from our place of residence and became refugees.

When we arrived in Nacogdoches, Isaac and I thought perhaps instead of setting up camp, we might instead board at the hotel downtown, given my condition. This sufficed for a time; it was nice to not have to be responsible for preparing meals, keeping a fire in the hearth, or hauling up water from the spring. Water, wood, and meals were all provided, albeit for a price. Isaac and I had more than one discussion supposing we could not return to our snug little cabin. A farmer at heart, he did not want to abandon the land he tilled, but practical as he was, he realized he might not have a choice, at least temporarily.

He offered his services to General Rusk should volunteers be needed to fight for the Republic, and then he set about finding work in town, given that we did not know just how long it would be before we would be able to go home – or if we would have a home to go to. He settled into helping build the small frame houses that were springing up around town, but we both yearned for our home. I longed to see our child – by now, I was imagining a boy with Isaac's green eyes and my own red hair – happily playing outside our cabin with his cousins, free from care, and ourselves, free from uncertainty.

To distract myself from worry, I joined my sisters-in-law in a daily sewing circle, where we applied ourselves diligently to preparing a trousseau for my husband's sister Izzie, soon to be my double-sister-in-law upon marrying my brother Kias. We had many hours of genteel companionship and laughter in the face of our troubles as we stitched up skirts and bodices, sleeves, fichus and pelerines.

Finally, the day arrived wherein we found an agreement had been reached between our representatives and those of the Indians who wished to retain control over our land. Our land!! It was ours, by honest purchase and by law! And yet they felt they could tell us whether or not we could have our land, our homes, our crops – it was enough to make my blood boil. The anger, however, was equally matched by joy at the prospect of returning home.

Isaac warned me, in that soft, sensible tone he had, not to get my hopes up too high, that the conditions stated we were to leave as soon as our crops in the fields had been harvested, and before the first frost of fall. I cared not – although, in retrospect, I should have – and eagerly found my place in our wagon for the trip home, where our baby would soon be born, and we would live, as the fairy tales promise, "happily ever after".

6

Massacre. Depredation. Devastation. Utter horror.

I wish I had no recollection of a single thing about that day, but I can remember everything.

Not everything all at once, not like I am reliving it moment to moment, but it comes in big snatches and wrestles me into submission, into exhaustion, into darkness.

I have no clear memory of how the day started, but I do remember our noon dinner. I was heavy with child, but insisting on helping as much as I possibly could with cooking and serving, and Mammo and Pappo (the names the grandchildren had given Miss Urcey and Isaac Senior) had given up on making me sit down and instead were directing me to the least strenuous of tasks. It was not much, but at least I felt useful.

Pappo went to take, as he termed it, a "little siesta" after eating. The habit was something he had picked up on from the Mexican men in Nacogdoches, and it seemed to him quite a sensible addition to his daily routine. He'd find a good spot under a shade tree with a little breeze blowing around it, spread out one of Mammo's good quilts, and make himself comfortable for the better part of an hour.

The tables cleared, the men wandered off to various tasks while the women chattered and finished cleaning. Mammo, Narcissa and I were debating crossing the creek to Nathaniel's place to check on Orleana and baby Eliza. They had missed eating with everyone, due, Nathaniel said, to the baby keeping Orleana up all night with teething and she wanted the two of them to have some time to sleep a bit.

To get to Nathaniel's cabin, there was a sturdy bridge over the creek bed, wide enough for a wagon and strong enough to hold two horses, so no need to be balancing on stepping stones or sinking into the mud. But, the hillside path to the cabin was steep and a difficult climb in my condition. Likewise, Narcissa hesitated to take baby Billie with her, as it was nearly his nap time. Mammo, like the good grandmother and mother-in-law she was, was ever mindful of the fine line between being a doting grandmother and a meddling mother-in-law.

We were deep in discussion when Mammo held up her hand for quiet. "Listen", she said.

We listened. Narcissa shook her head. "Should we hear something?"

I looked at Mammo. "We should, but..." I said gravely. "Nothing. Not a thing making a sound. Not even a bird."

Then we heard hoof beats. Lots of horses headed our way, splashing through and up alongside the creek. Horses following the creek meant men mounted on horseback trying not to leave a trail. If they were avoiding leaving a trail, they were probably up to no good.

· · ·

Should we ever be under threat of attack, whether by man or beast, the plan had always been to go to the canebrake that grew tall and thick by the creek and hide. I am not so sure it would have protected us from beasts – there were black bears, panthers, bobcats, all sorts of big things that could kill with just one swipe of a paw – but under the right conditions, one would be concealed from most people. But with riders coming up the creek, running toward it seemed like a bad idea. Hiding in the cabins was not smart either; the first place they would look would be the cabins, to rob, murder, or worse.

We headed east toward a cluster of big oak trees, with brambles and vines all around and in between them. Elbert had cleared a narrow path to the center of the grove to make himself a hideout for when he wanted to avoid chores. Luckily, as his big sister, I knew all about his secret spaces, and figured this would serve us well as long as no one looked too hard for three women and a baby. And Kias. He ran up to us, thinking as we were that the creek was not a wise choice and knowing about Elbert's not-so-secret secret space. He took Billie from Narcissa so she could make better time getting to that sanctuary, but to no avail.

Five mounted men, either painted Indians or painted to look like Indians – I was never quite sure which it was – bore down upon our little group. Kias thrust Billie back into his mother's arms and shoved her toward the trees, taking off running the opposite direction.

They hunted him down like prey. Guns drawn, guns firing, guns shouting terrible blasts and Kias never made a sound. He just fell. Forward. Rolled onto his back. Legs twisted askew. I saw his face. I saw his eyes. His beautiful, big brown eyes, open wide, the whites whiter than marble and the brown glistening still, still filled with fear. Filled with shock and dismay and utter bewilderment. He was wearing tan breeches, a plaid shirt of red and black, and braces buttoned at his waist. He had not had a haircut in so long, it was all tangled at the ends and he was trying so hard to grow a beard like a grown man – like the grown man he was. And his mouth was open. He never screamed, he just opened his mouth and there was nothing to come out. I crumpled to the ground, soundless myself. All the sound had left all the world.

Until there was more gunfire. I could not even begin to count the number of shots I heard. Someone told me later they found eighteen bullet holes in Pappo's body. That is one thing I do not remember. I do not remember looking at his body. I know Mammo found him in front of their cabin. I know we tried to move his body. I know he was too heavy for us to move – Mammo being older, Narcissa being tiny, and me being encumbered with an unborn child. Narcissa and I went into the house and brought out quilts to cover him. Mammo picked up firewood to weigh down the edges of the blankets. We started back to the oak grove, but we were just going in circles. Dog Shoot and a couple of other Indians from Chief Sam Benge's village came rode up and said they were sent to take us to their camp. Narcissa and Mammo refused, with Narcissa being sharp of tongue, and they got made and took off, leaving us alone.

We finally made it to the oaks. Pappo's little dog, Jack, followed us. The dog never barked and baby Billie never cried. We were tired, worried, hungry, grieving, and nigh on hopeless. The livestock, as best we could tell, had been stolen or scared off, so there were no horses or mules to ride. We debated what to do. It was pretty obvious we might well be the only survivors. I finally found my voice and ventured that we might could go to Sleeping Bear and Sophronia's home, but Mammo worried they might have been butchered too, on account of being friendly with us. I frowned, thinking of that. Fort Sam Houston was fairly close, on the other side of the Neches, to the southwest, but that was the direction we had last seen the murderers moving. We supposed they were headed to the Kickapoo village, but they might be headed to the fort just as easily. We were well acquainted with the route to Fort Lacey. It lay to the south and there were friendly Indian villages along the way – or at least, they had been friendly the last time we had passed through. It seemed to us that it would be the path most likely to get us to some semblance of safety.

7

We thought perhaps to travel under cover of darkness would be wise. The days were growing shorter and the night would afford us more time. The moon had been full only two nights ago; it had not waned much and gave plentiful light to the ruts cut by our wagon wheels on our previous journeys. We did our best to move quietly, remaining alert for any sound that might alert us of the presence of others. Narcissa's baby was quiet; thankfully, he was not yet weaned so he at least would not go hungry as long as her milk held. The dog stayed close to Mammo's skirt, darting between her ankles at the sound of a hoot owl. I placed my hand on my belly, needing to feel the familiar movements of the child within me, reassuring me of life and hope.

By dawn, we began to seek shelter. A protected place to sleep, gather something edible, fresh water – we found a spot about halfway between the trail and the creek running alongside it, where the ground dropped about a foot and a half to a flat grassy ledge before sloping to the creek. Narcissa set Billie down and edged her way to the creek for a drink. I kept watch while Mammo foraged for a pocketful of nuts – chinkapins and acorns - plus some chickweed. It was not much, for which I was grateful, because the taste was unpleasant. It passed for a meal, though, and we had fresh water, so sleep could come, not impeded by empty bellies, but only by anxiousness and grief. My senses were alert to every shift of wind, every sound of nature, every scent which might bring further calamity, or perhaps – hopefully! – rescue. The baby kept tossing and turning in my womb, mimicking my inability to find comfort in repose. I eventually turned on my side; Jack came and stretched out the length of my back, placing himself firmly against my tired boy and aching muscles. The warmth of his body seeped into mine, easy my physical pain and calming my turbulent emotions. The babe in my womb relaxed with his presence as well, for the kicking subdued. I was finally able to doze off for a bit, awakened all too soon by a prodding Narcissa, insisting it was time to begin our journey once more.

The trail was difficult to discern, even with a fair amount of moonlight. We were all becoming discouraged and irritable. After a few hours of stumbling along, Narcissa stopped to rest on a fallen tree, sitting and pulling Billie to her lap. "I am not going any further tonight. In fact, I am not walking by night any more. You two may do as you wish, but I am going to get started in the light of day, and if the Indians get me, so be it. I would just as soon chance it with them as with wolves and coyotes and panthers and God only knows what all else in these woods at night."

I looked at Mammo, my eyebrows raised, questioning her thoughts. She nodded tiredly. I sighed, rolled my eyes a bit, and nodded in agreement. Narcissa had been the one who pushed hardest to travel by night, and now she changed her mind. Experience had taught us that the best way to live with Narcissa in peace was to do things her way. We made our beds as best we could, my four-legged protector Jack taking up his place by my side once again, and thus settled, waited for the morning light.

We made a fair pace in the daylight. There was abundant water from the creek near the trail, and a few nuts and wild greens to be foraged. I contemplated gigging a few frogs and having a campfire to roast them over in the evening. That daydream of a hot meal was interrupted abruptly in mid-afternoon.

We arrived at a fork in the trail. Uncertain of which way to continue, we meandered first one direction a few yards, then the other, trying to discern what might lie ahead. One direction was overgrown, the other fairly clear. The clearer path seemed the safer choice. But as we returned to the cross point, an Indian appeared on the trail behind us, clasping a rifle. Pointed at us.

He motioned with the gun for us to take move forward upon the path to the left, the narrow one with scraggly underbrush. Narcissa screamed; the redskin ran toward her – my heart was beating wildly, I was terrified.

He stopped abruptly and showed us his gun; there was no powder in the pan, he could not have harmed us. By signs, he encouraged us to move down the path, heavily shaded by trees and curving into a dark woods. We stood firm and shook our heads. We had no intention of following him. We started down the open path to the right.

He ran in front of us and leaded his gun, pointing at us once again, with all seriousness.

We looked at one another in mutual dismay. "He may kill us if we continue, and he may kill us if we follow him," Mammo said. "We may as well just go ahead and follow him. It may buy us another day, or a chance to escape."

Not far from the curve in the path, where it seemed the woods grew more dense, we turned a second time into a clearing, with several huts and a multitude of Indians. Most, from what I could see, were painted for war. Cows were being slaughtered and meat was cooking on spits over open fires. Our escort motioned us into a shack on the edge of the encampment, then sat in the doorway, facing outward, his rifle across his lap. Were we prisoners, we wondered, whispering amongst ourselves.

Presently, a Negro woman approached the doorway and was granted entrance by our guard. She brought ample supplies of food and drink, and a bucket of water for washing ourselves. Narcissa and I asked her who she was, where we were, what they planned to do with us, but she would just shake her head and shrug. I wondered if she understood our questions in the first place. A man appeared next, a mulatto by my estimation, who conversed with the Indians as easily as with us. He assured us we were safe; we were in a place under the control of Little Bean, whose village we had frequently visited. Had we gone down the other path, he explained, about a half-mile or so, it would have meant death, for that village had sworn war upon the whites. The painted Indians I had seen were from that village, and we were to remain in the hut until he came for us the next day. The guard at the door had been part of a group of friendly Indians who knew of the trouble at our place, and knew there were women and children trying to find their way to white civilization.

Our Indian guard spent the night upon the threshold, rifle at the ready, to keep us safe from those who would do us harm.

We slept well upon pallets covered in deerskin, and had a good breakfast at daybreak. The camp was quiet; the singing and dancing had gone on until the wee hours of the morning. I suspected the 'wild Indians' were fast asleep and would be until at least noontime. Our new friends provided us with three horses, and sent us on our way to Fort Lacey long before the night's revelers awoke.

The sun had just set when we came in view of the fort. What a welcome sight! Sentries hailed us, but we could not hear them clearly or make ourselves heard in our excitement. "We are the women from Saline," we called out, "The Killough women from the Neches-Saline!" Finally, they heard us. The heavy doors to the fort swung open and we wept with joy.

8

We slept so deeply it was noon before any of us awoke. Mr. Lacey's wife, Dolly, and the Box ladies, Sally, Keziah, and Mary, brought us great bowls of stew and plenty of hot cornbread with freshly churned butter. I believe it was the best meal I have ever had in my life. They brought in fresh clothing for us, even a little well-worn dress for Billie, which was a smidge too large, but clean and nicely mended. To accommodate my condition, there was a generous shift that ended above my ankles and had comfortable loose sleeves.

My condition. The babe's movements had become fewer and further apart. I worried. Mammo said it was perfectly normal, that my time would be upon me quickly and the little one was simply resting up before making an entrance. She eyed my belly and said, "See how your weight has dropped further down your waist? It will not be long now." I felt reassured; she had given birth and attended births more times than I could count.

· · ·

Two days later, Nathaniel arrived at the fort with Orleana and baby Eliza. They were on horseback, and appeared to have fared better than our party. There was much commotion over this addition to the community; the men questioned him well into the night and the better part of the next day about the attack, the Indians, their journey to the fort and conditions along the way. Orleana, for her part, was her usual deferential self within Nathaniel's eyesight, although Mammo and I detected a change in her disposition. Where she had been cheerfully submissive, the thin smile of acquiescence was now strained, there were furtive glances toward her husband when he was otherwise occupied which showed distress, distrust, and confusion. She clung to Eliza as though the child was a lifeboat on a sinking ship. Mammo and I started to speak to her, but Nathaniel waved us away, claiming she was suffering from the shock of being attacked.

We let Orleana be. Nathaniel was in his element, with so many of the prominent men of Nacogdoches coming to hear his tale and hang onto his every word. The gentlemen made quite a fuss over him, having him repeat the tale time and again, which he did, adding a bit here and omitting a bit there. I thought it was odd the way his story changed, but Mammo and Narcissa took no notice. Narcissa was irate about something else entirely. "No one asked us about anything," she fussed. "We could have told them plenty."

"We did," I reminded her. "We told them the whole of it, as best we could, that first night."

She nodded. "I even told them that I recognized that awful Hawkins character under all that Indian war paint! That silly feathered headdress he was wearing slipped down over his nose, and mussed his paint up good. I am convinced most of those horrible murderers were men other than Indians. I think they were all white men and Mexicans! But now that Nathaniel is here, they will latch onto whatever he tells them and go off on a fool's errand, probably get one or two of them killed for their trouble." She huffed indignantly. "Men! All they care about is having an excuse to go out and shoot something or someone!"

By about the tenth time of Nathaniel's telling of the story, how he was watering his horse when he heard gunfire, then raced to his house to get Orleana and the baby, Narcissa had had her fill. Perturbed she was not the center of attention, she took Billie and went to stay with some friends in Douglass, halfway to Nacogdoches. It was a lot quieter in the compound after her departure.

Almost immediately after her exit, Nathaniel departed for Nacogdoches, to meet with even more important men in the political and military arenas. He took Orleana and Eliza with him; when he returned, he was alone.

The Box families were divided on returning to their own farms, about three miles north of the Lacey's. They had a rudimentary fort of their own, but on the whole, much smaller and not as well fortified. There was only one small cabin and a dugout within its walls; all the family's homes and fields were outside the fort. It was finally decided that two of the Box men, Stephen and his nephew, Roland, would ride out to scout the area and come back the next day.

Upon their return, they were riding fast to the gates,

frightening Sally Box so badly that she ran to her husband, knocking him to the ground. She began to beat on him with her fists, crying out "Pray, Johnny Box, do pray, if you ever did pray, pray now, for the Indians are coming!!"

She was very much relived when her son and brother-in-law dismounted, assuring us they were only having a good natured race back to the fort, and no Indians were in sight.

My waters broke soon thereafter. Mammo, Dolly and Sally made me as comfortable as possible with as much privacy as could be accommodated by so many people in close quarters. I labored long, trying to bear the pain as well as I had seen others bringing a child into the world, but I was overcome by agony as the hours passed. I lost all sense of time. My midwives came and went from my vision; cool compresses were applied to my forehead. They massaged my lower body with lard and gave me sips of tea, all in hopes of bringing my baby.

She was born. Mammo drew her from me, then turned so I could not see. I heard the sounds of the women, but not a babe's cry. I was frantic. Sally brought me a sleeping draught. I shook my head. She insisted.

Mammo pulled a chair to the bedside and sat heavily, taking my hand. "I am so sorry."

My mind spun. Sorry? I have seen my husband killed, our cabin set ablaze, lost everything except my baby — and then I realized my baby was lost as well. I screamed one final outpouring of anger, pain, and loss. Dolly held a motionless bundle out to me. I cradled her to my breast, tears running down my face onto hers. She had red hair and blue eyes and was perfect in every way, except she drew no breath and never would.

Mammo took her from me, placing her in the little cradle that had been prepared. I let Sally give me the draught, and hoped I would never awaken.

9

I stayed abed for a good while afterwards, then Mammo and I set off for Douglass to meet Narcissa and Billie. From there, we went to Nacogdoches and home to Alabama. That was Nathaniel's idea, to send us all back home. Not that it mattered to me; I had no care for where I went or what I did. I had a little bottle of laudanum and a spare to comfort me as the long nights approached. Jack, appointing himself to be my dog, stayed close to my side, as if he sensed my despair and wished to console me. At night, I held my wedding locket, where Mammo had placed a lock of my poor babe's hair. Isaac's love and our daughter's curls mingled in the locket between my fingers, every night, and with a drop of medicine upon my lips, brought dreamless sleep.

We arrived in Alabama in just a few days time. Patsy, Mammo's oldest daughter, made a big fuss and set up a room in her house for us with her best bed linens and fresh water in the ewers. Meals were sumptuous, compared to what we had become accustomed to in Texas – corn was no longer the staple morning, noon and night.

My body was recovering, but my heart was not. There simply was not anything left inside of me anymore. Ma was gone, Pa was gone, Owen was worthless, Elbert was off on his own, Kias was dead, my Isaac was dead, and our child never even took a breath. I hated myself I hated everyone around me I hate being pitied I hate the pity I felt for myself I hated God, I hated fate. All I wanted to do was turn back time - go back to before Ma died, when everything was normal. We might have been poor but at least I had life waiting for me. Now it is just death and death and death and more death. Why was I not dead too? I was just so tired of being alive. I was just so tired of pretending to be alive because I felt really and truly dead inside. The last little bit of me that was alive died when my baby died, and I was just wandering around, a dead soul in a might-as-well-be dead body.

All I could think was 'I have failed at life completely. Totally, utterly, completely. There is nothing left for me.'

I found myself wandering aimlessly around the countryside. The doctor Patsy had sent for insisted that exercise and fresh air would set my mind at ease, so she never paid much attention when I set out day after day. After about a week, I realized with a start that I was near the slave quarters of the Killough plantation that had belonged to my Isaac's Uncle James'. Dozens of pairs of brown eyes were following my every move, but not a body moved to accost me. I kept trying to remember something, and it kept slipping from my mind, just out of reach. Sallie. Sallie, who had stepped in after Mama died and nursed Elbert and mothered me until we were able to fend for ourselves. Which cabin was hers? Was she even still here?

I slumped to the ground and began crying. The tears came rapidly, hot and salty, accompanied by anguished sobs. Almost immediately, there were arms lifting me, holding me, rocking me, a voice shushing, "Baby, it alright. Sarah Jane, yo home now. Sallie rat here. Whatever it be, yo gwine be alright."

Sallie half-walked, half-carried me into the board and batten shack that served as her home. She set me on the bed, which was no more than a pallet of straw atop boards a few inches off the ground. The fresh sunshine smell of the clean quilt covering the rude bedstead helped quell my agony, and she handed me a gourd full of fresh, cool water.

"Chile, tell ole Sallie whut be achin' so bad."

I told her everything. How I used what she had taught me to make certain I kept from having a baby right off after getting married, how Isaac and I had built our cabin, planted crops, put money aside, and made plans for our future. I told her about the massacre, the long walk to the Lacey's, and the baby coming and never even crying once. How we buried her, among virtual strangers, and how tiny and blue she had been. How perfect her fingers and toes were and the strawberry hair that had a pretty little curl on top. I opened my locket to show her.

Sallie held me and stroked my hair, soothing me with love that could have only been matched by my own mother. I began to feel like myself again. Broken, but mending.

She sent me home with some herbs for tea, telling me

to take it every night, and for me to get rid of that nasty laudanum. I followed her instructions.

Narcissa's pa came and took her and Billie to his place in North Carolina. She promised to write regularly, and told us that she had no intention of giving up the homestead she and Samuel had in Texas. "It is Billie's inheritance," she said, matter-of-factly, "and it is the only thing he will ever have of his father's. I am going to make sure I keep it for him."

I thought briefly about what I would do about our – my – homestead. I could not bear the idea of returning, but neither could I bear the idea of abandoning our – my - home. Mammo said to give it time, that Nathaniel is handling things back there and to trust him. My stomach turned a bit at that. For some reason, I had never felt I could fully trust my brother-in-law, and that feeling had grown ever since he appeared at Lacey's fort with his ever-changing stories.

10

The first thing Mammo did when we got home was have herself named Administratrix of Pappo's estate. She sold the last bit of property they owned in Alabama, 176 acres for sixteen hundred dollars. The buyers were William Scott and his wife Flora of Pickens County. They signed the papers the morning of November thirteenth, and the Scotts turned around and sold it to William Hawkins that very afternoon, along with an adjoining ten acres they had paid a hundred dollars for – for fifteen hundred dollars. Now, that just does not sound very smart to me, to buy 186 acres for seventeen hundred dollars and sell it the same day for fifteen hundred dollars. But it was not my money, not my business. I kept my thoughts to myself and turned my attention to petting Jack whenever I found myself wanting to poke my nose in other people's business.

. . .

Letters came from Nathaniel, detailing all his legal doings. He was petitioning the Republic for restitution on all the losses of life and household goods, filing suit against Vincinte Cordova and Juan Cruz, and asking to be named administrator for the estates of Pa, his brothers, and George Wood, claiming they all died without a will or other papers, and died owing him money, so it followed that he was entitled to all the lands held, to keep or sell as needed to satisfy their just debts. I could not recall any promissory notes within the family, aside from the money George and Allen owed Reverend Bacon for the land. But then, I had tried to stay out of family doings as much as possible. It made life a lot simpler for me.

Now that I was caught up in the whirlwind, there was so much I did not understand. My head failed to comprehend how Mammo could be Administratrix in Alabama and Nathaniel could be Administrator in Texas of the same estate, but maybe it was because it was two different countries, that it made for two different estates. I wondered if George's brother Eli would have something to say about Nathaniel taking over George's estate, but I kept my mouth shut. The one thing I refused to do was to keep my mouth shut about was my right my Isaac's share, though, and I made it quite clear that I had every intention of claiming the land for my own. I was not going to be left widowed and destitute. Our right to our husband's property was one of the few points Narcissa and I ever agreed upon.

Nathaniel wrote that both Izzie and Molly had been killed in the massacre and he was claiming recompense for them in his request for restitution. Mammo was mightily grieved to lose her youngest daughter and beloved granddaughter. I grieved too, but it kept nagging at me that Dog Shoot had been adamant when he wanted to take us to Benge's camp that they had been told not to harm any of the women or children. He and the two Indians with him had certainly not harmed Narcissa, Billie, Mammo or me, although Narcissa had taunted him to the point of anger. On the other hand, bullets had been flying every which-away that day and they could have been shot, I suppose. I figured I would never know. But why would Nathaniel be due the recompense for Molly when she was Owen and Polly's daughter and they had survived and were still living on their homestead? About all I could suppose was that Nathaniel had turned the whole mess into a bird's nest on the ground for himself.

Nathaniel penned many lines about the battle he had fought against the Kickapoos under Captain Bradshaw, how he was shot through the shoulder but mended well, and about the small contingent who volunteered for burial duty, including John Middleton and Dr. Cannon, at our little settlement. They found the remains of four of our loved ones, three of which could not be identified. The fourth was Pappo, known by his gold tooth. They were laid to rest beneath an oak tree, about a hundred yards from Mammo and Pappo's cabin. About the same place Kias was killed. I hoped he had received a Christian burial. I want to believe he did.

We got letters from Narcissa too. Her pa had talked her into staying in North Carolina for a spell. More and more her epistles spoke of a Mr. Sammons, John to be specific. After a year of mourning, she became engaged to the cabinet maker, and I did not expect to ever see her again. I hate to say it but I had a happy smile at that thought.

. . .

And then, there were the letters addressed to me. They were few, but I clung to them. Sergeant John Sullivan was among the men at Lacey's fort when we arrived. He had been most concerned for my well-being, but in the most gentlemanly way, never presuming upon my person. He was the epitome of all that is good and noble in a man, and I deeply appreciated his offer of friendship. He had accompanied us as far within Texas borders as possible, as an official armed escort, with the blessings of General Rusk. Even during my darkest hours, he was a steady light who could be relied upon to give a ray of hope. As the months went by, and our correspondence grew, I began to anticipate with some small happiness our return to Texas. Of course, it might be that my opinion of him was favorably colored by the fact that he never failed to ask about Jack and say kind words about the animal who had now become my most dearly treasured friend.

11

When Nathaniel wrote his mother the news of Orleana's declining health, complicated by being in a delicate condition, we knew it was time for us to go back to our Texas homes.

Patsy's son Isaac Byars and Nathaniel's cousin Allen Killough, born of Isaac Senior's twin brother James, decided to accompany us. Allen looked so much like Nathaniel's brother Allen who had been killed in the massacre that once we arrived in Texas, lots of folks just figured he was our Allen, who had somehow miraculously survived. Once we got to Texas, he joined up with the militia and went to fighting Indians.

Mammo and I went and stayed with Nathaniel, who had moved himself into his parent's cabin during our absence. He had made scant improvements; in fact, it was a bit worse for the wear. We made do.

The baby came in due time, small but strong. Orleana named her Julia. I could not help but think of my own babe, how she would be a toddler now, with gleaming red curls. I had to stop and put such things out of my mind; thinking on them risked falling into melancholia again, and once of that was more than enough for me.

Julia was strong, but not Orleana. We buried her before Julia was properly weaned. Mammo and I fed the baby plenty of corn mush and buttermilk, and she grew plump and happy. Her big sister Eliza was nearly three years old, eager to help with her baby sister. It made me recall fondly the way Izzie and Molly had been, so many years ago. The thought of them haunted me, and I questioned Nathaniel time and again about their fate. He was adamant they had both been killed, but declined to say how, where or give a single detail whatsoever. Finally, he told me a story that Elizabeth had found Kias' body and wrapped herself about him, and seeing movement, one of the raiders had shot, thinking Kias was not dead yet, the bullets finding Izzie instead. It was a romantic story, but I knew better. I had seen Kias killed with my own eyes, and I had never been out of sight of his body until late in the evening, when the marauders had abandoned their task. I did not tell Nathaniel I knew it was a lie, but I think he could tell by the expression of my face. And Mammo's, who heard every bit. She caught my eye and just shook her head. I never pursued the question again.

I did pursue the issue of my land, my inheritance from my Isaac. Nathaniel had remained embroiled in the probate process for over a year now. He claimed Samuel's estate was indebted to him for a thousand dollars (I wondered how Narcissa would take that turn!) and that my Isaac's estate was comprised of a headright of six hundred and forty acres plus one hundred and sixty acres as his share of Isaac Senior's inheritance. All in all, it would be three hundred and ten dollars to settle my

Isaac's estate, the cost of paying for surveys and settling the bills on Isaac Senior's land. He recommended being allowed, as administrator of the estate, to sell some of the land to pay the debt. I promised to file a lawsuit against him if he dared sell one square inch of land without my approval.

Then I packed my things, called to Jack, and moved back into my own cabin. I would eke out a living from the land all by myself if need be.

Sergeant John N. Sullivan had no intention of letting me do so.

John Sullivan was a good and decent man. When he rode out to Nathaniel's place and found I had departed, he immediately came to my door, hat in hand, and proposed marriage. I was astonished.

"John, I am flattered. Truly, I am. But surely there is some young girl who could make you happier than I, who could give you children, and –"

He shook his head no. "Sarah, I am not a man who wants to raise a wife, much less children. I want a woman who can stand by my side, a woman with courage and conviction and compassion. A woman who can share my hopes and dreams, meager as they are, who can love me as I love her. I love you, Sarah Jane Williams Killough."

Jack nudged his muzzle at my skirts, pushing me toward John. I glanced down at the pup, wondering if he sensed more than I did. John placed his hand gently against my cheek and in a husky, half-whisper, added "Besides, who needs children? We have Jack."

So sensible and yet so sweet. I could not help but agree to marry him.

. . .

Not long before we were to be wed, we made a trip to Nacogdoches. John tended to buying goods to get my – our – cabin in good repair and lay in supplies for planting summer crops. We were getting a bit of a late start, but not so late we would not be able to have a decent harvest. For my part, I browsed through the dry goods stores and mercantiles, thinking I might perhaps find something pretty to mark the occasion of our wedding.

I entered the establishment of Mr. Thorn, a shop with high ceilings and shelves laden with everything imaginable. Candles, oil wicks, camphene, fabrics, notions, china, ironstone, cookware, washboards, lye soap – anything necessary and some things completely unnecessary. A girl – no, young woman – was finishing up her trade with Thorn and something about her seemed familiar. Her dress was clean, but plain and well-worn. Homespun, in a dull reddish-orange brown, probably produced by using some tree bark or maybe even the red clay that made up so much of our dirt. I felt a bit embarrassed by my own finery, ruffles and stripes in blue and white, protected by a freshly starched pelerine. I peered a little closer, and gasped as my heart began to flutter in my breast. She turned. Molly turned and faced me. "Mrs. Killough," she decried "how delightful to see you today!"

I was speechless as she hurried to my side to catch my elbow. "Shall we go out and talk for awhile? It has been so terribly long since we have seen one another." With those words, I allowed myself to be maneuvered from the mercantile and onto the broad sidewalk.

"I am dead, you know," she said companionably as she tucked her arm through mine.

"So Brother Nathaniel says," I replied acidly. "But you feel warm to the touch and I do believe I see you breathing, so either I am dreaming, or Brother Nathaniel is sorely mistaken." I stopped suddenly, my skirts swaying as I turned to study her face. "Mary Elizabeth, my little Molly dolly, it is you! I am not dreaming! How have you come to be here? Where have you been? And where, dear God, is Izzie?"

Molly just nodded. "Shall we wander down a bit further and find a nice shady spot away from everyone?"

We found a little place between the town's businesses and the well-to-do residences of the business owners. Molly told me in flat tones of all that became of her and Izzie after the raid. Tears came to her eyes as she recalled parting from her dearest friend and relation. "I have to believe she survived," she said in a half-whisper. "I have to trust the Almighty that I will see her again someday, if not on this earth, then in the next world."

We held hands for awhile in silence.

"What of you?" she asked.

"What indeed," I replied. "Your grandmother, Narcissa, Billie, and I had quite the adventure walking to Mr. Lacey's little fort with Jack. Once we got there, the baby came. She was still-born."

"Oh, Auntie, how terrible!"

What could I say? Terrible did not even begin to describe the experience, but I could not find any words that would. So I just stayed quiet for a bit and then continued. I told her about going back to Alabama, Narcissa going off to live with her pa, her grandmother and I coming back here, and Orleana having a baby and then dying herself. I told her what I knew of Nathaniel's wickering the estates and that I figured he was planning on using the tragedy to propel him into wealth and maybe even political office. "He is planning on running to be a Congressional Representative next fall, and he truly believes he can win a seat. But not if I have anything to do with it. You should have heard the story he made up about Izzie's supposed death!"

"No!"

"Yes. I knew it was a tall tale, not a shred of truth to it, but I let him tell it anyway. Your grandmother knows how much blather it is as well, but she will not speak out against him. I know she has no desire to go back to living with Patsy, and she feels useful helping him raise those two little girls. She is not going to leave them alone to be raised by him."

"I suppose we can only pray the truth comes out someday."

"Sooner rather than later is my prayer."

"Will you be staying here in Texas then? On your homestead?"

I blushed. "Yes. In fact, I am getting married on the seventh of next month." I then proceeded to tell her all about John, and our unusual courtship.

"I am so happy for you!"

"Molly, would you come live with me – us? Your grandmother will be so glad to see you, and know you are alive and well. She has had such fears about everyone; it would do her a world of good to have you back."

Molly shrank back. I realized how deeply the actions of Nathaniel had wounded her, how frightened she was of him. "I have an obligation to those who rescued me, who have kept me safe all this time. It is very kind of you, Auntie, and I would love to see Mammo again, but perhaps it is better if we leave things as they are. I am afraid Uncle Nathaniel can be a very dangerous man." She looked down at her moccasin clad feet. "Perhaps I am more Indian now than white. I do not think I can go back to being white, knowing what our people can do. And I do not want to be fully Indian either, for I know what Indian people can do too. But there is good in both races, and I want to be what is good. I think that is how the Almighty wants us to live, by seeking him and by loving one another. I love the people I live among, and I see the hand of God in all that surrounds me. I cannot depart that life." She raised her eyes to mine. "Please do not tell them you have seen me. I could not bear for Nathaniel and men like him to come hunting me, hunting the people I love. I have already lost one family to murder, please do not put me in danger of losing another."

"I could never endanger you or those you love." I promised.

12

Our wedding was simple. Elijah Payton read the vows over us. I wore that same blue and white striped dress with the ruffle on the bottom, with the locket that held the curl of my baby's red hair. Lavinia Eugenia, that was what I would have named her. That is what I called her in my heart, and I had her with me as I took a new name for myself, Sarah Sullivan. The Killoughs can, and probably will, continue to call me Sarah Jane, or Jane, but my new husband calls me Sarah, and I love hearing my name called from his lips.

John and I assessed what damage had been done to the cabin by fire, weather, and general neglect. Fortunately, when the marauders set fire to our cabins in thirty-eight, none of them ever completely caught fire. There were some insidious reminders, scorch marks on the walls and blackened rafters, but a bit of elbow grease took care of just about everything. The roof was missing some shingles, yet Isaac's froe still hung from the rafters in the loft. John had new shingles split and the roof repaired within a week, and I had the walls and floors scrubbed clean. By the time we had been wed a month, the cabin was weather-tight and cozy. Making new memories here with John helped ease the pain of losing Isaac and the dreams we had. I still had dreams, new ones, with a new husband, and surprisingly, that never diminished the love I had held for my Isaac.

Nathaniel ran for a representative seat in Congress in the fall of forty-one. He traveled around the county during the month of August, making speeches and debating his opponents, James Mayfield, Isaac Watkins, and Red Brown. When he returned he told us about some excitement in Nacogdoches. The same day he gave his speech there, Tuesday, the tenth – two days after stumping in Douglass - they had a trial that morning for two Negroes, a man and a woman, who confessed to having put Jameson weed in the coffee served to the Hyde family, the owners of the woman, Frances. William Goyens owned the man, Jack, who helped her. The jury found the man guilty the next day and sentenced him to hang on the twentieth; the woman was granted a change of venue. Nathaniel said Mr. Sterne and many others were quite upset with nearly all of the slaves in the area, charging them with much mischief and thievery of late. I told Nathaniel I was glad there were not many slave owners in our area, but I could tell that did not set well with him. Nathaniel had always aspired to being a big plantation owner like his Uncle James. But what truly upset him was the news on September sixth, when we were in Nacogdoches to see the votes counted. Out of hundreds of votes, he received only twenty-eight. James Mayfield was elected with two hundred and thirteen votes, and I noticed Mr. Sterne was beaming at the results. I was equally pleased.

Perhaps to make up for his disappointment in politics, he married Bethena Fisher on the twentieth of October.

I know Nathaniel's mama was happy to have Bethena in the family. It was another set of hands to help with the two girls, and keep up with the household chores. Nathaniel could have bought – and wanted to buy - himself a woman to do all that instead of getting married, but he minded his mama's wishes. Miss Urcey was just as set on not having a slave owning household as her son was on becoming a slave owner. She was not an abolitionist; she just felt slaves were more trouble than they were worth. Slaves would be just more mouths to feed, bodies to clothe, and would need tending when they get hurt or sick, and then what if they up and ran away? You would be out all that money and no further ahead on your chores. If you need more hands around the house, she said often enough, either do like your Papa and I did and have more children, or hire help when you need it. It is a waste of money keeping on help all of the time. Bethena did not give Nathaniel any more children though, so he was left to doing the farm work himself, with my John lending a hand when it was time to plant and again at harvesting. Nathaniel never did a lot of planting, though. He just pretty much put enough seed in the ground to grow food for the family to eat and a little extra to take to market. He had big dreams, but they were never dreams of being a good farmer. He wanted a plantation he could lord over, not labor over, but his mama stopped him at every turn. I do not have a clue how she did it, but she did. Or maybe it was because he was still all tangled up in settling the estates. It took him almost until Texas ceased to be a Republic and became a State before he was done with all the legal papers. Then the United States declared war on Mexico and our little patch of land seemed to just explode with new settlers.

Elam Tarrant was one of the first. He had volunteered in Mobile with the Thirteenth Alabama Infantry under J. Mitchell Withers. From Mobile, they had sailed to Mexico, done a little fighting for the term of their enlistment, and mustered out, setting off on foot from Mexico to Alabama. More than one man stopped along the way and decided to stay where his worn out feet had decided to stop. Elam married up with Dr. Dodson's widowed niece right quick and she started having babies right away, almost every year or so, it seemed. He started planting cotton, bringing in all sorts of slaves – some black, some mulatto, and some he claimed were Filipino. He and Dr. Dodson had the only Filipino slaves in the county, and it certainly was something to remark upon in the day.

About the same time, Johan Reierson took his own advice from the magazine he published, "Norge og Amerika", and started scouting out places in our neck of the woods. Before long, we had a passel of Norwegians industriously building homes and businesses all around us.

Then the McKee's showed up. I never was quite sure how that came to be, if it was through the workings of the Cumberland Presbyterian Synod, or the mysterious engineering of the Masons, or another remnant of the United States Army in Mexico. But here they were and here they stayed, and they made fast friends with Nathaniel. Nathaniel took another turn at being Justice of the Peace in forty-six; mostly he liked the air of importance it gave him, but in truth, the largest part of his job was just marrying folks.

John and I pretty well kept our distance from all the newcomers. We were friendly, but not chummy. We were both getting older, and without children to bring up or a big farm or a fancy business to maintain, there really was no reason for much socializing. We hired a farm hand or two seasonally, and we added an extra room to the cabin for their use. On the off season, we'd occasionally rent the room out to a traveler who wanted a more private accommodation than could be provided by the hotel one of the McKee's had built near the Neches-Saline road.

13

Our little settlement was only one of many with a building boom. The little speck called Gum Creek, about ten miles south, had become populated at a fair pace as well. Starting with Jackson Smith's house and blacksmith works, a druggist, post office, mercantile, dry goods, church, Masonic lodge and all sorts of other hallmarks of refined civilization began to flourish. For us, it cut a good fifty miles off the trek into Nacogdoches to shop at a well-stocked store.

I was in the dry goods shop in Gum Creek while John was busied with the horses at Mr. Smith's smithy. I had my eye on some sweet smelling soap, a treasure after years of making my own concoctions of lye, when I heard a clear voice call my name.

Molly had hardly changed. Her eyes were still a brilliant blue, her figure was a bit rounder, her blonde hair had darkened some and was parted in the center, plaited and pulled up and around her head. She held a young child on her hip, with brown hair and blue eyes.

He was fair skinned, wiggled a great deal, and pulled at her earlobes.

I approached her with a smile. "And who is this?"

"May I introduce my son, Samuel Houston Williams" she replied.

Only one thought went through my mind. "Williams?" How is it this child would carry his mother's maiden name. I could only think of one reason, and I was shocked.

She blushed, understanding my confusion, and whispered "It is not what you think. Terrapin took my name so we could stay in Texas." A bit louder, she said, where eager ears might overhear, "Yes. Matthew Williams is my husband."

She leisurely turned to a stack of newspapers, newly arrived from New Orleans. There were papers from New York and Boston, not too long past dated, and more recent editions from nearer locales.

Together, we scanned the New Orleans Bee. The salacious details of the Paris murder of a Ducesse, by her husband, Charles Laure Hugues Théobald, duc de Choiseul-Praslin for the love of his supposed mistress, Henriette DeLuzy, the recently dismissed governess of the murdered woman's own children, followed by his suicide before standing to account by his peers, captured my attention, mostly old news but with the added speculation that the Duc had survived.

We perused the details, drawing a shocked breath now and again as the intrigue grew of the nobleman's supposed absconding and rumored sightings of him in New Orleans, where he had relations. "Can you imagine a man being the hand of such evil in his own home?" I exclaimed.

"Of course I can imagine, and so can you," Molly

retorted. "At least, this poor fool acted on his own behalf, rather than hiring out the evil deed, and had the decency to remove himself from this world in atonement. May God have mercy on his soul."

"May God have mercy on him, but I pray He will show no mercy to Nathaniel." I lowered my voice, bitterness tingeing the tone. I looked at Molly curiously, recalling suddenly a bit of information John had relayed. "He received a letter from Mr. Parker some time ago, reporting you had been found with the Comanches."

"I was", she replied calmly.

"Whatever were you doing with Comanches? They are bloodthirsty savages! You know what they did to the Parkers, the Gotchers, the Websters, that poor Matilda Lockhart..."

"Perhaps from their viewpoint, circumstances were different." She spoke quietly, telling of finding Janie's son.

I was infuriated with my former brother-in-law. He had withheld the precise contents of the letter from everyone, except John, passing it off as a ruse for ransom money by a crazy old man. I had kept my promise to Molly to not reveal her circumstances to anyone, although it had been difficult when that letter arrived. And now to think of those children of George and Janie's being raised as Comanches! And maybe Allen and Bessie's children too!

Nathaniel was so wrapped up in being someone important, a landowner of thousands of acres, making a reputation for himself as a man of good moral character, a benefactor of the community, a man who could be implicitly trusted by one and all. What commotion would be wrought if Molly and the Wood's children were to appear and demand answers – and their rightful inheritance! I fumed. They were due that, and more.

"If only there could be some justice in this world, that I could witness, I would be somewhat consoled. If Nathaniel knew you lived, happily, and that Janie's little ones were healthy and strong, I think it would be punishment greater than any court could render. Nothing will change the past, but if his days were haunted, I would think righteousness had been served. Will you show yourself to him?"

"I am not ready to face Uncle. I may never be." She was still terrified of him. I sighed as held her little Samuel a bit closer, the softness of his baby hair against her lips, protecting him from the monsters that live among us.

To change the subject, I told her of the McKee family, newly arrived from Tennessee, headed by a slave-holding minister, and recounted how Nathaniel had even purchased a slave of his own, a young man to help with the farming, which had made his mama madder than a wet hen. Nathaniel, she charged, had his head in the clouds along with that McKee bunch. They had grand plans to create a fancy new town. Larissa, they were calling it, after the birthplace of Achilles, with a highfalutin school-house, elegant church-house, and even a big Masonic lodge. We both said we'd be surprised if it lasted, if they were ever able to build it at all.

Not long after harvesting was done for the season and the hired hands had vacated the extra room, a carriage I recognized from the McKee's hotel jostled into the yard. A fellow stepped out, looking like something out of a fashion catalog. He had on a tall hat, a black coat, striped trousers and the brightest red cravat I had ever seen. He ascended the porch steps, sweeping the hat from his head in an elegant motion. "Mrs. Sullivan?" I nodded. "My name is Jesse Duren. Innkeeper McKee has suggested you might be amenable to putting up a young lady for a spell." I was hesitant. Did this fellow take me for a woman of low morals? "She is a lady beyond reproach, I can assure you," he crooned, gesturing toward the carriage. "I fear the inn is too rough an atmosphere for someone of her delicacy and refinement."

I squinted a bit; my eyesight was not nearly as good as it had been years ago. I saw what must have been yards and yards of fabric, all brown and pink, ruffled all around, puffed sleeves and a tiny waist. She floated across the yard, approaching the porch. Beneath a pink bonnet, I saw brown tresses and green eyes, with a familiar shape to the chin and brow.

I felt faint. I stumbled forward "Izzie!"

Mr. Duren caught me.

14

Mr. Duren helped me to my rocker on the front porch. I closed my eyes and said a prayer. I felt soft hands taking my own old claws up and holding them. I was acutely aware of my shapeless house dress, gray hair, creased hands and lined face. I truly felt old for the first time. Weakly, I opened my eyes to face reality.

Izzie sank to the floor, holding my hands, not leaving my side.

Mr. Duren broke the silence. "I take it you are acquainted?"

Izzie nodded. "Allow me to introduce my sister-in-law, Mrs. Sarah Jane Killough."

I managed a feeble smile. "Sullivan, Sarah Sullivan. I married John on May seventh, 1840. We will have our tenth anniversary in the spring." I drew a deep breath, composed myself, and asked them to have dinner with me and John. And, of course, Izzie was welcome to stay as long as she would like.

. . .

The smokehouse held a good sized ham to grace the table that evening. I peeled and cut up some sweet potatoes to boil and mash with butter and ribbon cane syrup, and stirred up a pan of cornbread. I had some dried peas already soaking, so I cut up some sweet onions to flavor them and added a little bacon grease to the cook-pot. We would have as good a meal as a family could serve up on short notice. Izzie wanted to help with the cooking, but after a few missteps, I realized she had not experienced preparing her daily meals in quite some time. Someone else had tended to getting food on her plate; she was as inexperienced as a child anymore. So, I had her sit down and while I tended to the victuals, I told her a fair bit about what had transpired in her absence, and inquired of her own experiences. She demurred at first, then related some vague stories of New Orleans life, mostly of being a nursemaid to sickly folks in wealthy families. That explained why she lacked any cooking skills!

Dinner was a fine affair. I noticed Izzie taking stock of my John, and I stopped feeling quite so old. He is a good looking man, even with his gray hair. Mr. Duren was quite interested in our little community. John spelled out the brief history: McKee had laid off Larissa, bringing in not only a large contingent of his family and friends from Tennessee, but also encouraging Johan Reierson in settling a group of his Norwegian countrymen, including his brother Christian. The Olsen and Hansen men were talented woodworkers who had set up shop near the Reierson store on the town square. The McKees, for their part, in alliance with Nathaniel and others, set about establishing a Masonic hall, a Presbyterian church headed by Reverend McKee, a schoolhouse with the impressive moniker of "Larissa Academy" which they grandly planned to expand to a full fledged University. Their desire was to emulate a romanticized vision of Ancient Greece, replete with philosophers and scientists, mathematicians and linguists, musicians and thespians, all scholars and sophists. The town's founders prided themselves on being men of exemplary virtues, John concluded.

"Sounds to me as if what this county needs is some good old fashioned vice to balance out all that virtue," Mr. Duren mused.

"I reckon so," John replied. "About the only vice around here is old man Roddy selling whiskey next door to the Baptist preacher's place."

"Maybe you need another little town, with more 'interesting' entertainment, just within a stones throw." Mr. Duren pondered aloud. "I have heard first hand how vile Miss Killough's brother can be, and after meeting him today, I am of the opinion that he could benefit from a bit of rain this little Larissa parade." He paused, considering his next words. "Do you suppose anyone in the neighborhood would be willing to sell enough acreage to build a few shops and houses?"

John and I looked at each other. We had been married long enough that one could almost say exactly what the other is thinking. John nodded my direction. "As far as I am concerned, the land we have is all hers. She fought Nathaniel for her inheritance from her first husband, and the house and land are hers to do with as she pleases. If she wants to sell, then sell we will. We might even get the Sammons to sell as well. Narcissa had to fight Nathaniel to get her share too, and there is no love to lose between her and Nathaniel. It is a shame Polly and Jeff Wallace sold out last year and moved away; they had a good deal of land further west."

I had avoided mentioning Polly to Izzie. "I was waiting to find the right time to tell you. Owen passed awhile back. Polly married a fellow named Jefferson Wallace; they sold the place and took the boys to Brownsboro. Narcissa has a new husband, Mr. John Reed Sammons. They have a houseful of young 'uns. Little Billie is nigh grown now; just wait till you see him."

We agreed to visit the Sammons family come morning. Mr. Duren took the carriage back to McKee's inn and I showed Izzie to her new room.

15

Narcissa was a lot less bossy and self-centered since having more children. Being tugged at in every direction by one child and then another had taken a lot of the brattiness out of her. I almost felt sorry for her. Mr. Sammons seemed to not be a heap of help, and if anyone needed help running a household, she did.

I could tell by the way her hair was disheveled that she was already worn out, and it was well before noon. I took her by the arm and set her in a chair, then put a kettle on to boil. What that girl needed was a good strong cup of tea, a regular tonic. Of course, she was expecting again, and that was adding to her malaise.

John Sammons lumbered in, trailing East Texas red clay dirt in his wake. Narcissa looked at it and sighed. I knew she would have to sweep it up later; experience told her that asking him to wipe his feet at the door or leave his boots outside was a lost battle.

We sat around the little square table, crudely made for expediency with no care taken for being level or smooth. A cabinet maker by trade, Mr. Sammons did lovely, precise, and delicate work for paying customers, but was not so concerned with quality for his own family.

I served up the tea in noggins as Mr. Duren smoothly began his salesman's pitch. I saw Narcissa nodding, and her husband dipped his head in agreement. By noon, an agreement was reached to the satisfaction of all. John Sammons was eager to leave Texas, after discovering there would be no inheritance from his wife's former mother-in-law. Narcissa was equally eager to move to South Carolina, where she had relatives in Greenville County, where there were more civilized cities and towns, where life was not as harsh, and the reminders of that fateful October day were not lurking right outside her front door. Or inside her front door, for that matter. She readily transferred the homestead to me and John, so Nathaniel could never accuse her of selling out Billie's inheritance away from the family. We, in turn, handed over their section of land along with a good piece of our own to Mr. Duren for the establishment of a new town to compete with Larissa.

He called it Talladega, and the first thing he built was a saloon.

I insisted on Izzie remaining with us. I worried a bit about Nathaniel discovering her, but it worried me more to think of her going back into the wide world all alone. Mr. Duren was a married man, with a wife in Houston, and while there was nothing improper in their acquaintance, there was no need in flirting with gossip. When asked about the newcomer to our household, I simply told the old biddies she was my niece from Alabama and we expected her husband to join us in due time. Izzie herself had suggested she should go by her given name of Elizabeth, and put forth McGowan as a surname. She said it was the name of lady who had been most kind to her when she was in great despair. I knew better than to ask any questions.

Our little deception was to hold us in good stead, for to Elizabeth's consternation, she was with child. In desperation, she packed her little carpetbag and set off walking. I found her, sobbing, by the creek. I took her back to the house, put her to bed with a hot toddy, and declared she would remain. John and I would ensure the child had a proper home and upbringing. I pronounced her imaginary spouse deceased, and proclaimed her a widow to any who inquired. Few asked more than once.

I inquired once as to the paternity of the child; I was told it was a madman who had assaulted her. She implored me to press her no further. As with Molly, I respected her wishes.

16

Elizabeth had a terrible time those long months of carrying her child. I feared her mind would break. I arranged for Molly to visit for a few days and that pleasant company seemed to improve her demeanor. Her nights, however, were filled with terrors I can barely begin to imagine. Being in such close proximity to the site of our familial horror wreaked havoc on her fragile state. She saw things that were not there; she heard voices of those dead a dozen years. She spent increasing amounts of time wandering the woods and by the creek, picking plants and stripping trees of bark. She burned some, she left some to dry, and she soaked others in spring water to pull the oil from the flora. Sometimes, I caught her blowing smoke from a burning bundle of stems and leaves; other times, I saw her daubing water on the door and window sills. I had used nature's bounty to heal and help nearly all my life, but I had never seen anyone work as Izzy did. My very soul was scared by some of her practices. Truly, she had undergone some mysterious change after the massacre. If I did not know better, I would not have recognized her as the girl I had I had known so many years ago.

I thought perhaps when the baby came, her mind would snap back into place and she would be the bright, outgoing Elizabeth of old. Her water broke early one morning; by mid-afternoon, a son, William, was born. Her labor was blessedly easy; Mrs. Lockey McKee came to assist from the inn. We had no need to call for a doctor or a midwife. Elizabeth fell into a deep and undisturbed sleep afterwards. The baby nursed easily, quickly gaining weight and becoming a cheerful, chubby child that John and I delighted in parenting.

Not long after William's entrance into the world, Nathaniel's mama exited the world. She was followed quickly by Bethena, and Nathaniel did not seem terribly concerned about the loss of either. He started buying more slaves, mostly women, and in no time at all, most of them were having babies. Yellow ones, but all the nice ladies in town turned a blind eye to it, and focused on the poor widower with those two precious girls.

Samuel McKee, the innkeeper, passed away about the same time. Nathaniel never missed an opportunity to enlarge his fortune, and quickly married the widow McKee, the same Lockey who had helped bring William into the world. She already had four children, including a pair of twins, and soon she had two babies with Nathaniel. He finally got the son he had always wanted and named him for himself. The new baby girl, he named her for dear Orleana, his first wife. I always have wondered how Lockey felt about that, but I never quite got the nerve to ask her.

In between the burials and the wedding, Elizabeth took a fancy to a showman passing through, Ebenezer Harvey. John and I thought to put an end to it before anything ever began, but it only went as far as a thought. Before we knew what was happening, she had brought this man into our home, then up and ran off with him. He was a ventriloquist, amusing crowds by throwing his voice so it seemed animals and infants could talk, or even dolls. It was an entertaining show, to be sure, but to make a living at it, he had to constantly be on the move from town to town, from opera house to opera house. Thankfully, she left William in our care. I am afraid I could not have stood having her take him from us into that vagabond life.

She wrote to us; the first was to let us know they had been legally wed in Douglass, just outside of Nacogdoches. The next letters arrived from New Orleans; they had decided to settle there for a spell. She wrote about a new kind of church they were attending, something to do with uniting all religions with one spiritual approach, and people who communicated with the dead, just like she was able to see and talk to her papa, brothers, and Kias all the time she was carrying Willam. She had told her new husband about her 'abilities' and I suppose he got an idea or two that he could make some money off her by using his voice throwing to make it seem she was hearing even more voices. Such thoughts were unpleasant, and disrespectful of her marriage, so I put them out of my mind. But I wondered, more and more as time went by, if he had married her more on account caring for what he could make of her 'visions' and less on account of caring for her.

I tried to put my fears to rest and focus on raising

William. He was an intelligent, thoughtful, and considerate youngster, starting in toddlerhood. He required very little supervision; he was eager to be helpful, willing to listen and learn before attempting a task on his own. We sent him to a little day-school where he learned to read and write, cipher and get along with other children in the community.

Nathaniel's Larissa was bustling fairly well. The businesses were thriving, the church houses were full, there was a full roster of Masons going to the lodge meetings, and the college took up several buildings, including dormitories for both males and females. The school was chartered and under the responsibility of the Cumberland Presbyterian Church, although one did not need to be a member of the church to attend. Reverend Franklin L. Yoakum was named the President; Nathaniel and Mr. Thomas McKee were on the Board of Trustees. I reckon that was about as high up in prestige as Nathaniel ever went.

Elizabeth wrote she and Eben had moved to St. Louis, Missouri. She had become a 'medium', holding séances and giving messages from 'beyond the veil'. I just shook my head. I had never heard anything I in the Presbyterian church or the Methodist church along such lines. She seemed happy, though, and her marriage was all she had ever dreamed of; they had a nice house and had hired a lady to do the housekeeping and cooking. I had to smile at that; she had never been cut out to cook for herself or a husband.

. . .

Slavery, as Miss Urcey had always said, was more trouble than it was worth, and folks learned that the hard way. It divided a nation later on, but first, it divided Larissa.

The college needed something important to bring in students. They had quite a nice collection of specimens for the study of geology, mineralogy, physical and natural science, chemistry, botany, animal science, moral science and mental science. Math, Latin, Greek, French, Spanish, philosophy, rhetoric and logic were in the curriculum. But someone figured what really was needed to bring in students was astronomy and the biggest and best telescope money could buy.

Of course, that meant they needed to find the biggest and best telescope and get the money to pay for it.

I am not certain who had the connections, but somehow, the board managed to order, from a Dr. Fritz in New York, an eight foot long telescope with a four inch diameter, at a cost of somewhere between seven hundred and a thousand dollars, depending on who was bragging about the purchase. Supposedly, it magnified the night skies thousands and thousands of times over, and was even more powerful than the same instrument at Yale University. Very impressive, to be sure, and very valuable. As valuable as a good slave, literally.

The Board of Trustees could not raise the money for the telescope. The President of the College was determined to have it, even if he had to pay for it himself. So, the good Reverend Doctor Yoakum had Mr. Long take one of his best hands to Shreveport and auction him off. The proceeds from the sale of that slave, a young man named Daniel, paid for the pride of Larissa.

Miss Joiner, of the Female Department of the College, was not impressed. In fact, she was furious.

Miss Joiner was an abolitionist. What she was doing

here in Larissa, teaching at a college where just about all the students, faculty, trustees, and administrators were either slave owners or came from slave owning families, is beyond me. She probably should have stayed among her own kind, like-minded do-gooders. I was not keen on slavery myself, nor was John, but we knew when to keep our mouths shut and mind our own business. Miss Joiner had no such discretion. She was, in a word, outspoken. As much as she was cultured, talented and had many academic achievements, she was still a Northerner. A Yankee. She was born in Vermont and educated in Canada; why the trustees overlooked that in hiring her is beyond me. The year after they bought the telescope, they expelled her from her position.

Not that it really mattered in the long run. The class of 1860 was the only class ever to graduate from Larissa College. The War came along, the young men went to war, and the young ladies went home to await their return.

17

The War. Thank Providence John was too old and too sensible to go marching off battle. William was too young, at least at first. He had war fever, though, and wanted to fight. We told him time and again that the best contribution he could make to the war was to stay home and help raise crops and livestock to feed folks here and maybe have extra to send to the men at the front. With so many husbands and sons away, young boys William's age – children, really - were being called on to take on a man's workday, plowing, sowing, and harvesting on small farms like ours. The folks who owned slaves fared a bit better, since they had hands to do the farm labor, to run the sawmills, to drive the mules in a never ending circle to press the sugar cane, wheelwrights and blacksmiths and all the other functions a big spread needed to keep up the production of cotton, corn, and every other thing a living body needs.

Nathaniel did fairly well, but the imminent demise of the college weighed on him, I am certain of that. He had about a half dozen field hands or more at the start of the war, not counting the mulatto woman and her seventeen-year-old daughter who ran away before the war ever started. I never thought he put much effort into finding those two. He kept his crops growing and harvested, and sold a little timber here and there. Not too many people had money, though, to pay for what they needed, so he got by the way so many of us did, by trading and bartering. Eventually, he took to selling off his slaves. That was when I knew things were bad for him.

I heard through the local gossips that his health was declining. One of Lockey's sons was in bad shape as well. Consumption, the doctor said. Just a matter of time.

Corresponding with Elizabeth became increasingly difficult as the war continued. All I could do was pray she would be kept safe. We heard rumors and saw occasional newspapers where trouble in Missouri was reported. There was a real ugly thing that happened between William Quantrill's guerrillas and the Yankees in Kansas, not far from Missouri. But surely she was far away from those terrible happenings.

In sixty-four, William rode off to Jacksonville and joined up with Captain Lovelady's company that was part of the Eighteenth Texas Infantry. He lied about his age, probably the only lie he ever told in his life. He went to battle in Louisiana, along the Sabine and Red River, and stayed around Shreveport toward the end of the war.

He was in one of those battles when Elizabeth returned home, thin, angry, bitter, and exhausted. She had bought a slave in Missouri, with the agreement he would protect her and see her safely home, then she would manumit him upon arrival. I was floored. She signed the papers with John and me as witnesses. Daniel thanked her profusely and lit out, papers in hand, towards Nathaniel's house. I was too stunned to ask why, but all those years of yellow babies gave me an idea or two. I wondered too if he was that same boy Reverend Yoakum sold off, before the war, but I figured that would be too much of a coincidence. Still, stranger things have happened.

Elizabeth was ill herself. I thought at first she was just weak from such an arduous journey but it soon became apparent her whole body was given out. She was alive only by sheer determination. She intended to confront her brother before she died. Before he died.

John thought it best if he were to pay a visit to Nathaniel first. He promised not to tell Nathaniel of Elizabeth's arrival, only to ascertain his health and mental acuity. Nathaniel was sitting up, with a blanket across his lap and a fire in the hearth, even though it was late March and already warm. He asked John to witness the will he had just finished writing.

'I, Nathaniel Killough of the state of Texas and County of Cherokee, being sound in mind, do hereby make and ordain this my last Will & Testament in manner and form as follows

Viz: 1. I commit my body to the dirt and my spirit to Him who gave it.

2 After paying all my just and legal debts, I do

hereby give and bequeath to my daughter Eliza J. Matthews my negro women Epsy together with all her present and future increase, said woman now having three children, and said daughter Eliza J. Matthews being already in possession of said woman and children. My gift heretofore to my said daughter Eliza J. Matthews of a House and Lot in the Town of Larissa remains unchanged. I further give to my daughter Eliza my negro woman Jane and her youngest daughter Viana aged about seven years. I further give and bequeath to my daughter Eliza seven hundred and thirty eight acres, off of this Head Right, situated in the County of Henderson

I also give to my daughter Julia A.E. Chamblin my negro woman Pauline together with all her present and future increase, said woman now having three children, and said daughter Julia A. E. Chamblin being already in possession of said woman and children. I also give and bequeath to my daughter the lumber which built her residence in the Town of Canton together with some money to make her equal with her sister Eliza. I further give my Boy Alfred to my daughter Julia A. E. Chamblin. I further give to my daughter Julia my Head Right of six hundred and forty acres situated in the County of Vanzdant.

I further give to my son Matthew Nathaniel Killough my negro girl Emiline, and my negro Boys Sam and Jeff.

I further give to my daughter Orleana Cornelia my negro woman Mary and two girls Caroline, and Molina.'

John read the will, front and back, nodded and handed it back to him. "What of Lockey or your nephew Billie?"

Nathaniel's eyes clouded as he gazed into the fire. "I

suppose I will have to study on that before I sign the will."

I cannot say what happened when Elizabeth went to Nathaniel's home. All I know is, not too much later we got word he was dead.

Nathaniel was buried out near his pa and the three unidentified bodies that Dr. Canon and Mr. Middleton had laid to rest after the massacre. There was a nice turnout for the funeral. Elizabeth even came and stood off to one side, without tears, without remorse. That afternoon, she took to her bed. We interred her in the burying ground a week later.

18

After Izzie's death, life resumed for me and John. William came back from the war, no longer a boy, but a man with sadness in his eyes. He never spoke of what caused it; when I asked, he simply said "I did what I had to do. God help me if we ever have another war."

He managed to socialize a bit with folks his own age. There were plenty of young ladies eager to find husbands, and he had his pick of the belles. He settled on a sweet girl named Elvira who lived with her parents in Jacksonville. They set up housekeeping near her folks. Five children came along in short order, three girls and two boys. William joined the Masonic Lodge and worked his way up pretty high. John and I were right proud of him.

Billie, who was now styling himself "The Baby of the Massacre", came to live on Nathaniel's old place somewhere around sixty-seven. He was thirty years old, a little advanced for being known as a baby, I thought, but it brought him some notoriety and I suspect he made a dollar or two off of it. He practically made a career of avoiding working; he'd much rather sit and spin yarns. To one group, he would tell about how he had spent the whole of the War under General Hood; to another, he would spin a tale of sitting by his Uncle Nathaniel's deathbed, promising to keep all the Killough land and never do anything with it. Well, he was right on that point – he never did much of anything with it. But he must have had wings to be in Atlanta, Georgia with Hood and here in Larissa, Texas during April of 1864. As he got older, he filled the heads of his children with tales of how all of the land his daddy and granddaddy settled was rightfully his, and eventually, theirs. He cast aspersions on my character, Polly and Owen's, and the Wood family, trying to claim our inheritance as his – and the same for Nathaniel's own children. He hardly ever bothered to mention that there was a younger baby who survived the massacre, Nathaniel's own Eliza. I am not sure, but I think Eliza and her sister Julia, who inherited the most from their Daddy of what was left of our little settlement – Nathaniel had sold off quite a bit of the original settlement back in the forties, as he was bound and determined to create the town of Larissa – the girls just let Billie squat on the place, since they both had married well and had no need of being bothered with the property. Ah, well, that was their business, not mine. My title to my land was secure, and unbound by any deathbed promise to never sell or do anything with it.

Talladega never did make a go of it as a town. Larissa just withered and blew away like so much dust after the War.

The college closed down and most of its assets were sent to Tehuacana, where the Presbyterians were consolidating some other colleges. A few years later, there was a meningitis outbreak, which made a good dent in the population. The real death knell came when the railroad bypassed the town. After that, the need for churches or businesses fell off, and I reckon they will all fall to dust soon enough. Everything except the cemeteries. Those will endure, long past the memory of the towns.

After John died, I began to think on how much time I had left on this earth, and if I could continue to live on our farm, alone. I decided time might be short or long, but I had no need to stay by myself. I sold the place and moved to Jacksonville, about ten miles south. It had grown from being Gum Creek with just a few stores to a decent sized town and changed the name in honor of Jackson Smith. Once the railroad came through, and missed the town by a bit, they decided to dismantle the town and move it to be closer to the railroad to make it a thriving place. It sounds crazy, but where there's a will, there's a way, and that is just what they did. Took the buildings apart board by board and reassembled them a couple of miles to the east. They call it the 'new Jacksonville'.

Andrew Jackson Chessher has a grocery store in the new Jacksonville; his wife, Melvina, keeps herself occupied by running their place as a boarding house. I moved into a private bedroom there and help with the cooking and cleaning in exchange for part of my room and board. It is a welcome change for me; her kitchen is outfitted with a big sink and hand pump, a nice stove, and even an icebox. Looking back, I could have never imagined such luxuries in my time! Even now, as I am slowing down and getting near the end of my life, I can still do a few chores with ease on account of these modern inventions.

My time is coming, maybe not today or tomorrow, but I cannot imagine I will see the end of this century. I might not even see the end of this year. Time will tell. I think more and more on the life I have lived, and the people I have known. Some I have loved, some I have just tolerated. Most of them, though, the ones close to me – those, I have loved and still love, even though many left this world long ago. And I ponder on what is to come.

My mind turns back, thirty plus years, to my sweet pup Jack. He lived a good, long life and I miss him to this day. He was just a puppy when Isaac and I married, he made that long trek with the family from Alabama to Texas, stuck by my side as we walked away from the horrors, and stayed by by bed as my baby came into this world without so much as a whimper. He went back to Alabama with us, and returned again to Texas with me. When my John was bad sick not long after we married, Jack would go out and catch rabbits and squirrels, bringing them home for me to clean and cook, so we would all have something to eat. I made sure Jack always had a generous portion of whatever we had; he was more than a dog – he was my protector, my confidant, my companion, my friend. The night he died, I lay beside him on the floor in front of the hearth, stroking his soft coat as he struggled to breathe. When he was gone, I wailed. I was inconsolable for days, if not weeks. I cried more tears for Jack than I ever shed for a human being.

Izzie never said if she saw Jack and I never asked. I had no need of such reassurance; I always felt his presence. Now, as I approach the end of my days, I sometimes feel his weight press against my back, comforting me as in days of old.

Not long before Izzie died, she told me about the vision she had of what awaits after this life. Not a Heavenly Father's house with many mansions. Not a vision of Christ. Not even angelic countenances of her mama and papa waiting for her with outstretched arms at the pearly gates. She said that when we die, our souls burst forth in freedom from the mortal body in a blaze of colors, and travel into space where an enormous bright white orb pulsates as if it has a heartbeat. All the souls, of everyone everywhere who are dying at the same time, they are all different colors, and they are all are racing toward that white pulsing orb. They go in spirals, or in straight lines, some bouncing, some zigzagging - but always toward the big ball of bright white light. The colors fall into this white sun, and as they do, they are swallowed up by the light in a rainbow explosion of color, with blazing light and colors that are never seen on Earth. As the colored orbs are going into the light, other tiny white orbs break free of the larger, just as pure and perfect as the white light they come from. These speed out into the darkness; they are the new souls racing into the world to be born. The light is where all things begin and end; it is truly the Alpha and Omega, it is love everlasting, unconditional, eternal love.

Izzie said "I have no fear of judgment for we are our own judges, juries and executioners. We create our own prisons on this earth in these bodies. Once free of the body, we are truly free, we are immortal souls. The soul is simply a small piece of All That Is, of God, of the Creative Source from whence we all came and to which we shall all return. What I have done on this earth, I have done of my own free will. There have been consequences for every action I have taken, whether for good or ill. The same is true for everyone, the punishment for our actions on Earth is here on Earth, levied by man or by one's own self. There is no punishment of the soul; there is only release from mortal bondage into love and joy. What was of the human body is behind us once we cease to breathe."

I am not much of a seminarian, but her words rang true to me. If nothing else, she believed them. And as I think on it, so do I. I will add, though, that when my own spirit leaves this earth, I will be accompanied by one very special fice dog, and Jack and I will make that final, glorious journey together.

EPILOGUE

The historical account of Elizabeth Williams ends with a brief notation in the Reverend James Parker's journals. Nothing further is recorded of Sarah Jane D. Williams Killough Sullivan after the transfer of property to Jesse Duren for the establishment of Talladega. The final reported sighting of Elizabeth Killough was as she was rushing to hide in the canebrake along Killough Creek on October fifth, 1838. Over the years, the massacre site was largely forgotten, until during the Great Depression, when the Works Progress Administration undertook the building of a monument at the site of the Killough family burial ground. The monument, a towering obelisk, is constructed of native iron ore stone, like those covering the four unmarked graves of the men found by the burial detail after the massacre. As time progressed, legends and ghost stories have emerged regarding the massacre and burial ground. One of the more persistent is the tale of a ghostly Native American, on horseback, wearing the war bonnet of a Plains Indian chief. Odd, because none of the accused aggressors were of those tribes, nor were any Native Americans counted as killed in the massacre. In fact, the only known dead were white men in the Killough settlement. So, why would a Plains Indian chief be haunting the site? Perhaps...

1909

We put on quite a show in Fort Worth. The city hosted an indoor rodeo at the North Side Coliseum, an enormous building, slightly reminiscent of the old Alamo, but fresh and modern. My old friend Quanah insisted, as usual, I come along and be part of the 'Wester' spectacle. As usual, I agreed. It was good to get off the reservation, to travel, and dress as an Indian warrior again. We played our roles to the fullest – long war bonnets, bone breastplates, lances, making ourselves the popular image of the noble warrior. In truth, we were at war, although the war we were fighting now was one for the white man's dollars and, hopefully, a bit of respect as men.

After the rodeo, and before the next stop on our entertainment circuit, Quanah and I took our families on another of his expeditions to locate the final resting place of his mother, Cynthia Ann Parker. He knew she lay somewhere in East Texas; his white relatives were never very forthcoming in exactly where. We traveled into Anderson, Henderson, Smith and Cherokee counties, just as we had for several years. Friends along the way provided us with the best hospitality they could afford. One of those friends was Jeff Norris Killough, who was known by the name John.

When we first went searching though that part of Texas, many years ago, I felt a twinge of apprehension. I rarely felt such emotions, and Quanah suggested it might be a spiritual affliction. I agreed it did seem deep-rooted, and we thought that when we reached his friend's homestead in Bullard it might be good to fast and pray over the question.

Fasting and praying were not needed.

That was when I first met John Killough. Upon our introduction, a distant memory began to claw its way to the surface. Just as Quanah had led Montechema to the reservation, and from there to be reunited with his white family, recognizing the name "Hermann" from his brother's lips, so now Quanah was leading me to a white family, whose name was buried in my heart. The name "Killough" touched my ears with a near-forgotten familiarity.

John was much younger than I; I could not have known him from my childhood. Yet he bore a strong resemblance to my mother, and to her brother. I fought to recall the name. It was Biblical: Isaac, perhaps. Samuel?

I must have said the words aloud, for John's eyes grew wide, and he peered into my face intently. "Who are you?"

I struggled to recall. I had been trying to learn, or relearn, English for some time now. Words flitted though my mind, brushing against my tongue in an unfamiliar way. Leaf, bark, tree, trunk, branch, limb, wood. "Wood," I replied. "My name was Wood." I was relieved. Another word came, unbidden, yet insistent on annunciation. "Junior."

John rocked back as though he had been stuck. "George?"

I thought for a moment. A chord struck within me; I nodded.

"George Wood Junior. Well, I'll be blasted. You must be my Dad's cousin."

I was still trying to absorb the enormity of the moment. I must have, somehow, recognized something in the creeks, hills and valleys that reminded me of that day, that horrible day. The memory is still blurred, but I recall gunshots, Ma and Pa shooing me and my brothers into the canebrake, Ma carrying my baby brother on her hip. There were others with us too, but

I cannot remember their names or faces. Other children, other adults – and then Pa took off and there was more shooting. A bunch of men dressed as Indians - but they were white and brown, not red – stormed into the cane and snatched us up onto their horses. My mind refuses to let me remember much of anything else, not until I came to live among the People.

Now, here we were again. My English is greatly improved, and I enjoy our visits with my cousin John. "So, George, how about we go pay a visit to my dad?"

I have avoided this in the past. From what John has told me, many of my white family blamed the Indians for the massacre. I dared not think I would be welcome, with my long hair and buckskin breeches. But I'm getting older; this will be my last adventure with my friends. Perhaps it is time to touch the stones of my past.

We set out early the next morning, on horseback. John took me to the burying ground first, at my request. I wanted to see where my pa was laid; it burned in me the way Quanah's quest to find his mother did in him.

"Not really sure who is buried where, George. It was awhile before anyone could come back to find them and get them in the ground." *The four neat cairns of stone lay in a perfect line, facing east. Clumps of Bahia grass grew between the graves; a few random wildflowers sprung up here and there. There were newer graves as well; John pointed out the resting place of his Uncle Nathaniel, pretty much the sole survivor of the massacre, according to his dad. Of course, his dad and his dad's mother had survived, but John added that as an afterthought.* "Dad is still called "The Baby of the Massacre", even though he has lived more than seventy years."

"I must be nearly eighty or more myself, then," *I mused.* "Surely, I could not have been more than ten years old that day. I cannot recall how old I was, so I have no idea how old I am now." *Suddenly, I felt very tired. I sat down upon the ground, in the shade of an old oak. "You go on and get your dad. I will stay here and talk with mine."*

I watched him depart, knowing he would only find my shell upon his return. I had conferred with Quanah before we left that morning. "I feel this is the day," I told him. "Ask to bury me near my pa, just as I know you want to be with your ma someday."

My old friend nodded and bid me farewell, a single tear escaping from his eye

HISTORIC FIGURES

- Unknown surname, **Daniel** (unknown) Referenced in *Larissa* as the slave owned by Rev. F.L. Yoakum and sold to finance the purchase of the college telescope.
- **Attree, William** (? – 1849) Reporter for the New York Herald.
- **Barret, Francis Regis (Sister)** (1804 – 1862) Head of the New Orleans Sisters of Charity New Orleans Female Orphan Society
- **Bauer, John N.** (1810 – 1888) Prominent businessman in Jefferson City, Missouri
- **Bays, George** (1801 – 1869) - The first white settler in the Neches-Saline salt licks, arriving in 1823
- **Benge, Sam** (? – 1839) White or half-white Cherokee chief who was a signatory to the Houston-Forbes treaty
- **Big Mush (Hard Mush, Gatunwalie)** (? – 1839) Considered the war chief of the Texas Cherokees. Died in the Battle of the Neches, July 16, 1839
- **Blake, Bennett** (1809 – 1896) Arrived in Nacogdoches in 1835. Served under General Thomas J. Rusk in battles with the Indians in 1839 and 1841. Swore out affidavit claiming he knew Richard Parmalee's identity to be Richard Parmalee Robinson.
- **Box, John (Johnny) Morris (wife Sally)** (1780 – 1842) Settled between the present-day towns of Alto and Rusk in East Texas in the 1830s with several family members. In addition to cabins, they build a small log fort on a bluff west of Box Creek.
- **Box, Roland W. (wife Mary)** (1803 – 1851) Son of John M. Box

- **Box, Stephen (wife Keziah)** (1780 – 1844) Brother of John M. Box
- **Brown, John "Red"** (1786? – 1852) Democratic county and state official. Born in Ireland and arrived in Texas in 1836, settling near Nacogdoches. Lawyer and farmer.
- **Burleson, Edward** (1798 – 1851) Arrived in Texas in 1830. As a colonel of the First Regiment of Infantry in April 1838, quashed the Cordova Rebellion. In 1839, at the Battle of the Neches, defeated the Cherokee and allied Indians.
- **Castrillion, Manuel Fernandez** (? – 1836) Major General of the Mexican Army under General Santa Anna. After the Battle of the Alamo, he advocated for the humane and honorable treatment of a small group of captured Texans. His arguments were ignored and the prisoners were executed. Died at the Battle of San Jacinto.
- **Chessher, Andrew (or Anderson) Jackson (wife Melvina)** (1815 – 1889) Grocer and Justice of the Peace in both "old" and "new" Jacksonville.
- **Choiseul-Praslin, Charles Laure Hugues Théobald (wife Frances)** (1805 – 1847?) The Duc de Praslin, a French nobleman and politician, accused of the murder of his wife in August 1847. Most believe he died by suicide in the following days; others contend he fled to America and eventually South America, where he remarried and had a second family.
- **Choiseul, Charles** (1818 – 1862) French born, naturalized American citizen. Attorney. Confederate Lt. Col. for the 7th Louisiana Regiment.
- **Chouteau, Henry Pierre (wife Clemence Georgina)** (1805 – 1855) Prominent businessman in St. Louis, Missouri. Died in the Gasconade River Train Disaster.

- **Clapp, Theodore** (1792 – 1866) Originally a Presbyterian, he became a devout Unitarian, and established the "Stranger's Church" in New Orleans, Louisiana.
- **Coe, Daniel Bates** (1821 – 1902) Brother-in-law to Richard Parmalee Robinson by marriage to Cynthia Robinson on September 1, 1841. In 1851, partnered with Robinson in a livery stable and stagecoach service in Nacogdoches.
- **Cordova, Vincinte** (1798 – 1842) Alcalde of Nacogdoches prior to the Republic of Texas. He opposed Texas Independence and instigated the Cordova Rebellion in an effort to overturn the Republic. He attempted to negotiate with Cherokee leaders for their support; this partially lead to the Indians being implicated in the Killough massacre.
- **Crockett, David (Davy)** (1786 – 1836) Frontiersman, congressman, defender of the Alamo.
- **Cruz, Juan** (unknown) Along with Juan Flores, assumed leadership roles in the Cordova Rebellion.
- **DeBard, Elijah** (1810 – 1868) Doctor. Partnered with Chief Bowl in the manufacture of salt at the Neches-Saline.
- **DeLuzy-Deportes, Henriette** (1813 – 1875) Governess to the children of the Duc and Ducesse de Choiseul-Praslin from 1841 until July 1847.
- **Dodson, Elijah** (1807 – 1867) Doctor, slave-holder in Cherokee County, Texas.
- **Dog Shoot** (unknown) Cherokee Indian associated with Sam Benge.
- **Douglas, Kelsey** (? – 1840) Nacogdoches merchant and congressman in the Republic of Texas. Charter member of the Masonic Grand Lodge of Texas. He issued paper money in Nacogdoches, payable at either his store or his office in New Orleans. His notes circulated at about the

same rate as Republic of Texas currency. The town of
Douglass is named for him.

- **Duren, Jesse** (1804 – 1864) Land speculator who
  established Talladega, Texas. The town was known for
  having a saloon, gambling hall, and racetrack.
- **Edwards, Haden** (1771 – 1849) Early empresario in
  Nacogdoches. Along with his brother, instigated the
  Fredonian Rebellion. First Worshipful Master of the
  Milan Lodge #2 in 1837.
- **Ferguson, Jesse Babcock** (1819 – 1870) Church of Christ
  preacher who developed Spiritualist leanings during the
  1840s and 1850s. He was expelled from the Church of
  Christ for his evolving beliefs in 1857, and eventually
  became convinced of the doctrine of Universalism and
  was active in the Universalist faith.
- **Gover, Samuel** (1800 – 1885) With wife Isabelle Crain
  Gover, fourteen children and fourteen slaves, emigrated
  to Gum Creek/Jacksonville in the 1850's from Alabama.
- **Goyens, William** (1794 – 1856) An early Nacogdoches
  settler and businessman. He was a free man of color, born
  of a free mulatto and white woman. He was a blacksmith,
  wagon maker, freight hauler, innkeeper, gristmill and
  saw mill owner. He owned over 12,000 acres of land and
  several slaves.
- **Harvey, E. L.** (unknown) - The Northern Standard of
  September 17, 1842, announced the appearance of the
  "well-known and unrivaled" ventriloquist E.L. Harvey in
  Clarksville, Texas. Tickets were fifty cents each
- **Haughery, Margaret Gaffney** (1813–1882) New Orleans
  philanthropist known as "the mother of the orphans", of
  humble beginnings as an Irish immigrant, widowed, who
  had lost her only child, and supported herself as a
  washerwoman for the St. Charles Hotel before building a
  successful bakery business.

- **Hawkins, Benjamin** (? – 1833) Mixed-blood Creek Indian who settled with his wife Rebecca near Nacogdoches in 1833. Murdered, allegedly by rival Indians, for conspiring to bring a large contingent of Creek Indians to settle on lands occupied by Cherokees, Kickapoos and others under the Houston-Forbes treaty.
- **Hawkins, Williamson** (1790 – 1875) Alabama pioneer and owner of a two thousand acre cotton plantation.
- **Hazard, Clara** (unknown) Possibly an assumed name. A Philadelphia prostitute who worked with Helen Jewett.
- **Halvorsen, Christian** (1823 – 1874) Norwegian settler in Larissa. Initiated as a Mason into Larissa Lodge #57 on June 22, 1850.
- **Hotchkiss, Archibald** (1794 – 1882) Arrived in Texas about 1825, as a surveyor, interpreter, and land agent. Settled in Nacogdoches in 1834, and by 1835 was urging Lamar to remove the Cherokees from East Texas, while surreptitiously contracting with representatives of the Creek Nation to sell them the land covered by the Houston-Forbes treaty.
- **Hotchkiss, Atala** (1820 – 1871) Daughter of Archibald Hotchkiss. Married to Benjamin Phillips, widowed. One child, Catherine (Kate). Second marriage to Richard Parmalee Robinson, widowed. Third marriage to William Beck Ochiltree.
- **Hotchkiss, Rinaldo** (1818 – 1886) Son of Archibald Hotchkiss. Lawyer. Master Mason of Milan Lodge #2. Fought in several battles for Texas Independence, including the Battle of San Jacinto. Participated in both the engagement with the Kickapoo in October 1838 following the Killough massacre and the Battle of the Neches in 1839.
- **Houston, Sam** (1793 – 1863) Negotiated the Houston-Forbes treaty with the Cherokee. As General, commanded

troops in the Texas Revolution, securing the defeat of Santa Anna at the Battle of San Jacinto and establishing the Republic of Texas. He was the first popularly elected president of the Republic of Texas.

- **James, Frank** (1843 – 1915) Confederate soldier and guerrilla under William Quantrill and "Bloody Bill" Anderson in Missouri and Kansas. Older brother of Jesse James. In later years, part of the James-Younger gang.

- **James, Jesse** (1847 – 1882) Followed his older brother Frank into serving the Confederacy and acting as a guerrilla under William Quantrill and "Bloody Bill" Anderson. Following the war, was part of the James-Younger gang as a bank and train robber. He killed when shot from behind by Bob Ford for reward money.

- **Jewett, Helen** (1813 – 1836) Born Dorcas Doyen; known by many other names, including Helen, Ellen, and Nell/Nelly. A prostitute by trade, she was brutally murdered with a hatchet, her body was then set on fire in her bedroom. Richard Parmalee Robinson, a client with whom she had developed a close relationship, was soon charged with the murder. He was acquitted due in large part to the judge declaring the inadmissibility of testimony presented by the women similarly employed in the house. The trial was widely covered in the press, including the New York Herald, by reporter William Attree, who had met Miss Jewett prior to her death.

- **Joiner, E. L.** (unknown) Vermont born, Canada educated women's teacher at Larissa College. Her abolitionist sentiments led to her dismissal.

- **Lacey, Martin (wife Dorothy "Dolly")** (1789 – 1843) Sometimes spelled "Lacy". Settled in Texas around 1828 near present-day Alto, establishing a fort for the protection of his family, neighbors and travelers. He was

an Indian Agent, farmer, cattle rancher, merchant and
Indian trader.

- **Lacey, Cage** (unknown) Slave owned by Martin Lacey
- **Lamar, Mirabeau** (1798 – 1859) Elected vice-president of
  the Republic of Texas in 1836. In December 1837,
  opponents of President Sam Houston considered him a
  candidate to be the second president of the Republic, as
  under law, President Houston could not serve consecutive
  terms. There were two other candidates for the
  presidency, Peter W. Grayson and James Collinsworth,
  but both died by suicide prior to Election Day, assuring
  Lamar's victory. Under Lamar's administration, almost
  all Indians were removed from Texas and relocated to
  Arkansas.
- **Landrum, Willis H.** (1805 – 1865) Soldier and legislator.
  Commanded a company of volunteers in the Third
  Regiment of the Third Brigade in the Battle of the Neches
  in 1839.
- **Lehmann, Hermann** (1859 – 1932) Captured by Apaches
  as a child and adopted into an Apache family. As a
  teenager, he killed an Apache medicine man and chose to
  live for a year alone in exile on the West Texas plains. He
  then joined a Comanche band, given the name
  Montechema, and adopted by Quanah Parker. On the
  Oklahoma reservation, he was recognized as white and
  returned to his family in Texas. He did not recognize his
  mother or siblings, but did remember his name when his
  brother spoke to him.
- **Leveau, Marie** (1801 – 1881) Free Creole woman of color,
  renowned New Orleans Voodoo priestess, rootworker,
  conjurer, herbalist, midwife and hairdresser.
- **Little Bean** (unknown) Cherokee leader. His village was
  located near present-day Rusk, Texas.

- **Lockhart, Matilda** (1825 – 1840) Captured by Comanches as a child. Penetenka Comanches presented her to authorities in San Antonio in March 1840. She bore the marks of great torture, with bruises and sores all over her head, face and arms. Her nose had been burnt off to the bone, both nostrils showing and a scab formed over the end of exposed bone. The outrage of the citizens of San Antonio lead to the Council House Fight, resulting in the death of thirty Comanche leaders and warriors, as well as some women and children.
- **Long, W. T.** (1820 – 1889) Larissa resident who took Reverend Yoakum's slave Daniel to the market in Shreveport to be sold in order to facilitate the purchase of Larissa College's telescope.
- **Lovelady, W. H.** (1836 – 1902) Captain of Company K, organized in Jacksonville, of the Eighteenth Texas Infantry in the Confederate States Army.
- **Mayfield, James Shannon** (1808 – 1852) Lawyer, legislator, and soldier. Arrived in Nacogdoches County in 1837, where he began practicing law. He represented Nacogdoches County in the Fifth and Sixth congresses of the Republic of Texas.
- **McKee, Thomas** (1785 – 1866) Moved with his wife and at least six of their nine children from Tennessee to Texas in 1846. Was instrumental in establishing the town of Larissa and Larissa College, which began as a log cabin where classes were taught by his widowed daughter Sara Rebecca McKee Erwin.
- **McKee, Samuel Lessenbury/Lessenberry (wife Lockey/Lockie)** (1819 – 1852) Son of Thomas H. McKee, brother of Reverend Thomas Newton McKee. Arrived in Texas in 1846. Owned an inn at Larissa.
- **Middleton, John Washington** (1808 – 1898) Texas Ranger. Served in the Cherokee War. Volunteered for

recovery and burial detail following the Killough Massacre.

- **Nocona, Peta (wife Cynthia Ann Parker, "Naduah")** (? – 1860?) Comanche chief. Husband to Cynthia Ann Parker (Comanche name Naduah) and father of Quanah Parker. His dates of birth and death are uncertain.

- **O'Flaherty, Thomas (wife Eliza)** (1805 – 1855) Prominent businessman in St. Louis, Missouri, and one of the founder of the Missouri Pacific Railroad. A victim of the Gasconade River Train Disaster. Father of novelist Kate Chopin.

- **Opothleyahola** (alternate spellings **Opothle Yohola, Opothleyoholo, Hu-pui-hilth Yahola, Hopoeitheyohola,** and **Hopere Yahvlv**) (1778 – 1863) Muskogee Creek Indian Chief. In 1834, he sought to purchase a large portion of the land covered by the Houston-Forbes treaty in order to relocate his people there, as the territory had a indigenous plant which played an important role in traditional Creek culture. He gave $20,000 as a down payment, but was forced to abandon his plans by American, Mexican and Texan political maneuverings.

- **Page, Harriet** (1810 – 1902) Milliner and seamstress in New Orleans prior to 1836. She moved to Texas sometime before the Texas Revolution with her husband Solomon C. Page, who abandoned her and their children not long after their arrival.

- **Parker, Cynthia Ann "Naduah"** (1825 – 1871) Taken captive at age nine in the raid on Fort Parker in 1836, Cynthia Ann was adopted into a Comanche family and spent twenty-five years as an Indian daughter, wife, and mother. She was captured, with her young daughter, Topsana/Prairie Flower, by Lawrence Sullivan Ross in 1860 in an attack on a Comanche camp, and forcibly returned to her white relatives.

- **Parker, James (Reverend)** (1797 – 1864) Following the Comanche raid on Fort Parker in 1836, he devoted much of the remainder of his life to seeing that the family members taken captive were returned.
- **Parker, Quanah** (1845? – 1911) Son of Peta Nocona and Naduah (Cynthia Ann Parker). After many years of fighting against American soldiers, he transitioned to reservation life, becoming an outstanding leader of his people and a valuable ally to the federal government.
- **Plummer, Rachel Parker** (1819 – 1839) Abducted by Comanche Indians at Fort Parker in the same 1836 raid that saw five others taken captive: Rachel and James Pratt Plummer, Mrs. Elizabeth Kellogg, John and Cynthia Ann Parker. She wrote an account of her captivity entitled "Rachael Plummer's Narrative of Twenty-One Months of Servitude as a Prisoner Among the Commanchee Indians".
- **Quantrill, William Clarke** (1837 – 1865) Confederate soldier and guerrilla. His group included Frank and Jesse James.
- **Rey, Henry** (1831 – 1894) Free creole of color living in the Treme neighborhood. He worked as a clerk for Pitard's Hardware store. Following his father's death in 1852, he became interested in Spiritualism, attending private séance circles and recording the locations, dates, participants and communications received and names of spirits contacted during the sessions.
- **Reierson, Johan** (1810 – 1864) Norwegian colonizer of Texas, writer and publisher.
- **Reierson, Christian** (unknown) Brother to Johan Reierson.
- **Robinson, Richard Parmalee** (1817 – 1855) Tried for the April 1836 murder of Helen Jewett in New York City, he

relocated to Nacogdoches by August of that year, as incriminating evidence of his guilt was published following his acquittal. He dropped his surname upon moving to Texas, and became a Clerk of the Court, partnered with Mr. Roeder in a store, and by the time of his death from a mysterious illness, owned a stable, blacksmith shop, passenger coaches, horse teams and ran a stage line. He married Atala Hotchkiss Phillips. He died at the Galt House in Louisville, Kentucky in 1855. His body was returned to Nacogdoches for burial in December of that year.

- **Rose, Louis "Moses"** (1785 – 1851) Left the Alamo prior to the final battle. He is the source of the story about Col. Willam Travis drawing a line in the dirt with his sword.
- **Rusk, Thomas J.** (1803 – 1857) Soldier and statesman. In 1838, he commanded the Nacogdoches militia in suppressing the Cordova Rebellion. In 1839, he commanded troops in the Battle of the Neches.
- **Santa Anna, Antonio Lopez** (1794 – 1876) General of the Mexican Army during the Texas Revolution. Defeated and taken prisoner by General Sam Houston at the Battle of San Jacinto.
- **Smith, Jackson (wife Evalina)** (1814 – 1897) Blacksmith. Instrumental in establishing the community of Gum Creek, later known as Jacksonville.
- **Sterne, Augustus (wife Eva)** (1801 – 1852) German immigrant to New Orleans, Louisiana in 1817. Arrived in Texas in 1826. Colonist, merchant, land agent, legislator and diarist.
- **Tail "Utana" Benge** (1764 – 1838) A mixed-blood Cherokee warrior, whose brother Robert Benge, "The Bench", was considered the most notorious Cherokee of their time. They committed many depredations in and around Kentucky before Robert Benge was killed. Tail continued to be considered a "bad Indian" by many,

including Chief Bowl. He was killed in the Kickapoo
skirmish following the Killough massacre.

- **Tarrant, Elam** (1821 – 1893) After serving in as a
volunteer infantryman from Alabama in the Mexican-
American War, he settled in the vicinity of Larissa.
- **Taylor, William S.** (1795 – 1858) Attorney, legislator,
planter. Arrived in Texas in 1847. Elected to the Texas
State legislature in 1855 as a representative of Cherokee
and Anderson counties.
- **The Bowl (Duwali)** (1756 – 1839) Principal civil chief of
the Cherokees in Texas. His father was Scottish. He
brought his band of Cherokees to Texas sometime before
1822, settling along the Neches-Saline where they
established a salt works. He was killed at the Battle of the
Neches in 1839.
- **Thorn, Frost** (1793 – 1854) Empresario and merchant.
The first Texas millionaire. Operating in Nacogdoches
with Haden Edwards from 1825, their interests included a
general store, bank, salt mine, and lumber business. He
included Indians in his trading and landholdings.
- **Travis, William Barret** (1809 – 1836) Jointly
commanded the Texas forces at the Battle of the Alamo
with James Bowie.
- **Von Roeder, Rudolph** (? – 1839) Emigrated from
Germany to Texas with his family in 1833/34. Settled at
Cat Spring in Austin County, then moved to Nacogdoches
County. He was a merchant in partnership with Richard
Parmalee Robinson.
- **Watkins, Jesse T.** (1776? - 1837) Doctor. Arrived in Texas
in the early 1830s and was established in Nacogdoches by
1836. Father of seven children, including Reverend
Richard Watkins and Judge Jesse Watkins. He was an
Indian Agent, and according to his interpreter, Louis
Sanchez, he was captured and burned at the stake by a

band of Cherokees while en route to negotiate a treaty with Keechi, Caddo, and Tawakoni Indians. Watkins' son-in-law, Captain Robert Smith, shot and killed Cherokee Chief Bowl at the Battle of the Neches in retaliation for Watkins' death.

- **Watkins, Richard Overton** (1816 – 1897) The first Cumberland presbytery in Texas was organized in 1837, and Richard Watkins was the first minister ordained in Texas.

- **Watkins, Isaac** (unknown) Candidate for congressional representative, Nacogdoches County, Republic of Texas, 1841

- **Yoakum, Franklin Laughlin** (1819 – 1891) Physician, educator, Cumberland Presbyterian minister, writer and editor. Arrived in Texas from Tennessee in 1845. Served as President of Larissa College and taught classes from 1855 until its closure in 1866. He was a teacher of botany, geology and astronomy, and declared that if the school could not afford a telescope, that he would buy one himself. The purchase was funded by the sale of one of his slaves.

SUGGESTED READING

Cohen, Patricia Cline. *The Murder of Helen Jewett*. Vintage Books (July 1999)

Exley, Jo Ella. *Frontier Blood: The Saga of the Parker Family*. Texas A&M University Press (2009)

Ford, Fred Hugo and Brown, J.L. *Larissa*. Kiely Print Co. (1971)

Field, Rachel. *All This, and Heaven Too*. Chicago Review Press; Reprint edition (May 1, 2003)

Kirkland, Elithe Hamilton. *Love is a Wild Assault*. Shearer Publishing. (1991)

Lehman, Hermann, et al. *A New Look at Nine Years with the Indians, 1870-1879: The Story of the Captivity and Life of a Texan Among the Indians*. Leacock Graphics. (1985)

Moore, Jack. *The Killough Massacre*. Kiely Print Co. (1969)

Pinkerton, Gary L. *Trammel's Trace: The First Road to Texas from the North*. Texas A&M University Press. (2018)

Sterne, Adolphus and McDonald, Archie P. *Hurrah for Texas! The Diary of Adolphus Sterne, 1838-1851*. Texian Press. (1986)

Stuck, Goodloe. *Annie McCune: Shreveport Madam*. Moran Pub. Corp. (1981)

ABOUT THE AUTHOR

J. L. Anderson is a sixth-generation East Texan. Her great-great grandparents, Samuel and Isabelle Gover, moved from Talladega, Alabama to Gum Creek, Texas in the 1850's. Her lifelong interest in local history, legends, and ghost stories began with family tales of "the old days". When she doesn't have her nose in a book, she enjoys collecting fondue pots, surrounds herself with mid-century décor, and tends to a multitude of rescue animals.